The Cleaner of Chartres

The Cleaner of Chartres

SALLEY VICKERS

VIKING

an imprint of

PENGUIN BOOKS

VIKING

Published by the Penguin Group
Penguin Books Ltd, 80 Strand, London WC2R 0RL, England
Penguin Group (USA) Inc., 375 Hudson Street, New York, New York 10014, USA
Penguin Group (Canada), 90 Eglinton Avenue East, Suite 700, Toronto, Ontario, Canada M4P 2Y3
(a division of Pearson Penguin Canada Inc.)
Penguin Ireland, 25 St Stephen's Green, Dublin 2, Ireland (a division of Penguin Books Ltd)
Penguin Group (Australia), 707 Collins Street, Melbourne, Victoria 3008, Australia
(a division of Pearson Australia Group Pty Ltd)
Penguin Books India Pvt Ltd, 11 Community Centre,
Panchsheel Park, New Delhi – 110 017, India
Penguin Group (NZ), 67 Apollo Drive, Rosedale, Auckland 0632, New Zealand
(a division of Pearson New Zealand Ltd)
Penguin Books (South Africa) (Pty) Ltd, Block D, Rosebank Office Park,
181 Jan Smuts Avenue, Parktown North, Gauteng 2193, South Africa

Penguin Books Ltd, Registered Offices: 80 Strand, London WC2R 0RL, England

www.penguin.com

First published 2012
001

Set in 12/14.75 pt Dante MT Std
Typeset by Jouve (UK), Milton Keynes
Printed in Great Britain by Clays Ltd, St Ives plc

A CIP catalogue record for this book is available from the British Library

HARDBACK ISBN: 978–0–670–92212–3
TRADE PAPERBACK ISBN: 978–0–670–92213–0

www.greenpenguin.co.uk

ALWAYS LEARNING   **PEARSON**

For Ben and Rupert, with much love,
recalling happy times at Chartres.

Author's Note

While it is my hope that all the historical and physical details of the town and the cathedral of Notre-Dame in Chartres are accurately drawn, none of the characters portrayed there, or in Evreux, Rouen or Le Mans, are based on any person, living or dead – with the honourable exception of Malcolm Miller, who appears in these pages as the 'learned English authority'. In my researches, I benefited enormously from his wide knowledge and long experience of the town and the cathedral. Any errors found in the following pages will be mine and not his.

Chartres

The old town of Chartres, around which the modern town unaesthetically sprawls, is built on a natural elevation that rises from a wide, wheat-growing plain in the region of Beauce in central France. Visitors and pilgrims, who since earliest times have made their ways to the ancient site, can see the cathedral of Notre-Dame from many miles off, the twin spires, like lofty beacons, encouraging them onwards.

Five successive cathedrals have stood on this site; all were burned to rubble save the present cathedral, which grew, phoenix-like, from the embers of the last devastating fire. On June 10th, 1194, flames sped through Chartres, destroying many of the domestic dwellings, crowded cheek by jowl in the narrow medieval streets, and all of the former cathedral save the Western Front with its twin towers and the much more ancient crypt.

As the fire took hold, the forest of roof timbers crashed burning to the ground amid frenzied clouds of burning cinders; the walls split, tumbled and collapsed while lead from the roof poured down in a molten stream, as if enacting a scene of eternal damnation in a Last Judgement.

The reaction among the citizens of Chartres was one of uniform horror. According to contemporary reports, they lamented the loss of their beloved cathedral even more than the loss of their own homes. Perhaps this was in part because, as today, their livelihoods depended on the many parties of pilgrims visiting the town to pay reverence to its most venerated relic, the birthing gown of the Virgin Mary, a gift to the cathedral by the grandson of Charlemagne, Charles the Bald.

Three days after the fire was finally quenched, some priests emerged from the crypt with the marvellous cloth still intact. As the fire took hold, they had apparently snatched it from its hallowed place and retreated for safety into the most ancient part of the cathedral, the lower crypt, the province of Our Lady Under the Earth, incarcerating themselves behind a metal door which had held firm while the fire raged destruction outside. The missing men had been presumed dead. The holy relic presumed lost. When it was seen to have been restored, and its rescuers returned to safety, it was agreed that this was a miracle, a sign from Our Lady that the town should build in her honour an edifice even finer than before.

The new cathedral was completed within twenty-six years, thanks to the devotion and hard labour of the townspeople, who pulled together to create a building worthy of the Mother of God with whom their town had so fortunately found favour. The bishop and his canons agreed to donate the greater portion of their salaries to aid the cost of the building works. Sovereigns of the Western world were approached for funds, and many dug deep into their coffers to ensure that their names were attached to the noble enterprise, which would gain for them fitting rewards in the life to come. People from neighbouring dioceses brought cartloads of grain to feed the citizens of Chartres, who were giving their labours for nothing more than the love of God. The whole astonishing structure was conceived, designed and accomplished by a series of master builders, men of clear enterprise and shining genius.

But of them and their companies – the scores of talented sculptors, stonecutters, masons, carpenters, roofers, stained-glass artists and manual labourers who implemented their plans – nothing is known.

Nor was anything known of Agnès Morel when she arrived in Chartres nearly eight hundred years after the building of the present cathedral commenced. Few, if asked, could have recalled when she first appeared. She must have seemed vaguely always to have been about. A tall, dark, slender woman – 'a touch of the tar brush there', Madame Beck, who had more than a passing sympathy for the Front National, chose to comment – with eyes that the local artist, Robert Clément, likened to washed topaz, though, as the same Madame Beck remarked to her friend Madame Picot, being an artist he was given to these fanciful notions.

As far back as Philippe Nevers could remember Agnès had been around. She had been an occasional babysitter for himself and his sister, Brigitte. Brigitte had once crept up with a pair of scissors behind the sofa, where their babysitter sat watching TV, and hacked an ugly chunk out of her long black hair. Philippe had pinched Brigitte's arm for this and they had got into a fight, in which Brigitte's new nightgown was ripped by the scissors, and when their mother came home Brigitte had cried and shown her both the nightgown and the pinch marks.

Although their mother had punished Philippe, the boy had not explained why he had set about his sister. Agnès was odd, with eyes, he might have suggested, had he overheard Robert Clément, more like those of the panther he had seen at the zoo, pacing up and down its cage in a manner the crowd found amusing. Philippe liked Agnès in the way he had liked the panther and had hoped that it might escape and get a bit of its own back on the laughing crowd. With the sensitivity which, even at age six, was a hallmark of his character, he knew their mother would be quick to blame Agnès for the episode with the scissors. So he bore the unfair punishment in silence.

Professor Jones, had he been aware of it, would have been able to date Agnès' arrival quite precisely, since it was the same summer that his second wife left him. The weather had been uncharacteristically inclement, even for central France, which does not enjoy the dependable climate of the South. Professor Jones had taken a sabbatical year in order to embark on a long-cherished research project of documenting each of the supposedly four thousand, five hundred sculptures which embellish the nine great portals of Notre-Dame in Chartres. The work was to be definitive in the field and he had dared to hope that it would make his name. But the parochialism of the small town, the depressing steady drizzle and her husband's preoccupation with insensate figures of the long past had lowered Marion Jones's spirits, the very spirits which her husband had hoped to raise by bringing her to the famed medieval town.

This mismatch in taste and comprehension was only one of a long list of incompatibilities between Marion Jones and her husband. That summer, a renowned Japanese cellist visited from Paris to play Bach's Suites for unaccompanied cello at one of the cathedral's prestigious summer concerts. Marion, bored to tears by the life she was leading, wandered into the cathedral while the cellist was practising, and it was noted by Madame Beck that he was not unaccompanied when, a while later, he left the cathedral to return to his hotel. Not long after the concert, Marion took to making shopping trips to Paris, which is barely an hour's train ride from Chartres. The trips became longer, and more frequent; one day she left with a larger than usual bag and never returned.

Professor Jones waited mournfully, long after his sabbatical year had come to an end. Finally, giving in to despair, he resigned his university position and made a permanent home in Chartres, but not before a small parcel containing a wedding ring had arrived with a note telling him where he could 'stick his bloody sculptures'.

The current dean, the Abbé Paul, might have remembered Agnès' arrival since he too, at that far date, had only lately come from his seminary to serve as a curate at the cathedral. He had found Agnès under a man's coat, asleep in a convenient niche in the North Porch. Although the dean at the time, Monsignor André, a stern administrator, had let it be known that tramps should not misconstrue the nature of Christian charity by taking the cathedral for 'a doss house', the young priest found himself turning a blind eye to the intruder.

Paul's father was a Highland Scot who could trace his family line directly back to Lord George Murray, the general who had led the ill-fated Jacobite rebellion against the English in the rising of 1745. The general's descendant had met his future wife when she had gone with a friend to visit the festival at Edinburgh, where he had held a research fellowship at the university. The marriage was a successful one: but Charles Murray had succumbed, after a short fight, to his French wife's pressure to return to her native land in search of the light she bitterly missed in the long Scottish winters.

The strain of rebellion in him succumbed to his greater fondness for his wife and concern for her happiness. He gave up his study of Ovid's metaphors and became a respected Classics master at a school in Toulon.

But a measure of his father's dissident heritage salted the young Paul's character. The sleeper in the cathedral porch was a young woman; she looked peaceful. For all Dean André's strictures the young Paul could not bear to awaken her to what he guessed was a grim reality.

Quite how Agnès had managed since those days was a subject of nobody's speculation. She had made herself useful in the small ways that help to oil the wheels of daily life. She was an accomplished ironer, a reliable babysitter and was known to 'sit' naked for Robert Clément (the last activity making her less desirable to some in the first two capacities). She made a reputation as a conscientious cleaner, and Professor Jones, after a more than usually bad attack of moth had made lace of his slender wardrobe, discovered that she could also darn.

Agnès no longer had need of the shelter of the cathedral when the subject of her cleaning it came up. The weather, which twenty years ago had witnessed her arrival, was repeating itself. Streams of sodden visitors – in coach parties, families and couples, as well as those travelling by choice or necessity alone, not to mention the troupes of those seeking enlightenment, historical or spiritual – were playing havoc with the cathedral floor. The once pale paving stones, quarried from nearby Berchères-les-Pierres, after hundreds of years of footfalls had darkened and pitted, which made them, as the current cleaner Bernadette often remarked, 'hell to keep clean'.

Agnès was weeding the flower-beds before the Royal Portal when the Abbé Paul encountered her. A summer of steady rain had brought on both the weeds and Thomas the gardener's rheumatism. His wife had put her foot down and insisted he go to a spa for a cure. And, as was often the case when a temporary replacement was needed, it was Agnès who had come to mind.

Enclosed in wicker borders, which gave the impression of large square florist's panniers, the flowers, mainly white, had been chosen to enhance the summer evenings. Had Robert Clément been there, he might have observed that they also enhanced Agnès' dark skin as she bent to root out the weeds. But the Abbé Paul was a man of the cloth and no doubt it was simply friendly courtesy that made him stop to greet her.

'Good day, Agnès. I must say we are most grateful for your help.'

Agnès straightened a back blessedly free of Thomas's rheumatism. Although she was unaware that the Abbé had let her sleep undisturbed that first night she had come to Chartres, she nevertheless felt safe with him.

'I like them best at night.'

The Abbé Paul agreed. 'The scent is stronger then.'

'Yes, Father.'

'The weather has brought on the weeds, though?'

'Yes, Father.'

It was one of Agnès' virtues that she didn't say much. It made the Abbé Paul more inclined to be chatty himself though as a rule he was not a talkative man. 'I'm afraid it's making a filthy mess of the cathedral floor. All those wet muddy feet. And now, God help us, we seem to have lost our cleaner as well as our gardener. It's too much for Bernadette's knees, she says.'

Agnès stood, a trowel in one hand, an earthy-rooted dandelion, which she planned to add to her evening salad, dangling from the other. The green leaves against her long red skirt and her impassive brown oval face gave an impression, the Abbé Paul fleetingly thought, of a figure from a parable portrayed in one of the cathedral's stained-glass windows. A labourer in a vineyard, perhaps.

It seemed Agnès was pondering, for as Paul was about to utter further pleasantries and move on, she spoke. 'I will clean it if you like.'

'Oh, but I didn't mean . . .' Now he was concerned that she might imagine that he was approaching her as a skivvy rather than for the pleasure of conversation.

'I would like to, Father,' Agnès said.

The Abbé Paul paused. It would certainly help. The bishop

was exercised about the state of the cathedral, which meant that he was being harassed too. And Agnès was known to be reliable.

'I would like to,' she repeated, with emphasis.

'Well, if you felt you could . . .'

'I do,' Agnès said.

So it was agreed she should start that same week.

2

Evreux

Agnès Morel was born neither Agnès nor Morel. So far as names go she was not born anything at all. She was found wrapped in a white tablecloth in a straw shopping basket on January 21st, St Agnès' Day, with nothing to indicate her parentage except a single turquoise earring lying in the bottom of the basket, which might well have been dropped there by accident.

Agnès is the saint to whom young women pray for husbands, and, since Jean Dupère, who had found the baby, presumed the foundling's mother had none, he named the anonymous woman's daughter after the saint. In the way of those who unexpectedly find themselves doing a good turn, he felt a touch of pride in the poetry of his choice.

'Morel' was an afterthought – Jean's small way of passing on something of his own. He had a taste for morel mushrooms, and the child was discovered, a frozen scrap of a thing, in the logging area of the wood where he was gathering fuel for his fire and where in spring he was in the habit of going in search of this culinary prize.

Jean was a bachelor. His romantic propensities, though stimulated by this unusual event, stopped short of envisaging raising a girl child on his own. But he was a farmer and fairly practised at rearing blighted orphaned creatures. He took the baby home and fed her in the old shepherds' way, by dipping a knot of a boiled cloth in warm watered milk. When, the next day, he reported the find to the local police, they suggested that the Sisters of Our Lady of Mercy at Evreux would no doubt care for the child while the necessary inquiries about her parentage were being made.

The inquiries came to nothing. No local midwife or hospital reported anything untoward. No lone young woman was believed to have lately been delivered of a child. Jean was no longer a practising Catholic but he had been brought up in the Church and nuns struck him as a better bet than a state orphanage.

A shared faith need not entail a uniform character. The Sisters of Our Lady of Mercy were, variously, strict, stupid, sadistic, well-meaning, intelligent and kindly – the three former traits slightly outweighing the latter qualities, as is generally the case in any human group. To be fair, as a community they were tolerant of illegitimacy. After all, the man whose life to which they had dedicated their own also came of ambiguous parentage.

As Agnès grew older, and teachable, Sister Laurence, who often regretted that she had not married her cousin and had a child herself (the parents were dead set against this for genetic reasons and in the end the young lovers lost heart and capitulated), enjoyed telling the young Agnès Bible stories. An alert listener might have noticed a slightly subversive note in Sister Laurence's voice when it came to the story of Moses found in a basket, a tone which hinted that his discovery by Pharaoh's daughter was not entirely an accident. But, for all Agnès' appetite for stories, she appeared quite incapable of mastering the ability to read or write.

The nuns were, on the whole, as tolerant of this as they were of her illegitimacy. Sister Laurence put Agnès' deficiency down to her unlucky start. It was Sister Véronique, who was writing a commentary on Dante, who tried her hardest to teach the girl, for, as she was fond of saying, 'She is plainly bright', adding somewhat tartly, 'She laps up those tales.' (Try as she might, Sister Véronique had never been able to rid herself of a certain scepticism over the factual accuracy of biblical stories.) But, as for helping Agnès to read the tales herself, it seemed to be a hopeless task.

It was not that she was stubborn. She was an unusually industrious child and apparently willing to learn where she could. Everyone agreed she was first-rate at washing, ironing, embroidery and darning. The Sisters gave her their black woollen socks and stockings to darn with some relief. Sister Céleste, who had been in charge of the mending before, merely cobbled over the holes in their hosiery in an ugly mess.

In time, Agnès began to work in the orchards and in the vegetable garden, where a local boy helped out. And that was when her troubles began again.

3

Chartres

On the first Friday Agnès was due to clean the cathedral, Philippe Nevers met her on his way to the station. Time had changed Philippe from the tubby boy in short trousers who had quarrelled with his sister to a lean and lanky young man who wore the most up-to-the-minute fashion and jewellery in the contemporary taste. But he had retained his boyhood manners.

'Good morning, Agnès. That's a very pretty skirt. You're out early.'

'I'm cleaning the cathedral now.'

'So you're wearing blue to match? Tough work, isn't it, cleaning in this weather?'

Agnès smiled and agreed and continued up the hill.

Behind a wreathing veil of summer mist, incalculably different from the autumnal mists, the tops of the two cathedral spires were aiming at a heaven the whole edifice beneath them was there to invoke. She paused to catch her breath before the three grand bays of the Royal Portal.

The solemn elongated figures of the bearded prophets and patriarchs, the dead kings and braided queens who give the name of Royal to the doors, stared inscrutably down from their perilous pedestals, their hands – such as had been spared from the depredations of time and the ferocity of revolution – raised as if in formal greeting. Above them on the tympanum, Christ, in his aureole, awaiting the glory of his second coming – but now so imprisoned behind scaffolding as to give an impression of some detained felon or caged wild animal – also raised an elegant right hand.

Agnès raised her hand of flesh and blood in an answering gesture. 'I hope, Lord, you have a better time this time around.'

She turned to walk along the north side of the building, to the porch where twenty years ago she had come to rest. Above her – now as then – Job lay on his comfortless bed of ashes, plagued by a grotesquely grimacing Satan.

Inside the cathedral, the musty air seemed to be perfused with a faint odour of onions. What caused that? Something to do with years of human sweat, she supposed. An alert sparrow took the opportunity to nip through the open door into the cathedral. It struck out across the empty nave chittering triumphantly as Agnès went round to the vestry, where the cleaning equipment was stored. She put on an orange overall and filled the bucket with hot water. Today was the labyrinth day.

Victor, the janitor, had already been in to see to the chairs that on most days obscured the famous labyrinth, which was set into the floor of the nave just inside the West Doors. Agnès stood looking at the pattern made by the path which, moving regularly forward and back on itself, traced eleven circles to frame an open corolla of petals at its centre. A cross was adumbrated by the bands of black marble that marked the turns in the path. It was clever, she reflected, the cross, being composed not of the stones that made the path but of those that marked its absence. Around the large circle of the whole, a pattern of cogs gave the impression of some mysterious clock.

The cathedral lay as if asleep, utterly quiet save for the sporadic pinking of the sparrow, which appeared to have found a convivial mate. Agnès took off her shoes. Moving to the entrance of the labyrinth, she began to tread the spiralling path.

★

Walking up the rue aux Herbes, Professor Jones witnessed the face of the upper part of the cathedral's South Transept lighting up to a pale honey. The sun, in a brave sortie, had made a bright gash in the clouds. The lower part of the transept, waiting its turn in the long programme of cleaning, was still grimy. Impervious to the dashing sunlight, the smoke-darkened stones made, with the paler ones above, for a strange piebald effect.

Really, the professor thought, taking a seat under the awning of his regular café, the weather this summer was almost as bad as that of his native Wales.

Without needing to be summoned, a waiter appeared with a small tray of café crème, a basket of fresh baguette, a slab of pale butter and a dish of apricot jam. *This* was not Pembrokeshire, the professor reflected. He had never got over his acute pleasure at taking his breakfast in France.

Opposite him, secure on a row of high niches well above the pedestrian world, weather-beaten bishops brandishing crosiers peered beakily down. Professor Jones stirred the coffee – to which, unmindful of his diabetes, he had added three lumps of sugar – and looked back up indifferently. He no longer cared a damn who they were. He had long ago lost interest in the majority of the four thousand, five hundred (if that was the true number) statues it had once been his ruling ambition to identify. Nowadays he cared for only a few familiar ones – the long elegant angel on the south-west corner, for example. It was a replica, of course. The original had grown too fragile to withstand the effects of the weather – a condition with which the professor, had he thought about it, might have sympathized.

When he had finished his breakfast, the professor left some euros on the table and moved across to one of the benches with the remains of the baguette. A former professional colleague from University College had recently visited and told him that the sparrow population in London was in decline. Something to do with the noise of the metropolis's traffic drowning the mating call of the male birds, his colleague surmised. What a very good reason not to live there, the professor had retorted. With the loss of all human company, save the very rare visitor, he had become greatly attached to the friendly little birds.

The neat grey-headed chocolate-backed male sparrows and their modest brown-flecked mates bobbed about consuming crumbs at the professor's large sandalled feet as he studied the angel bearing a sundial. It seemed a prosaic gesture for a heavenly body and yet somehow, he reflected, maybe it was fitting that a messenger from God should act as an agent of time.

What did it say in the Book of Revelation? Professor Jones had abandoned his Christian faith with his short trousers but he had not forgotten the teaching of his chapel upbringing. 'There shall be time no longer,' the angel of Revelation said. Time no longer. Is that not what death is, thought Professor Jones. For since the world is known to us only through our experience of it, does its existence not, in some crucial way, come to an end when we do? And is not heaven, then, merely the fact of non-existence? The loss of the fear of loss, which haunts and casts its shadow over so much of human life.

Inside the cathedral, Agnès, now on her knees and assiduously cleaning the path of the labyrinth, heard the Abbé Bernard, one of the elderly canons, opening the great West Door. For some months now, he had elected to take on the task of personally opening the cathedral to the public. There was no call for this for a man in his position but he had been an integral part of the life of the cathedral for so long that no one liked to gainsay him. He marched in, gown flapping, and seeing Agnès stopped short, his old freckled hand reaching nervously for the rosary at his waist.

'Bernadette?'

'She's left, Father. Father Paul asked . . .'

'Yes, yes, I remember, of course.' The Abbé Bernard was growing more and more afraid that he might be losing his mind. 'So today is Friday?'

'Yes.'

'I know that. I speak rhetorically.'

Taking advantage of the open door, a swallow made a dramatic entry, skimming the ear of the Abbé, who cursed heartily and hurried to shut the door. 'God damn it, we are not an aviary.'

A hopeless war was constantly being waged by the cathedral staff against the regular influx of birds. In former times, families of swallows had been annually raised in a nest built beneath the lancet window of King David and the suicide of Saul. Finally, the bird droppings became so great a nuisance that the bishop ordered that the nest be destroyed.

Agnès, on hands and knees with a scrubbing brush, ignorant of all this, her cotton frock making a cornflower pool around her, watched the swallow cutting an oblique curve through to the choir. Birds, she had heard on the radio, were older than humankind, the oldest of any species – perhaps the only surviving version of the dinosaur.

Outside the sun was winning. The high banks of coiled cloud were attenuating to let in stretches of purest blue. Professor Jones had dropped into a morning doze. He was five years old again, sitting beneath the keys of an upright piano at his mother's feet, as she sang in the Welsh tongue that had long since left his waking mind. If he sat there long enough she would scoop him up in her soft white arms and carry him to bed. Nestling against his mother's warm bosom – made slightly uncomfortable by the spikes of Sunday brooches of jet, bought during her parents' honeymoon at Whitby – Professor Jones on his bench sighed in a peaceful contentment that he was unlikely ever to know so completely again.

4

Evreux

'Agnès is looking very healthy these days,' Sister Laurence declared. 'It's nice to see her filling out. The garden work must be doing her good.'

Sister Véronique, who had merely glanced at Agnès to see what Laurence was on about, looked again more searchingly. Before taking the veil, she had been a headmistress of a girls' school and was accustomed to assessing the girls' weight, whether for signs of anorexia or more troublesome conditions. She collared Agnès at the first opportunity and demanded to know when she had had her last period. The reply did nothing to calm her fears.

'I don't know, Sister. Some time ago.'

When Sister Véronique reported her suspicions to the Mother Superior, the Sisters were collectively appalled.

'She is so young, couldn't we, in the circumstances . . .' Sister Laurence, who was only ten years older than Agnès, falteringly suggested but was reproved sharply by the Mother Superior.

'You cannot have forgotten, surely, Sister, that to interfere with nature is a mortal sin?'

Agnès was not yet fifteen. As far as they knew, she never went out. The number of men visiting the convent premises was necessarily limited. How could this violation possibly have occurred?

Agnès herself was vexingly unclear. Asked about possible boyfriends, she only shook her head and insisted she hadn't any. In the end, Sister Véronique, irritated by this impasse, summoned Frédéric, the boy who helped with the garden. Meeting with his persistent denials of any wrongdoing, she became assertive. 'Don't try to deny it. Only you could have done this shocking thing to our little Agnès.'

Frédéric's posture of denial became more intransigent. He fixed Sister Véronique with a cool grey Norman eye and asserted that he wouldn't touch a bastard retard if you paid him.

Sister Véronique lost her temper (a sin she had frequently been advised to overcome), made as if to whop the impertinent boy round the head and, according to Frédéric's mother, would have done so had he not had the presence of mind to duck. Sister Véronique, the indignant parent continued, had pushed her son out of the room 'swearing like a trooper'.

The mother had gone up to the convent to threaten the Sisters over their 'foul language and disgusting accusations', about which, she informed them, she was planning to write to 'the authorities'. Fierce words were exchanged. Frédéric was dismissed from his garden duties, and it was later found that he had expressed his resentment by stealing a pruning knife.

None of this did anything to help Agnès. In due course, she was packed off to a local nursing home, known to be discreet in such matters, where she gave birth to an underweight boy child who was mercifully removed from her before she could feed him or apparently had a chance to bestow on him a name.

Agnès returned to the convent from her sojourn at the nursing home quieter and more biddable than ever. The nuns congratulated themselves on their tactful handling of the sad affair. Sister Véronique tried again to interest her protégée in reading. (She herself in her secular days had embarked on her study of Dante as a means of recovering from an unhappy love affair with the History mistress.) Agnès meekly accepted the large-print book describing the life of St Thérèse of Lisieux.

But later, burnt fragments were found in the dustbin by the girl who had been recruited to help with the heavy work while Agnès was recuperating.

About three months after Agnès' return from the nursing home, a piercing caterwaul issued from the kitchen garden. Several of the Sisters hurried outside to find Agnès screaming and wildly tearing at the bodice of her dress as if it concealed some venomous snake or other deadly creature.

Nothing was seen or found either on or under her clothing; nor could anyone get the girl to make any kind of sense. She was finally persuaded to come inside and take a calming tisane of lime flowers. The Sisters conferred anxiously but agreed that this was an inevitable nervous reaction to the unfortunate birth.

Some weeks later, Sister Camille noticed drops of what looked like blood on the floor of the bathroom. It was not the time of the month when those of the Sisters who were still fertile underwent their communal period. Nor had any Sister complained of a wound. Various sharp instruments began to go missing. Several Sisters complained that they couldn't find their nail scissors. Sister Laurence did not report the loss of her razor, since it was a secret with which she dealt with an embarrassing vestigial moustache. But Sister Camille was open, even cantankerous, about the disappearance of her pinking shears and the cook reported the loss of a new carving knife.

Agnès continued reticent and hard-working. If anything, she seemed to want to do more for the Sisters than before, even offering to goffer the wimples they wore on certain feast days, a task so skilled that it had hitherto been reserved for the local laundress, who had been trained to the task through an ancient laundering connection to the convent. The girl was often seen in those days walking in the orchard gathering the many windfalls from the apple trees. But this gave no cause for alarm. It merely showed a love of nature, coupled with a proper sense of housewifely thrift. A series of delicious *tartes aux pommes* confirmed this diagnosis. Since her return, Agnès had made friends with the cook, who was giving her culinary instruction.

There were, however, certain disturbing events. The door to the hutch, where rabbits were kept to supplement the convent's diet, was found open, not once but twice, after the first lot of escapees had been replaced. More sinisterly (if less widely deplored), Sister Véronique's current work on the symbolism of the rose in Dante's *Purgatorio*, which she had left unguarded on a library table, was defaced. Examination indicated that excrement had been smeared over it. Tempers ran very high indeed when Sister Véronique, understandably outraged, began to accuse the community of neurotic envy of her scholarship.

All speculation was brought to an end when one night the Mother Superior, feeling a more than usual draught in her room, rose from her bed and put on the light to find Agnès standing there, stark naked and carrying a knife. Mother Catherine had once held a senior position in the Diplomatic Corps. She was a cool-headed woman and asked Agnès, quite briskly, to hand the knife over immediately. Mother Catherine told the doctor afterwards that the girl had stared at her, then, naked as she was, had made 'a quite extraordinary curtsy', after which she collapsed senseless before the Mother's bare feet, still clutching the knife.

It was not the missing kitchen knife (which in fact the cook had purloined) but the pruning knife from the garden shed.

5

Chartres

As is the case with all French cathedrals, Notre-Dame is owned by the state, which is responsible for its repair and the extensive and costly programme of restoration. At the same time, its use is granted to the Roman Catholic Church, and it serves both as the local parish church and the seat of the very ancient Bishopric of Chartres. It is therefore subject to two ancient masters, God and Mammon, who reputedly have differing aims.

The cathedral clergy could hardly resent the quantities of visitors possibly seeking spiritual enlightenment. Visitors brought money. As Friday was the day that, between March and October, the famous labyrinth was uncovered, it was also the day when the largest numbers arrived. The site was popularly supposed to have been a former haunt of druids, and inevitably this encouraged modern pagan worshippers and other believers in the strange or the bizarre. However much the clergy may have frowned privately on an interest that was not generated by a genuine Christian spirit, the modern pilgrims spent large sums at the gift shop, where mythic accounts of the labyrinth were on sale, along with its image on postcards, calendars, key-rings, paperweights, pendants, earrings, mugs and mouse mats. All this made a valuable contribution to the vast sums required to keep the cathedral going, never mind its perpetual need of repairs.

Along with other Chartres locals, Agnès had occasionally dropped by on Fridays, to watch the sight of the pilgrims treading the labyrinth path. Some came in groups and walked the route to the centre according to a privately agreed pact; they handed flowers and little notes to each other as they passed; frequently they wept or stopped to hug or hold each other, often in a massed group embrace, when they finally reached the centre. Some moved according to what looked like a set of martial-arts rules, slowly and carefully, deliberating each footfall. Many walked with half-closed eyes. Some sank to their knees en route and visibly prayed – or uttered lines from poems or mantras, causing a human traffic jam to build up behind them. These pilgrims generally shed their shoes to tread the cold floors barefoot (the state of their soles was uppermost in Agnès' mind when she came to clean). Others, less ethereally inclined, simply followed the path because it was there.

Later in the day, when the more intense pilgrims had mostly departed, children often arrived and ran or skipped around the spiral. Jesus' injunction to suffer little children to come unto him was evidently not uppermost in the early-morning labyrinthers' minds. More than once Agnès had witnessed irritation, especially from foreign pilgrims, if one of the local children, brought by their mothers to shelter from the rain, for instance, created a noisy distraction.

On that first Friday that she came to clean, Agnès had already finished washing the labyrinth when the Abbé Paul found her with a knife, picking off the candle grease on the altar that stood before the black pear-wood Virgin. 'No need to do that, Agnès. That's Victor's job.'

'Sorry, Father.' She dropped the knife hastily into her apron pocket.

'No need to be sorry. I'm here because I'm told we have a candle crisis. Can you credit it, the candle-makers are on strike?'

It was well recognized that years of candle smoke were responsible for the blackened state of the stonework, and for this reason a bulk delivery of environmentally friendly candles arrived regularly on Fridays. Their purchase by the visitors also provided a useful addition to the cathedral funds.

Disregarding his own words, the Abbé Paul scratched at a blob of intractable grease. Candle grease for some reason is irresistible. 'We're going to have to find another supplier in a hurry. God alone knows where.'

He hurried away, raking with his fingers his still-black hair, while Agnès, in her overall, resumed her work.

She began with the floor of the sanctuary of the pear-wood Virgin, who, imprisoned in her stiffly tinselled frock, looked mildly down as if to say she wished that she could enjoy again the simplicity of Agnès' dress. From here, Agnès moved slowly round to the ambulatory. The colours of the stained-glass windows – blue, red, green and violet – danced before her on the yellowed limestone, which from years of wear bore the patina of old marble. She passed the Virgin's celebrated veil (demoted from its former status as the Holy birthing gown but duly honoured in a ceremonial ark of gold) and stopped before a lancet window that, in its lower panes, depicted a man in green displaying what seemed to be a bale of cloth.

'He's showing a customer a fur.'

Startled out of her reverie, Agnès dropped the mop, which clattered to the floor, splashing the trousers of Robert Clément, who had come up behind her. Not that the wet marks were likely to cause any fuss. Robert's trousers were habitually as daubed as his palette.

'What are you doing here, my pretty?' he demanded.

Robert's family was obscurely connected to the painter Renoir's. Unkind people suggested that this legacy had encouraged a degree of arrogance in Robert that his painting did not warrant. But this was unfair. Robert dined out on the connection but essentially he was a realist and never made the error of confounding the famous artist's talent with his own.

Many years ago he had discovered that money was to be made by reproducing scenes from the cathedral stained-glass windows to sell to the many tourists who visited the town. He was therefore a regular in the cathedral, which he unconsciously regarded as a kind of ready annexe to his studio.

Agnès said nothing. She liked to look at the windows but she liked it best when, her eyes unfocused, the cathedral appeared to her a haze of jewelled light. But Robert liked the sound of his own voice, and regarded himself as something of an authority on the windows. Undeterred by her silence, he began to expound.

'This window is dedicated to St James the Great. The story is he was the brother of Jesus –'

Rather to his surprise, Agnès interrupted him. 'I know.'

'It's fanciful nonsense but then all this is, in its splendid way.'

'Why is the fur there?'

'The furriers and drapers of the town paid for this window.' Robert was delighted that he was in a position to instruct. 'If you look, you can see their signatures in the bottom panels.'

Agnès gazed at the window. At the top, the putative brother of Jesus was about to be beheaded. It looked more as if he were about to be knifed in the back.

Quite unaware that he had failed to get her attention, Robert continued. 'Most of the windows were endowed by the local merchants. There are some quite bizarre matches. The Miracles of the Blessed Virgin was given by the butchers. There's a bloody great hunk of meat ready to be butchered alongside all her miraculous deeds. It was a kind of advert. Trapped audience. Something to rest your eyes on when the preacher was rambling on.'

Agnès smiled as if interested. When Robert had gone, she would come back and look at the window undisturbed. She bent down and began to try to scrape away a piece of chewing gum which had been trampled into one of the interstices of the stone.

'Here, use my knife. Gum is the very devil to get off. I'd guillotine anyone found dumping it.'

'Father Paul said it was one of the reasons Bernadette left.'

'I wondered what had happened to old Bernadette?'

'I think it was her knees.'

'You look after yours, then. They're very pretty. I hope they're paying you decently, Agnès.'

Agnès smiled but said nothing.

'Mean as hell, the Church. Remember, I always need you as a model. Indecent payment guaranteed.'

Agnès smiled again and Robert, finally capitulating to her silence, plonked himself down on one of the wooden benches and began to draw.

Mopping as she went, as if in a dance with a singularly thin and passive partner, Agnès made her way round to the wine growers' Zodiac window, which needed no interpretation.

There was January with three faces, looking three ways – past, present and what was to come. Beside him Aquarius, the water-carrier, seemed to be pouring out the water from his pot. And there was Capricorn, as a strange goat-fish, beside the man feasting on Christmas fare. Was she a goat-fish or a water-carrier? According to Sister Laurence, she could be either.

Outside the cathedral, Professor Jones was engaged in the strangest endeavour. Money had come to him through his father, who had manufactured a variety of novelty biscuits in the shape of a bear, known as 'Bicky Bears', which at a time when children were barely catered for had proved immensely popular. As a result, Ewan Jones had been able to send his son to a minor public school, from where, much to his parents' pride, for they had come from very humble origins, the boy had gone on to read art history at Swansea University.

The two senior Joneses were killed in a car crash, while test-driving a Jaguar (the latest result of their newfound prosperity). Their untimely death left their son, an only child, richer, thanks to Bicky Bears, by several millions. His first wife requisitioned half the legacy when she filed for divorce. This, plus the fact that he had come to the conclusion she had only married him for money in the first place, left a sour taste in the future professor's mouth.

Earlier in his life, Professor Jones had been persuaded to consult a gypsy fortune-teller, who opined that he and money would 'never get on well'. The loss of his second wife caused him to brood. The gypsy's vaguely phrased warnings began to play on his mind. He became convinced that the only path to happiness was to give away his money; but to good causes. The problem was in settling on which.

One cause readily to hand was that of the teams of beggars who hung about the cathedral hoping to benefit from its heightening effects on the visitors' sense of charity. That these local mendicants were generally ignored might have troubled the cathedral clergy since the promotion of Christian charity was supposedly their task. In fact, they rather deplored the professor's efforts since it encouraged the vagrants. But what could they do? Also, as the bishop hinted, it wouldn't do to reprove a potential benefactor who might be persuaded to help out with the repair fund.

When Agnès finished for the morning, she left by the South Door and at the bottom of the broad steps met Professor Jones, who had completed his morning round of superstitious disbursements. The professor was glad of the chance encounter. Agnès had a pleasing smile and was not likely to tattle about him, as he feared many of the women of Chartres were prone to do. Madame Beck for example. Professor Jones, had he been able to summon up the knowledge, was frightened by the flashes of malice that he unconsciously detected in that person's little blue eyes.

'Hi there, Agnès.' Professor Jones tried his hardest to adopt the language of youth, unaware that, like too much make-up on an older face, it was merely ageing.

'Hi,' Agnès returned. The warmth he felt for her was reciprocated: each intuitively knew that, from the other, there was no question of any attack.

'I was wondering,' the professor went on, racking his brains for something he could reasonably ask, 'if you would come and help sort out my papers.' Ah, that was the thing! She might help with the paperwork which hung about his untidy apartment in menacing heaps and piles.

Agnès was glad to be offered employment. It was not so much that she needed the money; it was that for her own reasons she was in need of occupation.

Madame Beck, stationed at her lace-curtained watchtower, observed the shambling figure with the once-red-now-silver-and-auburn hair and the woman in the cornflower-blue dress as they walked together down the rue aux Herbes towards the professor's apartment in la place de la Poissonnerie. When they had vanished from sight, she picked up the phone and dialled the number of her friend, Madame Picot.

6

Rouen

The local doctor, who was summoned by the Mother Catherine to give his opinion on Agnès' state, diagnosed a case of catatonia.

'What is that?' Sister Laurence asked. She, in particular, was anxious over their charge.

'Dementia praecox,' said Sister Véronique shortly. 'Otherwise known as schizophrenia. But I doubt it myself. It's post-partum depression or I'll eat my St Augustine.'

Happily for her, Sister Véronique was not required to consume *The City of God*. The Mother Superior went with Agnès in the ambulance, which took her to the St Francis Psychiatric Clinic at Rouen, and after some protracted negotiations managed to recover the pruning knife. Mother Catherine was strong, and had once in a mood of frivolity challenged Sister Véronique to an arm-wrestling match. But Agnès held the knife in a grip so tight that even the Mother's famed force could not prise her fingers from it.

'Why the pruning knife?' the Mother asked once she had safely recovered the implement. Agnès made no answer. She simply lay there impassive, with an unnerving sightless golden gaze.

Told of her history, Dr Deman agreed with Sister Véronique. 'The loss of the child, coupled with her own history of motherlessness, this alone is enough to account for such a reaction.'

Mother Catherine chose to take offence. 'We have been nothing but a community of mothers to her.'

Dr Deman was tactful but adamant. 'Nevertheless, the effect of the dereliction of the biological mother cannot be under-estimated. Nor can the loss of a child.'

But at this Mother Catherine put her well-laced foot down. 'There could not have been any question of her keeping the child. She is not yet sixteen. Barely fifteen, in fact.'

Dr Deman brought the conversation to a close saying that in any case they would keep Agnès in for a while, and Mother Catherine left with the pruning knife and an admonition to him to keep a careful eye on the girl.

When her tight-sleeved dress was, with difficulty, removed, marks of severe cutting were exposed on Agnès' forearms, breasts and thighs. Many were recent. But some were scars of long standing. Dr Deman followed the gentler and unfashion-able methods of early psychiatry (in which he was not well supported by medical colleagues, who considered them re-actionary) that held that rest, good food and good air were the best nurses for states of mental disquiet. He placed Agnès in a ward with three other patients, all cases of what he surmised to be temporary catatonia.

His instructions were that the upper windows were to be left open to ensure a constant influx of air (the upper windows being too small to allow anyone to climb out), and the patients were prescribed first milk, if necessary in feeding bottles, and then nourishing soups, which were to be spooned into their mouths only if they made no protest. Otherwise they were to be left in peace. It was his contention that catatonia was a method of escaping the unendurable harassments of life and that the royal road to its cure was to let the patient be.

Whatever the truth of the theories, they seemed to work

with Agnès. After a fortnight of this treatment, she rose from her bed in the pure cotton nightwear with which all Dr Deman's patients were issued and asked for bread and cheese.

Dr Deman was delighted. He ordered that she be served exactly what she had asked for, together with some of the local gherkins, because in addition to the good effects of cotton next to the skin he placed some faith in the healing properties of vinegar.

The gherkins were a lucky inspiration. Agnès had formerly shown a great partiality to them, and their arrival on a plate of fresh baguette and ripe Brie gave her the first taste of pleasure she had had since her enforced spell at the nursing home. She wolfed down the bread and cheese and asked for more gherkins. Dr Deman saw her in his consulting room that same afternoon.

7
Chartres

Madame Picot, like Madame Beck, lived in the old town, that part of Chartres that lies within the city walls. Both women had been left comfortably off by husbands who had also left them comfortable apartments.

Madame Beck and her husband had owned the restaurant beneath their apartment in a picturesque house which stood on the south side of the cathedral close. After her husband's death, Madame Beck had leased out the restaurant. Her continued residence above it made it easy for her to monitor the lessees and ensure that the leasehold conditions were properly met. Much of the rest of her time was spent discussing, in detail, with Madame Picot the domestic affairs of Chartres.

Madame Picot's husband had been a tax consultant. She was richer than Madame Beck but lived in the lower part of town, a less historic, and thus less desirable, area than that of her friend.

'I hear the price of the house in the rue du Lait has doubled again. Such a pity Auguste didn't buy it for you when he could,' was Madame Beck's opening shot when she came to take afternoon tea with her friend that Friday.

'He was concerned about the woodworm, dear. Very practical, was my Auguste. He didn't want me having to worry about repairs when he was gone.' (It was one of Madame Picot's fanciful assertions that her hard-headed late husband was 'psychic' and had successfully predicted the year of his own death.)

Madame Beck's apartment was in the upper storey of one of Chartres' ancient fifteenth-century timbered houses. A popular subject of tourists' photos but known to be the very devil to insure and maintain.

'But a great investment, my dear. Auguste would surely have wanted you to have that. Claude always said, with our house in that position we'd never want for cash. Not that I need it. The interest from the restaurant lease does me very nicely.'

'A biscuit, dear?'

'Thank you, my dear, no. As you know I try to watch my weight.'

Madame Picot, who was inclined to run to fat, bent to caress her elderly Pekinese. 'Who's a sweet girl, then? Show Aunty Louise your new collar. My daughter sent it from Japan. The jewels are real.'

Madame Beck looked down at the little dog with dis-approval. 'They look to me semi-precious.' She did not care for dogs and she had no living children.

'Semi-precious is real, dear. See, this one is garnet.' Madame Picot's plump white hand played with the dog's collar.

Madame Beck's little eyes narrowed. 'Of course they get them cheap over there.'

There was a moment's silence while each friend withdrew to examine her artillery.

Madame Beck decided that the moment had come to apply their knives to weaker victims. 'I saw Professor Jones with that Morel woman this morning. They were going off together, very chummy.'

Madame Picot, less overtly adversarial than her friend, could none the less usually be relied on to rally to a joint attack. 'I wonder what her game is?'

Madame Beck sniffed. 'Money! What else? The man is fool-ish with it. I see him giving it away to the beggars hanging about the close. They should put a stop to it.' Without noticing what she was doing, she reached for a biscuit and then, collecting herself, snapped off a tiny portion. 'I'll just nibble at this corner, if you don't mind.'

Madame Picot smiled. 'Of course, dear. Just as you please. How is the smell from the restaurant?'

Madame Beck, who had been plagued with the output of the extractor fans, which she could not countermand since they were a requirement of EU health-and-safety regulations, gave a thin, pale-lipped smile. 'I am having someone in to estimate for air conditioning. Of course it will be expensive but they say it will solve the problem completely.'

Professor Jones was showing Agnès the papers, or rather he was showing her a portion of the papers, since the bulk of them were stuffed away in cupboards or jammed into drawers where they could not present a face of perpetual reproach.

'I need some help in sorting these.'

He was aware of the debilitating cost of procrastination but lacked the will not to pay it. The papers, many still unattended to since his parents' deaths, exacted from him an almost daily punishing emotional Dane Gold.

Agnès assessed the stacked piles of folders, loose sheets and manila envelopes, which for her harboured no harrowing ghosts. Maybe the professor wanted her to dispose of them? But no, he was talking about which she should put where, so it seemed that reorganization was what was being asked for.

'They're mostly in French so you shouldn't have any trouble.'

Agnès nodded and smiled, and the professor, anxious to get off the topic as soon as possible, offered to make her a cup of tea.

Professor Jones, having taken Agnès her tea and a stale Petit Beurre, left her to commence the Herculean task.

'I'm just off to the shop to get in some soup. Anything I can get you?'

Soup was a disturbing memory. 'No, thank you, Professor.'

It would never have crossed the professor's mind that Agnès could not read. Quite possibly, even had he been aware of this fact, he would still have enlisted her help. That she was unable to fathom what was in the papers did not greatly bother Agnès either. She had not attended to the professor's plans for organizing them into some rational scheme because she had intuited his fundamental terror of the whole enterprise. He was unlikely to be the best judge of how to deal with them.

She began by taking anything which looked like a letter out of its envelope. The envelopes were grey with dust and were the first items to be disposed of. Agnès went to the kitchen and found a refuse sack.

When the professor came back with his soup – one leek and potato, the other mixed vegetable – Agnès said, 'We need some boxes.'

'Boxes?'

'It would help.'

'I wouldn't know what to buy.'

'I'll buy them,' Agnès said. 'It won't cost much.'

Pleased to have another opportunity to offload some money, Professor Jones handed her two fifty-euro notes.

'That's too much, Professor.'

'No, no, take it. Boxes might be pricey.'

Madame Beck, on her way back from Madame Picot's, passed the shop that specialized in fancy stationery and, catching sight of a figure in a blue dress inside, decided that she urgently needed envelopes.

'Good morning. It's Agnès, isn't it?'

Agnès, examining boxes for colour and size, turned and saw

two little pale blue eyes that shifted rapidly from side to side as they took her in.

'Good morning. Madame Beck?'

'That's right. I saw you with Professor Jones this morning.'

'Yes?' Agnès assessed a red box.

'You clean for him?'

'No, Madame.'

Unused to dealing with reticence, Madame Beck paused. 'Of course he would need help living alone. Such a shame about the wife. You know about her?'

'No, Madame.' Agnès picked up a yellow box.

'She ran off and left him.'

Agnès was appraising a bright pink box that she thought might do for photographs.

'Oh, yes,' said Madame Beck. 'Ran off with a Chinky boy who played the fiddle. I saw it all.'

Agnès addressed a passing saleswoman. 'Excuse me. Do these come in any other sizes?'

'You do clean?' asked Madame Beck. It sounded like an accusation.

'Yes, Madame,' Agnès agreed.

The saleswoman, who had gone off to inquire, came back to say that they also did a larger and a smaller version of the pink box.

Madame Beck was suddenly taken with an idea. 'Because I was looking for someone to help me out.'

Agnès removed another box from the top of a pile. She now had too many to carry back to the professor's in one go.

'So,' Madame Beck continued, the unusual resistance giving her an appetite for the chase. 'May I ask you to come round to see me?'

Agnès returned the pink box to the top of the pile and made towards the counter with Madame Beck almost running after her. 'How about tomorrow? I live over "Beck's", our old restaurant, you know, mine and my late husband's, by the cathedral steps.'

'Tomorrow is Saturday, Madame,' Agnès said, presenting the pile of boxes to the girl at the till.

'Oh, I see.' Madame Beck was now seriously ruffled. 'Monday, then. Shall we say ten?'

Agnès had one close friend in Chartres: Terry, the local dog-walker. Terry came from a sprawling Newcastle family, where she had been nurse to five younger male siblings, and the touch of genius which is in us all was in her case for handling dogs.

She had come to France as an au pair to escape her family and had married a much older Frenchman, who, on their wedding night, had sat at the end of the double bed and wept.

'He said, "Oh, Thérèse, *chérie*, I think we have made a terrible mistake,"' Terry had confided in the early days of her friendship with Agnès. 'He was, is, I should say, gay. I was only nineteen and pig ignorant. I was just grateful someone wanted me. I didn't want to look beneath the surface.'

Terry was small and stocky and took some obscure consolation in believing she was ugly.

'But you have such pretty eyes,' Agnès had said during the first days of their acquaintance.

'Eyes only take you so far. I looked like a boy then, which is presumably why he thought he could make a go of it. Poor guy! He tried his best but the wedding night was the biggest flop, if you'll pardon the pun. But we're good friends now. He lives with his boyfriend, Raphael, in Toulouse. I visit them sometimes.'

Ten years on, Terry and Agnès were having supper together at their favourite haunt, the jazz café.

'Why does the old cow want you? That's what I don't get.' Terry speared a plump spear of blanched asparagus.

Agnès shrugged. 'I guess she wants help cleaning.'

'There'll be nothing to do.'

'There's always something to do,' Agnès said. She described a little of her day at Professor Jones's. Only a little, as she didn't want to betray the professor, who, she had grasped, was growing less and less able to handle his own affairs. 'He's lonely.'

Terry, however, didn't want to be diverted. 'He should get a dog. I reckon she wants to check you out. I know her. She's often round assassinating people's characters at Picot's when I collect Piaf.'

Agnès helped herself to a few slices of sausage and some gherkins. The idea of being 'checked out' made her uncomfortable.

'Piaf doesn't like Beck. They're bright, Pekineses. Not my cup of tea, mind you, too yappy, but you have to hand it to them – they're bright. That one is anyway. She's nosy too,' Terry, who, in the days when she had dogs herself, had always had terriers, continued. 'Beck, I mean, not Piaf – though Piaf too come to that. When François and Raphael were staying with me old Beck met us one night when we'd all had a few. She couldn't take her eyes off us after she saw us all holding hands. Raphael kept kissing me and then kissing François. She couldn't work out who was sleeping with who. Mind you, neither could I.'

8

Rouen

Dr Deman was of the opinion that it was counterproductive to refer directly to any 'episode' a patient might have suffered. When Agnès entered his consulting room in the clinic, he gestured towards a comfortable chair.

'Sit, please. You are enjoying our food?'

'Yes.'

Agnès looked around. The room was painted a pale lilac, a colour Dr Deman believed was calming to the nerves. On the wall hung soothing photographs of trees, birds, flowers, a mountain lake and behind his desk what looked like a map of a maze.

'I was wondering,' Dr Deman said, after a pause during which it became clear that Agnès was going to say nothing, 'why you think you are here.'

Agnès' pale tawny eyes opened a little wider. 'Because of the baby.' She looked, he thought, like a starved young lioness.

'The baby?'

'My baby,' Agnès said with some firmness. 'Where is he? He must be hungry.'

'Ah,' said Dr Deman, miserably aware that this was going to be nasty. 'You have a baby?'

'That's why I'm here,' Agnès said.

'Does your baby have a name?'

'But of course. He is called Gabriel.'

Dr Deman wrote the name in the file on his desk and then

appeared to make a further note. In fact what he made was the doodle of a pair of elliptically slanting eyes. It was an image he tended to draw when anxious or distressed.

'Gabriel is the name of an archangel. Did you think an angel was the baby's father, perhaps?'

The tawny eyes fixed him with candid surprise. 'Of course not.'

'So the baby came . . .'

'He was found,' Agnès explained. 'I found him.'

'You found him where?'

'In a basket. In the orchard.'

'Forgive me for asking all these questions, Agnès. But could you tell me when this was?' He glanced at the notes. The child had been born on January 29th.

Agnès' smooth brow knitted. When was it? She couldn't be sure. January the twenty-first, she decided. Yes, that was it. Her son was Aquarius. Born on the cusp.

'Do you know what month it is now?' Dr Deman asked.

Agnès was very surprised to learn that it was late July. She was also alarmed. Gabriel must be very hungry indeed. She must go to find him at once. Efforts to distract or waylay her were wholly unsuccessful. Finally, despite Dr Deman's philosophy, they had to sedate by injection.

'I wonder,' Dr Deman said on the phone to Mother Catherine, 'if it might be possible to invite the man who found her to come to see me. It might help us to establish some reality for Agnès. You have his details?'

Mother Catherine did have his details, though she was not keen to pass them on. Jean Dupère had been something of a nuisance, coming up and pestering them about the girl's progress. More than once, she explained to the doctor, they had had to send him away with a flea in his ear.

Jean Dupère, however, when Dr Deman phoned and explained who he was and what was wanted, said he was more than happy to drive over to St Francis's. He arrived rather early, an elderly, scraggy man, with a moustache, red-veined farmer's cheeks and a prominent Adam's apple, who sat turning his felt hat on his knees as he waited for Dr Deman. But once inside the consulting room he became quite garrulous.

He described the circumstances of his finding the baby and how she came by her name. 'I was out getting in firewood from my neck of the woods and I found her where the morels grow in season. I like morels. Agnès was after the lady saint.'

'How long would you say she had been there?'

'Couldn't be long, doctor, or she would have passed away in that perishing cold. Newborn that day, by my reckoning. I'm no expert, mind, with human births.'

'And you took her to the Sisters when?'

'Next day. I went to report it to the police and they said best to take her there while they made inquiries. They didn't find anything so she stayed there. Seemed best.'

'And you saw her there? You visited?'

Jean Dupère frowned and resumed the turning of his hat. 'I reckon they didn't think I should. I wanted to but –' He shrugged.

'You didn't see her at all as she grew up.'

'Seemed best not to.'

'But you tried.'

'The Mother asked me not to come. Seemed best to do as they said.'

'Did Agnès know that you'd tried to see her?'

'I left it to the Mother. She seemed all right. But –' He hesitated.

From behind his desk, Dr Deman, sensing a revelation, leaned forward encouragingly.

'I found this,' his visitor continued. He produced a matchbox from the pocket of his jacket and handed it across the desk. 'It was in the basket when I found her.'

Dr Deman opened the matchbox and took out a single earring.

'I was going to give it her for a present when she turned sixteen.'

Jean Dupère was not an avaricious man. He came from old farming stock and was cautious and slow. He had not passed on the earring when he took the baby to the Sisters because he had not known what was finally to become of her. If he had not handed it over when it was agreed that the child should remain under their care, it might have been because a small part of him wanted to retain a share in the child's future himself.

The plan to surprise her with the little turquoise drop had evolved in his slow but not unimaginative mind as he sat long evenings in his kitchen alone. He had been abashed – even a little hurt, had he allowed himself to recognize the feeling – by the Sisters' reluctance to allow him to keep in touch with his foundling and was looking forward to a small moment of drama when he turned up with this gift from her past on her sixteenth birthday.

But he was a decent man and not inclined to self-dramatization.

'Maybe best she has it now.'

'If you wish.'

'Can I see her?' The memory of his finding the little girl had, with time, become one of those episodes to which his mind returned with more rather than less wonder. Increasingly, it held for him a mysterious enchantment.

The note of suppressed longing was unmistakable and Dr Deman had his own views about the nature of the Sisters' care.

'Of course. But I plan to say nothing for the time being

about who you are. She's, let us say, she's not been well. We're taking things slowly.'

'Surely.' Jean Dupère's red face had lit up with shy delight. His little Agnès. He was going to see her again at last.

'Little Agnès' was lying on her bed in her white cotton St Francis nightgown. As usual, she was staring into midair, apparently at nothing. She was heavily sedated, as this, to Dr Deman's continuing regret, was the only way they had found to control her efforts to do herself harm.

Jean Dupère looked down at the placid oval face, dressed by a fan of long black hair. She looked like the Sleeping Beauty in the story told him long ago by his grandmother in the red-tiled kitchen which was now his.

'She always like this, Doctor?'

Dr Deman cleared his throat. 'It will – I should say, we hope – it will pass.'

Agnès' rescuer stood there, turning his felt hat in his hand. There had been mental illness, his mother had confided, on his father's side. 'Reckon I'll be off, Doctor.'

'Thank you for coming,' Dr Deman said. He felt depressed by this encounter. Hoping to salvage something from it for them both, he added, 'Why not give her the earring while you're here?'

Dr Deman handed the matchbox to the man beside him, who stood with it unopened in his big red hand and then handed it back again.

'Not much point is there, her being the way she is now. You give it to her, Doctor, when she's ready.' He turned, making to leave the room.

Partly to delay him, Dr Deman said, 'I don't suppose you know what happened to the basket?'

But it was too late. Unwilling that anyone should witness his brimming eyes, Jean Dupère, hastening to the door, failed to hear him.

'The basket?' Mother Catherine asked sharply, when Dr Deman rang her. 'I've really no idea. I imagine we put it with the others in the pantry. I'm sure it's long gone.'

'I just feel anything we can bring to bear on Agnès' history . . .' Dr Deman began to counter and let the sentence trail away, for he found the whole case, and his failure to make any headway with it, dismaying. History appeared to be repeating itself in this poor girl with a peculiar vengeance.

Damn the woman! Damn religion! He tried another tack. 'Do we know who adopted the baby?'

Mother Catherine felt it her place to become trenchant. 'It was all carried out under the strictest protocol. Naturally, we were not informed. I would have thought you would know this, Doctor.'

Dr Deman did know it of course.

9
Chartres

'And then there is the china,' Madame Beck said, indicating a mass of ornaments crowding the mantelshelf in the salon. 'It must be dusted each week and once a month washed. Perhaps you would like me to write this down?'

Agnès said she would remember it. She had appeared on Monday at 10.15 a.m. at Madame Beck's after she had finished at the cathedral.

Madame Beck was waiting for her. 'We said ten, I believe.'

'I'm sorry, Madame. I got delayed.'

Madame Beck had observed Agnès coming out of the South Porch. Her lips pursed, as a fisherman's might when he feels he is about to land a big catch.

'Next time I would be obliged if you would ring me. I might have gone out.'

'I don't have a mobile phone, Madame,' Agnès replied. 'Where would you like me to clean?'

Madame Beck's apartment was carpeted throughout, which could be easily dealt with by vacuuming, but there were a large number of 'knick-knacks', some quite cumbersome. A Breton spinning wheel, for example, and various copper kettles, pots and long-handled warming pans. These, in the days when the restaurant below was still under the Becks' management, had hung on the walls and in the many niches of the restaurant dining room.

The spinning wheel, Agnès was warned, was 'extremely

'fragile'. She must take great care while dusting it. The copper pans required a special polish. And then there was her collection of antique china dolls.

'These are extremely valuable. I would ask you to take most especial care with them. So you'll come tomorrow?' Madame Beck's eyes darted like little wintry blue fish.

Agnès promised that she would come when she had finished her other job. She was careful not to say what that might be.

Agnès had been cleaning the cathedral for about a week when she began to feel that she might have to do something about the Abbé Bernard. In recent months, the Abbé had fallen into the habit of sitting each morning before the figure of the black pear-wood Virgin, with whom he conversed, sometimes loudly, startling the early-morning visitors who had come to the venerated statue expecting to pray in peace and quiet.

Bernard, who had taken his name from the saint of Clairvaux, had entered the priesthood at eighteen. He had worked diligently at school, but for all his application his marks never placed him higher than halfway in the class. Still, everyone agreed he was industrious, honest and, for a boy, very devout.

His father had died when he was just fourteen, and his mother, a woman famed in the community for her piety, was thrilled when he announced his intention to enter the priesthood and began at once to advertise the news at their church.

Bernard's ruling aim in life was to try to make things better for his mother, whose loss of her husband came as a particular blow, since she had also lost Bernard's twin sister at birth. His mother and father had been sweethearts from the ages of thirteen and fourteen respectively. Bernard sometimes wished she would marry again – she was a handsome, big-boned, blonde woman and he had observed men casting approving glances at her. But his mother was determined to remain loyal to her dead husband and sought Bernard's approval for her saintly resolution. 'You would not want me forgetting Papa's memory. Such a good father as he was.'

What could an only son, and surviving child, do but agree? The priesthood was Bernard's compensating gift to her for all that she had lost and undergone. He left the matter of his faith in God's hands.

And until lately God had played fair by not raising any troubling questions about His existence. Then, at 103, the apparently indomitable mother died.

Circumstances had brought Bernard and his mother more than usually close. He had formed his ambitions to fit his mother's for him. It was for her that he had never married (for he would never want her to be bothered by another woman coming first in his affections); he had entered the Church for her, because he wanted her not only to feel proud of him but to be able to boast about him to her friends; he had kept his own friends to a minimum so she should never be neglected on his few holidays.

His mother had been a monumental presence. Now she was gone, and into the great void made by her departure there rode, like the four horsemen of the Apocalypse, anger, terror, confusion and, most deadly, a harrowing despair. Anger that she had abandoned him; terror that without her he would not be able to survive; confusion about the emotions her departure stirred in him; and despair that not only his mother but his God seemed to have deserted him.

Bernard, of course, had a spiritual adviser, Father Dominique, a Benedictine monk of famed theological sophistication. 'Remember our Saviour's words on the cross,' Father Dominique offered when Bernard confided his low spiritual state. '"My God, my God, why hast thou forsaken me?"'

The words did nothing to strengthen Bernard's flagging

spirits. Rather, they had a newly hollow ring to his inner ear. He had accepted them obediently all his adult life as a necessary part of the story of the passion of Christ but he now felt that the so-called Son of God may have been right to ask this question and that it was a question that had not been adequately answered. If He had a father in heaven, then what kind of a father was this to subject a son to a horrible torturous death? Slowly but surely, the thread of belief which Bernard had spun around him all his adult life began to unwind.

Bereft of immediate support, and unwilling to approach the Abbé Paul – whom he had counselled when the dean was still a young man – or the bishop – an upright but emotionally aloof man with an instinctive aversion to anything that smacked of the psychological – Bernard had taken to asking the help of the Blessed Virgin Mary, who was, after all, a woman and a mother. A mother, it seemed to the Abbé Bernard, was more likely to understand his condition than any man.

When Agnès first began to clean, Bernard had been disconcerted by the change in the regime but gradually her studied quiet began to soothe his nerves. He found in Agnès an apparently more willing listener than the Virgin, whose presence had also become a matter of encroaching doubt. As a result, he had taken to buttonholing Agnès and following her about as she mopped, dusted and polished her way round the cathedral.

His anguish went to Agnès' heart, for she knew something of what he was going through. One morning, unable to bear her own reticence a minute longer, she straightened her back from bending to polish the rail before the pear-wood Virgin, and said, 'If God is so good, then why have all these people remembered in this cathedral died for Him? Why would any good person want their loved ones to die?'

Bernard in mid ramble stopped, stared at Agnès and then, to her dismay, began to weep. His mother, his father, Annette, his little twin sister, whom he had never even seen, all gone into the dark and maybe for nothing or to no one. The bleakness of this prospect seemed to him unbearable.

Agnès let him cry for a while and then went over and put a hand on his shoulder. He was considerably shorter than Agnès, which made him seem to her more than ever like a hurt child. 'It is only what I sometimes think. Often I think maybe it is because death is good that God allows it.'

The Abbé Bernard turned upon her beseeching red-rimmed eyes, eyes that, had she been conscious and in Dr Deman's consulting room at the time, might have reminded Agnès of Jean Dupère's. 'You think so?' he asked eagerly.

It was almost a relief to get to Madame Beck's, although Madame Beck did not ask Agnès if she would like a cup of coffee, as her other clients did, or even tell her to take water from the fridge should she need it. Instead, she presented Agnès with a pair of polythene shoe covers.

Agnès knew these from the nearby swimming bath where she went with Terry, and wondered if Madame Beck had gone there especially in order to appropriate them for this purpose. 'No need for those, Madame. I take off my shoes when I clean.'

Madame Beck looked down at Agnès' long brown feet in her red sandals. 'Nevertheless, I would prefer you to use them.'

She showed Agnès into her bedroom, the walls of which were closely hung with pictures of holy saints and photographs of Madame Beck and her departed husband in various attitudes of beaming uxorious delight. A number of antique dolls, with china faces and limbs, lay at the foot of the bed, which was vast and heavily counterpaned. Above the bed there was a Dutch landscape with a windmill worked in coloured wools, which Madame Beck had made while waiting for her husband to propose.

'I would like you to strip the bed, vacuum the mattress and then turn it before putting on the clean linen.'

The linen was pure, Madame Beck explained. The following week she would require Agnès to wash and iron it. She listed a number of other tasks that Agnès was to perform. Agnès listened without comment before setting to work. At the end of the two hours they had agreed on, she found Madame Beck in the kitchen, drinking coffee and listening to her favourite radio programme.

'I can work an extra hour, Madame, or do the rest next time I come.'

'How much have you left to do?'

'The salon is all done. And the bedroom.' The mattress, horsehair, had all but defeated her.

'But the bathroom?' Madame Beck had asked her to clean the grouting in the tiles, for which task an old toothbrush had been provided.

'I've cleaned it, Madame, but for the tiles I'm afraid there was not enough time.'

When she had gone Madame Beck rang Madame Picot. 'She's slow,' she said. 'Didn't do half what I asked her to.'

'Lazy?' Madame Picot was inclined to laziness herself.

'Time will tell,' said Madame Beck with a certain satisfaction. 'For the moment I'll keep her on.'

10

Rouen

Had Dr Deman been married and with a family to go home to, he might have been less preoccupied with his work. As it was, he tended to hang around after his formal working hours, making a nuisance of himself with the cleaners, who had their work cut out already negotiating the piles of papers on all the surfaces of his office, without having to negotiate the office incumbent too. Like many easily abstracted men, Dr Deman entertained the delusion that he was unusually organized.

Occasionally, to get out of the cleaners' hair, and to avoid the trouble of shopping, he took his dinner at the staff canteen. He was enjoying a glass of wine with a good helping of their *porc aux pruneaux* when a couple of nurses sat down at the table next to him. One, whose face was familiar, smiled.

'Good evening, Dr Deman.'

'Good evening, Sara. Late shift?'

'No, we've just come off. And you?'

'I've finished too.'

'Sorry. How rude of me. You know Maddy Fisher? Maddy, Dr Deman.'

Dr Deman was mildly pleased to be introduced to her companion. He had noticed her about – a tall, dark Australian girl, with good bones, who, he surmised, had only lately come to work at the clinic. The two nurses were discussing the Australian girl's recent employment.

'Maddy was working as a nanny before she came here,' Sara explained.

Maddy went on to describe how she had filled in as a nanny after leaving her husband, who, in a fit of romantic optimism, she had married following a brief affair. 'It was a mistake – we both agreed. He's a nice guy but I wasn't ready for it. Still, it means I can work here.'

'Before she came here she was the nanny to Kelly Moonshine,' Sara confided.

Dr Deman, who did not follow popular music trends, hadn't the faintest idea of the significance of this name but he nodded knowingly. He was enjoying the company of Sara's friend.

'The boy was adopted,' Maddy continued. 'She's quite a bit older than him so they couldn't have kids themselves. Shall we get some more wine?'

Dr Deman, who was about to fetch a plate of cheese, suggested that he get a bottle for the three of them.

'How old was the child?' he asked, when he returned with a bottle of the best Bordeaux the canteen rose to.

'Nearly eight months when I left. Handsome kid. She's Colombian and if looks were all he could have been her own flesh and blood.'

Dr Deman had studied Agnès' face and features, and it seemed to him that she surely had some Algerian or gypsy blood in her. 'Really? You don't know where they, er, got the child?'

'I gather they used a backhander to get him from somewhere local. We weren't supposed to know all that but, you know, people talk.'

Sara said, 'That's awful.' Dr Deman poured Maddy more wine.

'Well, money no object, you know how it is with the rich. They were OK. It wasn't a bad job. Sweet little boy and it's a lovely house. A small château it was once. But, you know, I'm a nurse, not a nanny.'

Dr Deman cut himself a considered slice of Reblochon. 'Where is the house exactly?' he asked.

The six-month lapse of time when a child could be legally returned to the birth mother had long passed. But Dr Deman nevertheless drove the short distance to a large, isolated house in the countryside, easily found from Maddy's description, and spent some time patrolling its surrounds.

On one such patrol, he met a young blonde woman with a small child in a pushchair. Dr Deman smiled at the baby, who, with a child's quick instinct, sensed an ally and returned a radiant toothless beam.

'What a charming little boy.'

The young woman stopped and eyed him. Dr Deman was an attractive man and when he cared to he could rise to being quite charming himself. 'He's not mine. I'm the nanny.'

'How old?'

'Eight months, coming up to nine.'

'The parents must be proud. He's a lovely child.'

The nanny sized up her interlocutor. 'They don't see much of him, to tell you the truth. Don't know why they bothered to adopt.'

'He's adopted?'

'She's too old for kids. They wanted one that was, you know, kind of coffee-coloured, the kind they'd make if they could make their own.'

Dr Deman tried to repress any sign of his instinctive repugnance at her tone. 'Not so easy to find a child that fills that bill.'

The nanny became confiding. 'Rumour is they slipped money to some local nursing home.'

Dr Deman was not quick enough to wholly master his

response, and the woman, aware of something amiss, became alarmed. 'You a reporter? Because if so I said nothing.'

'Not at all. I was merely interested.' He made a polite farewell.

Later he could not have said what brought him to do this but perhaps for lack of any alternative way of handling this potentially disturbing information he wrote the address down in Agnès' file.

Chartres

Although Agnès could neither read nor write, she had a marked numerical ability. In the class for backward children at the local school near the convent, as with all the other slow learners, she was largely given up on, until an enterprising student teacher noticed her. She had observed the small girl concentratedly counting out tiddly-winks and placing the different colours in a series of complex designs. The student, who was to become the kind of teacher with ambitions for her pupils, took to the pretty girl with the appealing eyes and made the child her special project.

As a result Agnès could read ten- or even twelve-figure numbers, including those with decimal points, and could add, subtract and multiply very efficiently in her head. She could also do long division and plot a graph. Perhaps she could also do algebra, though the student teacher had left before her young student's talent could be further tried.

Agnès began her assault on the professor's papers by sorting the letters according to date. When the professor put his head round the door a little later she inquired, 'Have you any other letters?' She had divined the contents of the drawers.

By the end of two weeks, seventy-five years' worth of letters had been neatly clipped together according to the year, filed in transparent folders and placed in three yellow boxes, each of which was labelled with the dates of the correspondence. The boxes, she decided, would fit on the shelf at the top of the wardrobe.

'I think you could store them in there, Professor. I've cleaned it out.' Agnès indicated a number of plastic bags filled with clothes. 'I don't think we should bother with the charity shops.'

'How about the beggars by the cathedral?'

Agnès, who knew several of the beggars by name and was aware that even they might turn up their noses at the professor's matted jerseys, said she could try but she thought that maybe the clothes were best thrown out.

Before she left, the professor insisted on giving her a glass of white wine.

'I'm sorry it isn't cold – seems to be something wrong with the fridge. God knows where my wine glasses have gone. Frankly, I'm incredulous, Agnès. However did you manage all this?'

Agnès accepted the tumbler of wine and some stale salted biscuits from a chipped plate with 'Welcome to Aberystwyth' still just discernible to those who could read. 'It's easier when it's not your own stuff.' She tried to resist her urge to wipe over the glass, which was bleared with grease. Failing, she gave the lip a surreptitious scrub with her overall.

'But still, you're a genius. When can you start on the rest?'

'I'll come tomorrow morning if you like when I've finished at the cathedral.'

The Abbé Bernard was not merely losing his faith; he appeared to be losing his wits as well, and there was only so much that she could take, Agnès decided, of his mounting distress. She was an early riser, so in order to limit the time she would be exposed to his misery she must get there well before he was likely to arrive.

In any case, she loved the cathedral in its state of desertion, the only movement within its great space her own, or the shadowy flight of the odd sparrow. The tremendous height of the ceilings, the noble lofty columns – like lichen-covered trees – the succession of soaring arches, affected her profoundly and the jewelled brilliance of the stained glass, re-created in the ephemeral butterflies of light which played over the grey stone, lifted and brightened her darker thoughts.

Because of the restoration programme, the whole of the choir was closed off and half of the ambulatory behind. A complex of scaffolding had been assembled for the work on the ceiling plaster. The day after she had completed the filing of the professor's letters, Agnès entered the cathedral to find she was not alone. A man was there. A man with an open knife in his hand, sitting bold as brass on the marble dais by the silver altar, right beside the sign that forbade people to mount it.

She stopped dead and a bolt of fear flashed down her sternum. 'What are you doing here?'

The man put down the knife and looked at her for some seconds before replying.

'You're the cleaner. I've seen you.'

'Where?' The alarm flashed down her sternum again.

For answer, the man jerked his chin towards the scaffolding. 'Up there you can see most things.'

'You're one of the workmen?'

'I'm part of the team.'

'I see.'

'You always get here early?'

Habit made her cautious. 'Now and then.'

'We're behind. Restoration works are always behind so I'm going to be in early from now on. Get the benefit of the morning light before autumn.'

'I see,' Agnès said again. As if that was sufficient excuse to allow him to penetrate her sanctuary at this hour.

The man smiled. He had a long lean face, of a slightly mournful cast until he smiled. 'I'm Alain.'

56

'I'm Agnès.'

'That's a pretty name.'

Agnès, embarrassed, nodded.

'Would you like some sausage? I was having a spot of breakfast.'

'I've eaten.'

The man smiled again. 'I don't plan to get in your hair.'

'It's none of my business.'

'You needn't fret. I'm not chatty myself.'

'Nor me,' Agnès said, further embarrassed at being read.

'I can see that. I'm on your patch. But don't worry, there's space enough for the two of us.'

Agnès went to find her cleaning materials. When she came back there was no one on the dais, but she could hear whistling from above.

When the Abbé Bernard arrived, Agnès was about to leave.

'Off already, Agnès?'

'I've finished the work for today, Father.'

The Abbé Bernard scrabbled at her forearm. 'I dreamed last night that my mother was drowning in a duck pond. Mud, thick mud. Maybe worse. Maybe . . . and I stood there watching. I did nothing to save her.'

'It's a dream, Father. It happens when people die.'

The Abbé Bernard looked at her with scared exhausted eyes. 'Should I be feeling guilty?'

Agnès gently detached his hand from her sleeve. 'That happens too, Father, when people die. You will get used to it.'

12

Chartres

Professor Jones had been utterly absorbed since he opened the yellow box on which Agnès had stuck a label bearing the dates 1935–1955. There, before his eyes, lay the first twenty years of his life, neatly assembled in transparent folders. He took out the top letter, which was written in blue ink on blue-lined paper.

'My dear Bronwen,' the professor read. 'The news of little Owen's timely arrival last evening brought us the greatest joy.'

The professor turned the page to see who had written to his mother to celebrate his birth. He read the signature in the clear cursive hand: 'Mother'.

Nana. His Nana with whom he had gone to stay as a little boy. 'Da and I are so thrilled,' he read on. 'We shall be making the journey, God willing, to see you all as soon as you tell us to come. Meantime I am knitting away in the blue wool. Annie has taken back the pink I got in, in case, though we all said it would be a boy and praise the Lord he is.'

The professor's eyes began to prick. Days of heavy scones, thick with cream and running with blackcurrant jam, a pony which bit him with big yellow teeth when he tried to feed it a carrot, rain on warm grass wetting his socks, a cut foot from a broken bottle in a rock pool, sardine sandwiches, sand in his socks, roly-poly down a hillside – the revenant years began to fill out as he read.

Agnès had not been able to follow a strict system. She had put together all the letters which looked as if they came from the same hand in the order of their date. On the few occasions when there was no date (luckily the professor's correspondents tended not to depart from the correct etiquette of letter-writing), she appended them, clipped together, to the back.

Nana Williams had always followed the proper forms so every letter written, either to her daughter or, later, to her grandson, was there filed in chronological order.

'My dear Owen,' he read. 'Here is a ten-shilling postal order for your birthday. Grandda and I hope you will buy something for the train set. Grandda suggests maybe a turntable or some signals. We hope you will soon be coming on the big train to Aberystwyth to see us. Phoebe' – their black-and-white cat, Owen Jones, alone on his single divan in the faraway town of Chartres, remembered – 'is looking forward to seeing you.'

'She's a cow,' Terry said categorically. 'I can't think what possessed you to take her on. You should get out while you can.'

She and Agnès had been for their weekly swim. Agnès, naked, was rubbing herself down with a towel. 'It's work.'

'Do you need it? You never spend a sou as far as I can see. What are you saving for?'

But if Agnès was saving for anything she didn't say.

'I bet the pay's really mean,' Terry, slightly sulky, said. Like many apparently well-intentioned people, she was prone to take offence when her advice went unheeded. Looking at Agnès' naked body, she relented. 'Why don't you pose some more for old Robert? He pays well, doesn't he?'

Agnès shrugged. 'I do but –'

'Is he a lecher?'

'Not really. It's more . . .' But she didn't complete the sentence because Terry would not understand. Sitting so still for hours, with or without her clothes, brought on dark thoughts.

'How many jobs have you got now, anyway?'

Agnès collected her thoughts. 'My old regulars, the Duchamps, the Poitiers and there's still Madame Badon. Then there's the cathedral and now Madame Beck.'

'And the professor.'

'He's not "cleaning".'

'I don't know what you'd call it, then,' said Terry, who had seen the plastic bags stuffed with the contents of the professor's wardrobe. 'How much do you charge these days?'

'Twelve to fifteen euros. Depends when I took them on.' The truth was Agnès operated a sliding scale. The Poitiers, with five kids, could not afford more than ten euros an hour and even then she sometimes waited a week or so before being paid.

'I hope you've made old Beck pay top rate.'

Agnès, who had already agreed, without demur, to Madame Beck's proposed rate of ten euros an hour, said that she had.

'How much you charging the professor?'

'I don't know,' Agnès admitted. 'We haven't discussed it yet.'

When Agnès got to the professor's apartment, she found the yellow boxes on the floor where she had left them.

'I've been reading through,' the professor confessed. 'Things I'd quite forgotten. People too. It's amazing what one forgets.'

Agnès, who felt it might be a relief to forget, nodded. 'We'll leave them there for the moment, then. Should I get on?'

'Do. Do.' The professor went back to perusing two letters, each with a Scottie dog embellishing a corner, that he had received from Lorraine Partridge, a girl he had met at university. She'd had thick brown wavy hair, he recalled. And a light blue bra. He'd once got to the bra, after some effort and a lot of courage, but had not managed to unhook it, though with hindsight perhaps she was less unwilling that he should undo it than he had understood at the time. The professor sighed. So many wasted opportunities.

Agnès had determined that today was the day to begin to tackle the photographs. These she had amassed from a variety of hiding-places – envelopes, notebooks, old albums with black-and-white childhood snaps (taken, in fact, by the professor himself with a Brownie camera given to him by Nana and Grandda) – and arranged in piles in the study. It would be easier for her to order these than the letters since it involved no reading. Some, obligingly, had dates on the back in faded ink or pencil. But many Agnès could group by studying the characters.

There was the white-haired old couple who appeared first with a well-cocooned baby on the woman's lap, a baby that over a period of time translated itself into a youthful professor, first in long shorts and round spectacles, later into a youth in long trousers and a bad case of acne. From a picture taken at a beach – of the white-haired woman, a younger woman who looked like a daughter and the unmistakable young professor with plump bare legs and a shrimping net – Agnès deduced that a number of tiny black-and-white photos with crimped edges were of the same beach and thus belonged in the section for the old people.

As she was arranging these on the professor's desk, the professor himself came in.

'My God. St Govan's Beach. Now that truly takes me back.' He began to shuffle through the pile and picked out one of the photos of the white-haired woman. 'That's my grandmother, Nana, we called her. My mother's mother. She was, oh, would you know what I mean by archetypal, Agnès? She was like a grandmother in a story-book – always baking something, always kind.' She had smelled of Coty's talcum powder. Talcum in a dark pink canister with gold writing on it. Once, before they had had to leave, he had sneaked into her bedroom and found the tin and had sprinkled it on his stomach to remember her by. His parents had complained of the smell in the car all the way home. 'Do you use talcum powder, Agnès?'

Agnès shook her head.

'I expect your mum did, though. Look, that's my mother. My God, but she looks young.' He held out a photo of a serious-looking young woman with long, dark, waved hair wearing a waisted suit and a jaunty little hat set slantwise. 'She looks like the heroine of a war movie. She might have been too. My father had just missed being done in at Dunkirk.'

Agnès said, 'Maybe we shouldn't file these away. Maybe we could make something with them.'

'How do you mean?'

'On the wall,' Agnès said, looking at the dingy paper which contributed to the general pervading gloom of the professor's study. 'We could put your family pictures up there.'

Agnès returned to the stationers, where she bought three rolls of paper on which pictures and photographs could be tastefully stuck to form a collage. They spent the afternoon together making up a sheet celebrating Nana and Grandda.

'That's Grandda.' A man in a beret wheeling a wheelbarrow. 'That's me in the wheelbarrow. He loved sweet peas, Grandda. I used to give him the seeds for his birthday.' In a large packet, with pictures of the flowers they would become. Pink, mauve, blue and dark crimson flowers, which bloomed to give the sweetest scent. The professor, who could no longer smell any living flower, smelled again the heavenly scents of childhood.

The bells of the cathedral chimed for vespers. 'I'll have to leave soon, Professor,' Agnès said.

13

Chartres

The bells that Agnès heard that summer evening from Professor Jones's apartment were the same bells that she had heard when she arrived, twenty years earlier, and friendless, in Chartres. She had come, mostly on foot, sometimes accepting lifts from lorries, once from a couple who had seemed kindly enough, until at a petrol station the man had scuttled a hand up her skirt and she had had to make hurried excuses and leave. The lorry drivers were more decent. Generally, they offered her a piece of their cheese and baguette or a drink of their wine and told her how lucky she was that she was in their cab and not with some of the other fellows they could name.

The latest of these lifts dropped her one evening at the turn-off from the Le Mans road. At the first crossroads she heard the bells.

Like the pilgrims of former times, she walked the last part of the way, following, as they had done, the twin compass points of the spires. And if, thanks to the lorry drivers' decency, she was not as weary and footsore as the pilgrims, she was perhaps more heart sore. She could not have put into words what she was searching for but a spy-hole into her heart would have revealed that it was a safe haven she craved.

Her first real sight of the cathedral came as she was walking up the rue de l'Horloge, where she was met by the face of the sixteenth-century clock whose forty-eight wavering gold rays in the figure of the sun mark the passage of each half-hour. To her left a rain-drenched statue of a tall woman with long hair gleamed in the rays of the clock's real-life counterpart as it began its long summer descent below the horizon.

Agnès was used to the cathedrals at Evreux and Rouen. Sister Laurence had often contrived to take her to the cathedral at Evreux, and later she had occasionally gone to mass in Rouen with some of the more devout nurses at St Francis's. The lofty grandeur of these edifices promised prospects less alarming than those offered by the majority of humankind. And the expression on the face of the long-haired statue was sympathetic. Agnès climbed the steps to the porch and entered through the double doors.

What met her eye was a sight she was later to say that she hoped she would see as she was dying. The dazzling darkness was transpierced by a panoply of jewelled light. Before and, turning around, behind her, in the dim, high amplitude she saw the rose windows of the South and North Transepts, where brilliants of ruby, sapphire, emerald and gold traced diamonds, circles, squares and ovals, enclosing the forms of marvellous beings: angels, prophets, kings and queens, the Mother of the Mother of God and the Mother of God herself, each bearing in her arms her holy child.

These astonishing wonders were outstripped in their beauty only by the extraordinary lapis-blue of the Western Rose, which, now illumined by the light of the setting sun, seemed to offer a foretaste of a heaven she knew she would never see.

The service of vespers was starting. The priest had invited God to come to his aid and the congregation had echoed him, 'Lord, come quickly to help me.'

The sentiment exactly matched Agnès' need. She had been adrift for four months. She was weary, very weary. She would cast her lot there in Chartres and live, if she could, with whatever returns that might bring her.

*

The immediate returns to Agnès of that first day in Chartres were unpromising. Apart from some bread and a morsel of pâté and half a tomato, courtesy of the last lorry driver, Agnès had not eaten for twenty-four hours. She had a little money left from her last job, as a dishwasher, enough for a bottle of water and a baguette. That was it. There was certainly not enough for a room for the night.

Agnès walked about Chartres waiting for people to retire to bed. She lingered too long near the tables of an outdoor restaurant, hoping to forage some uneaten food, so that the manager, observing her, told her to move on. She tried asking at other restaurants if they needed any help with washing up. But all the answers were negative save for that of one man, who invited her into the kitchen and then pushed her against a fridge door and shoved his tongue into her mouth. Finally, depressed and exhausted, she salvaged some rotting peppers and a half-eaten croissant from the floor of the covered market.

As night was falling, she made her way back up towards the cathedral, whose majestic shape in the departing light seemed to offer a harbour of consolation. On the North Porch, she discovered a niche between the central and right-hand doors, and there she covered herself with a heavy coat, which smelled of wood smoke, and curled up like a cat between the strong arms of the cathedral's pillars. For the first time for many months, she slept a sleep free of marauding dreams.

Dawn breaking through her closed eyelids brought awareness of the stiffness of a night spent sleeping on stone and the sharp returning pangs of the cruel hounds of anxiety. But, on sitting up and putting her hands for warmth into the capacious pockets of the coat (for the mornings that summer were chilly), Agnès found to her surprise a ten-franc note. Unaware that the young Abbé Paul had tucked it there as she slept, she felt that it was some sort of sign left to her by the coat's ghostly owner.

The thought gave a fillip to her spirits. She had passed a small, unassuming café near the market the previous evening. She would go there, buy a coffee and use the *toilette* to wash herself and comb her hair.

The café still served coffee in the old way, in bowls, and the warmth of the china under her cupped fingers was a further source of comfort. With a fresh face, clean hands, tidy hair and the good-tasting caffeine inside her, Agnès felt she could take on the day.

A courageous outlook will often attract its own rewards. The café proprietor had been taken to hospital for an emergency hysterectomy, the young woman who served Agnès her coffee confided. She couldn't, the young woman admitted, complain. It was an emergency, after all, not Madame's fault, she wasn't blaming her, the bleeding had been terrible – but it meant she herself was not going to be able to take her holiday with her boyfriend, which was pissing him off no end. But what could she do? There was no chance of getting anyone else to run the place at such short notice.

Within half an hour Agnès was behind the counter being shown, by Christelle, the confiding waitress, how the till worked, told where the bread and pastries came from and whom to ring if they were late. She was introduced to Aziz the cook and Nini, who did the dishes and cleaned.

'The only thing,' Agnès said, 'is my clothes are being sent on so I've nothing to wear. And with my place falling through' – she had invented a domestic situation which had turned out badly – 'I've nowhere to sleep.'

Christelle said that was all right, Agnès could sleep at her place while she was away. She wasn't as skinny as Agnès, worse luck, but she could let her have some clothes as long as Agnès didn't mind them hanging off her a bit.

Agnès didn't mind. She spent the next night on Christelle's

sofa after a meal cooked by Christelle's boyfriend, who was full of gratitude that thanks to Agnès his holiday dreams had not been dashed.

When Christelle returned from her holiday, very brown and her low-cut t-shirt even tighter across her magnificent breasts, she announced that Madame had asked to see Agnès.

'What does she want?' The hounds of anxiety, temporarily in abeyance, came snuffing round again.

'Oh, just to thank you, I think. You've run the place beautifully. Loads of regulars said.'

Madame was as good as Christelle's word. 'I can't keep you on in Christelle's position, obviously, but I have to take it easy for some weeks so if you wouldn't mind helping us out?'

Among the regulars enthusiastic about Agnès was Robert Clément. In fact, it was chiefly his words of praise for Agnès' competence which had secured her the further employment. Madame had a soft spot for Robert, who had charmed her into letting him use the café to hang his paintings with a commission of a mere five per cent.

'You ever modelled?' he asked one morning as Agnès served his bowl of coffee. 'For an artist, I mean, not magazines.'

'No.'

'Like to try? I'll pay double what you get here.'

Agnès smiled and shook her head but on his third time of asking she said, 'What would I have to do?'

'Nothing. Just sit. You can keep your clothes on if you prefer.'

But Agnès was willing to sit without as well as with clothes. The café work became permanent; various other odd jobs began to come her way. After some months, she found she had developed a life, of sorts, in Chartres.

14

Rouen

The news of the attack reached Dr Deman through the most mundane and yet also in a sense the most unlikely of sources, the local regional paper. Dr Deman read *Le Monde*. He was by no means a regular reader of the local rag. He happened on it by chance, left in his outpatient waiting room, and only as he was about to chuck it in the waste bin did he notice the headline.

NANNY IN CHARGE OF POP STAR'S BABY STABBED!

The angry black letters sounded a warning note in his memory, which was only strengthened when he examined the photo of the victim, a young, long-haired blonde.

'Yesterday afternoon,' the newspaper report excitedly ran, '23-year-old Michelle Boyet was out with her charge, nine-month-old Caspar Louis Bonaparte Howell, son of the singer Kelly Moonshine and her fiancé, the property developer Jeff Howell. An unknown assailant surprised Mademoiselle Boyet from behind and stabbed her repeatedly in the back. An attempt by the assailant to remove the child was thwarted by François Chicot, the driver of a passing van, who reported that the attacker's face and neck were swathed in "a black scarf" but claimed that it "looked like a young woman". Mademoiselle Moonshine and Mr Howell hurried from Paris, where the singer was recording. Baby Caspar escaped unharmed. Mademoiselle Boyet is in hospital, where her condition is said to be "critical".'

A white fear prickled across Dr Deman's stomach. From his locked cabinet he picked out Agnès' file and read the last entry.

'Still refusing to believe that her baby has gone. Seems calmer, however. Have recommended continuing with the walking.'

Beneath this entry, he saw the address he had so thoughtlessly written in the file.

It was about eight, maybe ten kilometres away, an easy enough walk from the clinic by someone sufficiently determined. But how could Agnès possibly have read her file? The cabinet was kept locked and the key was on the ring in his own pocket. No, this was sheer paranoia. Agnès was too passive, too docile, to have done this thing. There was no way she could possibly have found the address. Also, thank God, he suddenly remembered, she couldn't read.

But, nevertheless, a few days later he summoned Agnès to his office. She sat there, as usual, her face impassive, waiting for his questions.

'How are you today, Agnès?'

'Very well, thank you, Doctor.'

'Still sleeping better?'

'Yes, thank you, Doctor.'

'And how are the walks going?'

'Very nice, thank you, Doctor.'

'You walk far, do you, Agnès?'

But to this Agnès made no answer. She just gave one of her habitual smiles.

Perhaps because of the suspicion he was trying to suppress the smile looked to Dr Deman today slightly sinister. Without quite meaning to, or rather without consciously forming the intent, he said, 'Agnès, a young woman was attacked last week with a knife. I don't suppose you know anything about it?'

Agnès sat there, the smile still on her face. Dr Deman produced the paper and held it out quite pointlessly, since Agnès could not read. 'Here. The woman was out with a baby. Her charge. She's a nanny. Not the mother of the child.'

To his dismay two great tears began to roll down Agnès' thin cheeks. 'He is my baby.'

'Agnès, did you attack this young woman? Please consider your answer carefully because if you tell me that you did I am bound to report it.'

There was no time for him to pray that she would keep silent. 'He is my baby,' Agnès repeated. 'She had my baby.'

Nothing so dreadful had ever before happened to Denis Deman.

'He is not your baby, Agnès,' he pursued weakly. 'That baby is called Louis, I mean Caspar.' It crossed his mind that Caspar Louis Bonaparte was a terrible conjunction of names.

Agnès stared at him in wonderment. 'He is Gabriel.'

'No, Agnès,' Dr Deman was almost crying himself, so furious was he with himself for allowing this catastrophe to have occurred. 'Not Gabriel. Caspar, Caspar, Caspar. He is not your son.'

He was by no means a bad man. Indeed, he was, by and large, a good man and a conscientious doctor. But a part of him was now concerned that his carefully prepared paper on the re-visioning of psychotic care through diet, air, rest and gentle exercise would be laughed to scorn once word about the consequences of his treatment got out.

'He is my son,' Agnès said simply. 'He was waiting for me.'

The report of the psychiatrist appointed by the court, after extensive police questioning, confirmed that Agnès was of unsound mind. She could not be safely permitted to continue at the clinic under Dr Deman's care. Although nothing concrete had been found to connect her to the assault, patently she was a danger. A danger to herself and, quite possibly, to others.

Dr Deman saw her once before she was taken to the psychiatric hospital where she was to be detained. He had set himself two tasks and the first was to apologize. 'Agnès, forgive me. If I had been more watchful this would never have happened.'

Agnès, now heavily sedated again, merely looked at him with dulled leonine eyes.

But there was a further torture Dr Deman had prescribed himself. 'Agnès, can you tell me. Where did you get the address?'

Silence.

'Agnès, was it from me? Was it from your file you got it?'

But for all his stricken pleas he could get nothing out of her and he left, more sick at heart than he could remember, before Agnès was taken off to a secure hospital in Le Mans.

15

Chartres

Agnès had come to expect to find Alain somewhere in the cathedral when she arrived there to clean. At whatever hour she came through the North Door he seemed to be before her, his presence signalled by cheerful whistling or humming. She tried a couple of times to beat him there, but even at 5 a.m. as she entered she heard the now-familiar sound of his whistle. He appeared to have taken to heart his pledge to keep out of her hair. A couple of times she saw his shadow reflected in the arches above the ambulatory, alongside the white overalls of his later-arriving mates. But she didn't for some while re-encounter his solid person.

The effect of this was to make her curious. She almost regretted his reticence now it was so readily granted. So it was not entirely an unwelcome surprise to find him once again sitting on the dais of the silver altar when she arrived one Friday at her usual hour of 6 a.m.

'You've caught me at breakfast again. Want some sausage?'

Agnès shook her head.

'Well, it's here if you change your mind.'

'You get here early,' Agnès suggested. For her the remark was a bold one and she blushed.

'I sleep here.'

'In the cathedral?'

'I have a sleeping bag up there.' His expression reflected her solemn one for a moment and then broke into a grin. His slightly pointed eye-teeth gave him the look of some feral animal. 'I'm teasing. I've a little room at the Hôtellerie Saint-Yves. I'm a lark like you, and like you I like the cathedral to myself.'

'I'm sorry if I interrupt your peace,' Agnès said.

Alain stopped smiling and looked at her. 'Have some sausage. It's excellent. I get it from the stall in the market. And there's wine. Or coffee. I bring a thermos. It saves going up and down.'

'OK. Thank you.' She accepted a couple of slices of sausage cut expertly with his penknife. 'What do you do up there?'

'We're cleaning back to the original thirteenth-century surface, where it still holds. A surprising amount does, maybe eighty per cent in the ambulatory. Where there are gaps we restore.'

'How is it done?'

'The restoration or the cleaning?'

'I suppose I meant the cleaning.'

'You really want to know? Or are you being polite?'

'No.'

'With patience, mainly. First of all we vacuum off the accumulated grime. Most of that comes from centuries of candle smoke. Then we apply chemical compresses to lift off the more engrained dirt and the grease. There's a lot of that. Then there's a further cleaning process at the micro level, a sort of gentle abrasive technique, not unlike what fashionable women have done to their skin, I hear. Probably not unlike what you do for floors. Just a bit more refined.'

'I don't "do" anything.'

'You clean.'

'That's not important.'

'Cleaning is important.'

'Not the kind I do.'

He looked at her again. 'Everything that is done well is

important. That's the basis of all this here. All this' – he waved his arms like a conductor energetically leading an orchestra to a final crescendo – 'was built by people who believed that they worked for the glory not of themselves but of God. Or the Mother of God, I should say.'

'I like cleaning it,' Agnès allowed.

'So do I. So, we're colleagues. Both cleaners if not for the Mother of God at least for her finest establishment on this earth.'

'Today's the day I clean the labyrinth,' Agnès said, emboldened.

He jumped up. 'I know. Victor came in last night to clear the chairs. He's taking his mother to Paris this morning to the heart clinic.'

They walked down the nave and then stood, side by side, looking down at the strange old design.

Alain said, 'Odd thing, isn't it, to find in a church?'

'I like the pattern.'

'Maybe the neural pattern of the brain.'

'Really?'

'It's as good a guess as any. It's the pattern that makes it fit in here. If you look about it's all circles and squares, octagons and pentagons, diamonds and triangles. And crosses of course. But crosses are not just crucifixes. They're axes.' He crossed his forefingers and she noticed again his hands. Workman's hands.

'Yes,' she said. 'The windows too.'

'Well, see,' Alain said, 'look around you. It's all shapes. Look at those columns – they alternate, see, some octagonal, the others round. All the proportions here are based on geometric principles but it's just that bit enough off centre to be natural – which is why the whole effect feels so immediately satisfying. Our faculties sense it subliminally before we consciously register it. The master builders who were in charge would have been skilled geometers as well as architects.'

Agnès looked down the empty nave at the grey-green columns rising like a regulated avenue of sturdy ancient trees to a heaven of cross-ribbed vaults above. And then down at the oddly compelling pattern on the floor.

'With so much to look up at, it's funny that for this you have to look down.'

Again he looked at her, but this time with a face that spoke admiration. 'That's a very shrewd observation. I'd not thought of it. And believe me I've thought a good deal about this labyrinth.'

'I was told it was a maze.'

'No. A maze has deliberate tricks in it. False trails. Dead ends. This is a labyrinth because there is only one path. A long and complicated one but only one.'

'Why is it here?'

'Maybe because of what you say. To make sure among all this exalted stuff we also keep our feet on the ground. Who knows? No one does, really. Of course there are theories, most of them guesswork. Half of them crazy. You know the story?'

The door through from the West Portal creaked, heralding the arrival of the Abbé Bernard.

Alain winked at Agnès. 'Better get back to work. See you around.'

The Abbé Bernard had been increasingly plagued by bad dreams which woke him early each morning. Sometimes he awoke in tears. In all cases, he knew the dreams had been about his mother. Once she came as a great tabby cat with cruel claws and draggled, matted, wet fur. Once as he had known her when he was a boy, in a hat dressed with blue flowers, a hat which had quite left his conscious memory. More than once he had learned to his horror that she was not dead at all, and had never been, but was trapped in her coffin underground. His nights were made hellish by her sepulchral calls.

He was very glad to see Agnès in her yellow turban headscarf and leaf-green skirt.

'Early bird, eh, Agnès?' The Abbé Bernard gave what he imagined to be a jaunty laugh.

Agnès smiled acknowledgement. She did not want to admit that she was in fact later than usual lest he come in earlier to find her.

'I wonder,' said the Abbé Bernard, 'if I might confide to you a dream I had last night. I was in a train . . .'

Madame Beck watched Agnès leave the cathedral by the South Porch with the Abbé Bernard. The silly old fool was clutching her arm, almost as if they were familiar friends. When Madame Picot called round for tea, this being Madame Beck's week to host this ritual, Madame Beck said, 'Is it right, that girl cleaning the cathedral? She never goes to mass. Bernadette was a regular attender.'

Madame Picot, who was not much of an attender herself, sighed and remarked that this was the way the world was going. Young people, she attempted to expound . . . But she was not allowed to complete her wisdoms on the mores of the young.

'All the more reason for the Church to set a good example. There are plenty of good Christian women who would be glad to do that job. I wouldn't mind betting that missy there is a Muslim. She has the look.'

'But what can you do about it, dear?' Madame Picot picked out the least stale-looking biscuit from the plate which her hostess had provided. She much preferred it when Louise came over to hers. Her tea was better than Louise's – her daughter sent her English leaf tea from her London visits – and she didn't have to leave Piaf, who sometimes expressed her displeasure by dragging her nails on the Persian carpet. 'I mean, you weren't thinking of managing the cleaning yourself, were you, dear?'

'Don't be absurd, Jeanette. Of course, I don't mean myself. I might have a word with Father Paul, or the Bishop. Father Bernard is going soft in the head. I wouldn't be surprised if she doesn't set her cap at him along with Professor Jones. Men are idiots at that age. A nod and a wink from anything in a skirt and they lose their heads.'

Naturally, she was not thinking of her own late husband.

16

Chartres

Professor Jones was utterly absorbed in reacquainting himself with his childhood. More than his childhood – his whole past life.

Agnès had filled several pages of the sticky paper with photographs from the collection: his grandparents, parents, uncles, aunts and cousins, and then later his first schooldays. Various photos of animals had also been found and stuck on a sheet of their own: Phoebe, Nana and Grandpa's black-and-white cat, his twin cousins' dogs, Pitch and Pine, his own pair of budgerigars, Salt and Pepper, a rabbit belonging to his other cousin Jane, called Muffet – or maybe it was Moppet? – and a mysterious parrot whose place in his former life remained an obstinate blank.

He was as sure as he could be that he had never owned a parrot but neither could he connect it with any other member of his family.

The scenes stirred his memory as profoundly as a madeleine dipped in linden tea, as he put it to Agnès one afternoon. 'I don't know if you've read any Proust, Agnès?'

Agnès said that she had not.

'I've never cared for him much but you know this memory business he went on about has something in it. He dipped a cake, a madeleine actually, you know those little' – Agnès nodded to indicate that she did – 'well, he dipped one into his tea one day, with his mother I think it was, which maybe accounts for it, because suddenly all his childhood came flooding back. Well, not all, or not at once – bits of it. Waiting for his mother to come and kiss him at night, as far as I remember. It's a long time since I read it, if I did read it at all. I couldn't have read it all, I think – maybe the first two volumes. But the thing is it was all there, all his past, just waiting for the right prompt. I suppose pictures are even more of a prompt than cake.'

Agnès said she supposed they might be. She agreed that certain tastes did bring back memories and went on defrosting the professor's fridge, which on investigation had proved to be a micro-Antarctic. An open bag of frozen peas and diced carrots had spilled into the icebox, giving an impression of a tutti-frutti ice cream run amok in the massive icy overspill that had formed.

Her afternoons at the professor's had convinced her that he was badly in need of help. His apartment, chosen by his absconding wife, and fundamentally a pleasant one, was suffering from years of neglect. Very little that was meant to function functioned. The fridge, the iron, the cistern, the washing machine, even the telephone receiver were all in a state of disrepair. The iron, covered in what looked like caramel, she had been obliged to throw out. It was clear to her that the professor would hardly notice if between her sessions of archiving work, as he was now referring to it, she put a few things right in the apartment.

She had started on the fridge, if only because she had to sample the results of its deficiencies in the tumblers of warm white wine which the professor, anxious to express his gratitude, thrust upon her. She would really rather not drink it at all, but she knew that to refuse gratitude can be taken as a kind of insult. As she wielded a warm knife, slicing off chunks of tutti-frutti ice, the professor launched into the details of a holiday at Laugharne, in Wales.

'It is what Dylan Thomas based his *Under Milk Wood* on. You know Dylan Thomas?'

Agnès shook her head.

'Great English poet. Welsh, I should say. The Welsh would shoot me hearing me say that. I was nine, no, hang on, ten it must have been and my cousins Gwen and Gareth were with us there. The twins. They were my Aunty Mary's – my father's sister, she was a great knitter, Mary – G and G we called them, sometimes Gee Gee, which frankly they didn't like. I don't blame them, do you?'

Agnès said that she didn't.

'You know, I'm sure it didn't but in my memory it rained every day and we didn't mind because the rock pools were full of finds – winkles, anemones, goby fish. Shrimps of course. Plenty of those. Gwen was a demon shrimper. We boiled them up in a billycan on a primus stove. D'you like shrimps, Agnès?'

Agnès said that she did.

'Gareth, now, he wasn't such a keen shrimper. He wasn't as patient as his sister. Boys aren't, you know. He and I got into trouble because we went into a cave and nearly got cut off by the tide. Our parents smacked us both. I remember it because we knew we had it coming and we vowed not to cry. I think I did. You could do things like that to children then.'

The professor's eyes indicated that he might be missing those far-off libertarian days.

'Where are they now?' Agnès asked.

'Who?'

'Your cousins.'

'Oh,' said the professor vaguely. 'I'm not sure. Gwen became a nurse, no, a physiotherapist. She worked with strokes, I seem to think. She must be retired now. I can't remember what happened to Gareth. An accountant maybe?' He frowned, unwilling to be hauled away from his lost idyll by the problematic present.

'Maybe you should find them,' Agnès suggested. 'If you liked them it seems a shame . . .'

But the professor's expression suggested that he found this idea bizarre so she returned to hacking at the ice.

When she had finished, she said, 'I could ask Victor to take a look at the cistern if you like?'

The professor, however, was too preoccupied examining a black-and-white Brownie photo of himself on a sturdy pony to respond. 'Now that was in Suffolk. We stayed in some coast-guards' cottages. There was a local artist, I remember. Paxton Chadwick. Odd name, Paxton, but you don't think of that as a child. I don't know how my parents knew him. Maybe through their Labour Party connections – in those days they were still socialists. He was certainly left-wing. Maybe a communist. They were pretty ardent socialists once, my parents – my father's father was a miner, and his father too, so they would be. The Welsh are, of course. I remember Paxton Chadwick had a shock of white hair and these blue, blue eyes. In fact, now I think of it, it was through him I got interested in art . . .'

Madame Beck had arranged for a man to come and give her a quote for an air-conditioning system, with which she hoped to combat the problem caused by the restaurant's extractor fan. As a result, that Tuesday Madame Picot went to hers for tea.

'I'm afraid I had to bring Piaf, I hope you don't mind, my dear. Terry was supposed to collect her at lunchtime for her second walk, but she's running late. I told her to pick her up from here.'

'If you wouldn't mind keeping her on her lead, dear. I've just had the carpets cleaned.'

'Of course, my dear. I've brought us some *pâtisseries*.' Madame Picot passed a crisp white bag of peace offerings to Madame Beck, who took it purposefully into the kitchen.

'I'll just put the kettle on, dear.'

Madame Picot made her usual appraising survey of her friend's salon. The arrangement of small china dolls on the little scallop-edged table caught her eye. A new one? A little brown china doll with a lace bonnet and bootees. How odd that Louise had this passion for china babies when she so disliked real-life children. And dogs too. The mantelpiece was crammed with them.

As if in response to her mistress's thoughts, Piaf strained at her lead and yapped so that Madame Beck's vigilant ear was alerted.

'Please make sure she doesn't scratch at the rugs, dear.'

'Of course, my dear. Sit, Piaf! Good girl.'

But Piaf, who, like many intelligent dogs, had a mind which could intuit the true state of her owner's, started rebelliously forward. Madame Picot lunged heavily after her, knocking the table on to the carpet so that the little brown doll fell on to the tiled surround of the fireplace.

A loud ringing of the doorbell obscured the sound of breaking china. Hearing Terry's voice at the door, Piaf yapped again.

For all her girth, Madame Picot could move swiftly. She bent to pick up the fallen dolls from the carpet, replaced them quickly on the table, scooped up the head now neatly severed from the body of the brown doll and stowed both body and head in her handbag. 'Here's Terry for you, Piaf. We're coming, Terry. Good girl.'

Madame Picot talked more animatedly than usual over tea and left rather early.

'Your consultant will be arriving. I'll get off, my dear, I have a bit of shopping. I hope you enjoy the *éclairs*.'

'Oh my dear, I quite forgot them. Never mind, they'll keep until next time.'

Madame Beck had bought the brown china doll only the week

before, on a visit to her trichologist in Paris (certainly, she did not want it known locally that she had a problem with thinning hair). She had observed the doll in a regular haunt of hers, a shop which specialized in antique toys.

In her youth, Madame Beck had been a handsome woman with a fine head of thick hair. It was her splendid mane, caught in the light of a September sun, which had first drawn the eye of Claude Beck, when she had walked into the Parisian café where he was working as a waiter. She had ordered a coffee and a *croque-monsieur* and by the end of her snack he had proposed a future meeting.

It is true that from that moment the liaison had been steered predominantly by the future Madame Beck, Louise Cartel as she then was. But Claude Beck had been proud enough of her when she pushed him at last into a firm engagement to purchase a small but costly hoop of diamonds. She was a shrewd businesswoman and the head with the magnificent hair was, he had discovered, well screwed on. When he finally got his own restaurant going, she would be an asset, he believed.

And indeed she had proved an industrious partner, supportive of him when the bank foreclosed and they had to shut down their first restaurant; working with him, day and night, to set up a successful business in Evreux. Claude Beck had a marked flair for figures. In a later age he would surely have gone to study mathematics at university and made, perhaps, a very different career. And Louise Beck, besides being a workhorse, knew how to drive a hard bargain. Together they formed one of those business partnerships that are born to flourish.

It was the very success of this that had tarnished the relationship. An incipient vanity in Claude Beck bloomed alongside his enterprise. His eye, never too faithful in the first place, began to rove more widely and conspicuously. Coterminously, his wife began to lose her looks.

The thick black glossy hair, of which Louise Beck had been so proud, began to shed, first in combfuls, then distressing handfuls. When she first nailed her suspicion that her husband had a mistress (in fact, had she known it, at the time there was more than one), she developed serious alopecia.

Claude Beck was too lazy – or too mean – to divorce his wife. And she was too frightened, and too concupiscent, to cut her losses and make a stab at going it alone. Gradually, over the years, she accommodated her husband's infidelities by denying them to herself. The new restaurant they set up in Chartres, after selling the one in Evreux for a tidy profit, became an instant money-spinner. Situated where it was, visitors attracted to the cathedral could sit outside, or under the striped awning if the weather dictated, and feed their physical tissues while they continued to feast their eyes on the great Gothic masterpiece.

A fiction of a contented uxorious partnership developed to suit both parties. When Claude Beck died, at the house of his latest mistress (a house he had given her the money to buy), the affair was hushed up so successfully by Madame Beck that in her own mind her husband had gone to his eternal rest in the vast conjugal bed in which, in the latter years of their marriage, he had rarely passed a complete week.

Quite how she had come to be a collector of china dolls was a question Louise Beck could not herself have answered, any more than she could have owned to the state of her marriage or the accumulated resentment which was its poisonous legacy. Perhaps by now she was simply in the grip of the mania which besets collectors who care more for the number of their acquisitions than for the inherent value of each. For whatever reason, at times of stress Madame Beck would commonly reward herself with another doll purchase.

The trichologist's report had been discouraging. Despite his expensive treatments, and her diligent nightly applications of a lotion for which he had promised much, the bald patch at her parting had grown noticeably larger since her last visit. The brown doll with its lace bonnet and jabot had caught her eye on her way back to the rail station, after the trichologist had admitted that the fabled new treatment had not worked as well as he had hoped it might.

Two days after Madame Picot's hasty departure, Madame Beck noticed that her new doll was missing. Her thinning hair was the outward index of a festering misery in Louise Beck. The inexplicable disappearance of her latest means to counter this sad state thus touched a particularly sensitive nerve.

17

Le Mans

Dr Deman had not been able to bring himself to visit Agnès in the secure psychiatric hospital in Le Mans. He was one of those souls who, lacking the necessary ruthless touch of self-preservation, should perhaps never have become a doctor at all. His guilt over Agnès grew rather than diminished. When, while searching through his desk for a mislaid letter, he came upon a small matchbox, which had got pushed to the back of the overcrowded drawer, he opened it with feelings akin to those of a more prescient Pandora.

The earring entrusted to him by Jean Dupère lay there reproaching him, with its single turquoise eye. He'd forgotten it. Or, rather, he had not forgotten it. He had kept it to give Agnès when she was well on the way to recovery, a recovery that, thanks to his negligence, she might now never achieve. The discovery of this further mark of his dereliction persuaded him it was time to take some days of long overdue leave. He wrote to the psychiatrist at the hospital to whom he had sent Agnès' case notes, announcing his intention to visit.

The reply was a little encouraging. Dr Nezat reported that Agnès had settled in quite well at the hospital and she, Dr Nezat, would be happy for him to come to see his former patient.

Dr Deman made the two-hour journey to Le Mans in his old Renault. He was not a bad driver but when preoccupied he was inclined to be careless. Distracting thoughts of what he would find when he reached the hospital caused him to veer across a lane, narrowly escaping collision with a petrol lorry.

He arrived at the hospital already in a distraught state and had trouble finding a parking space in the car park. Finally, he squeezed the car into a space that he hoped was not illegal. For all the world he felt like driving straight back to Rouen.

Dr Nezat turned out to be a short, stocky woman with shapely calves and a well-lipsticked smile. She was the sort of woman whom Dr Deman generally found reassuring, since experience suggested she was unlikely to try to mother him (an approach to which he was allergic). He relaxed a little on meeting her and she asked him if he would care for a coffee.

'Thank you. How is she?'

Dr Nezat, with her back to him, took time to fill an electric kettle from the small tap.

'A little more adjusted to reality.'

'Has she said anything about the child?'

'I have Nescafé myself. But I can fetch you coffee from the canteen if you prefer.'

Dr Deman said he was happy with instant.

When Dr Nezat had made the coffee, she said, 'A great deal about her own baby. Nothing about the one involved in the assault.'

'And she knows . . . what, exactly?'

'She knows that she no longer has the child. Understandably, that makes her very sad. But sadness is not a psychiatric condition.' Dr Nezat stirred her cup as if to emphasize the wisdom of this point.

'Indeed not.' Dr Deman felt mildly affronted. It was a wisdom he himself was in the habit of imparting to others.

'I took the precaution of bringing along her file with the notes you kindly sent on to us.' Dr Nezat opened a file on her desk. 'Do you mind if I smoke?'

Dr Deman said that he didn't mind. Although he had given up smoking as a student, he felt he could do with a cigarette himself.

'I see,' said Dr Nezat, lighting up a Gitanes and failing to offer her guest one, 'that the last time you saw her was before the incident.' She bent to peer more closely at the writing. "Still very obsessed with Gabriel. Seems to be sleeping better and gaining weight." That was the last time you saw her?'

Dr Deman felt himself flush. 'No. Naturally I saw her after the episode. When she seemed to want to confess to the crime.'

'You didn't write it up?'

'I dare say I did.' Dr Deman began to feel that his sense of reassurance in this woman had been misplaced. 'Sometimes I write notes on a pad and transcribe them later. Probably in view of the general consternation . . .'

The truth was that a disturbing episode in Dr Deman's fevered memory and a factor in his guilt was that he had removed the final page of Agnès' notes – on which he had transcribed the address which he believed had led to the near-fatality. He had set fire to the page with a shaky hand in his own fireplace. The act weighed on his soul as if he had been responsible for the attack himself. More so perhaps. For he had become increasingly convinced that he had been the unwitting agent of the crime; that, somehow, Agnès had got hold of this information and deciphered it, though by no means could he guess how she might have contrived this. He could not have said whether it was Agnès or himself whom he was protecting.

'What, in your view' – Dr Nezat blew a contemplative cloud of smoke into the fuggy air of her small office – 'I would be interested to hear, is the likelihood that she did commit the crime?'

'I don't know,' said Dr Deman hopelessly. 'I don't feel I know much any more.'

Dr Nezat shot him a withering glance, conveying that this was no way for a trained medic to speak, and said that if he was ready they could see the girl now. She guided him through a long corridor, smelling of cooking vegetables, into a room which was painted a shade of eau de Nil. A colour that induces melancholy, Dr Deman reflected.

He had braced himself for a surprise but was nevertheless shocked to the teeth at the sight of his former patient sitting at a table with some other young people.

The pale gold, oval face, which had sometimes called to his mind the features of a young Renaissance Madonna, was now huge, moonlike and disfigured with acne. The leonine eyes seemed almost to have disappeared in folds of flesh. My God, he thought, she must have gained about two stone.

'Agnès?' Impossible to avoid altogether a note of question, for in a matter of months she seemed to have been transformed into a quite other being.

Agnès stared at him and then gave a slow shy smile. Only then did he get a glimpse of the young girl he had known. 'Doctor?'

'How are you, Agnès?'

'Fine, thank you.' So nothing had changed there.

'What are you doing?'

'Making a wallet.' She held out to him a rectangular piece of maroon synthetic leather punched along two sides with holes. Dr Deman took it gingerly.

'It's her occupational therapy,' said Dr Nezat loudly behind him. 'We're very good at it, aren't we, Agnès? Last week she made us a lovely shoulder bag.'

Dr Deman stayed less than fifteen minutes with Agnès, during which time conversation was sporadic and stilted. She answered his cautious questions with polite platitudes. She had always done so, but previously – although maybe this was his

89

own delusion, for Dr Deman was aware that delusions were by no means the prerogative of patients – he had always had the feeling that something of his concern for her was communicated.

After five barren minutes of question and answer, during which he felt like a particularly brutal interrogation officer, there seemed to be nothing more to say. After another ten minutes of further profound discomfort, he bade his former patient goodbye.

Dr Nezat invited him back to her office, where she smoked another cigarette and did not offer him coffee.

'What treatments is she on exactly?' Dr Deman asked feebly. Whatever it was he was likely to be against it.

'The usual anti-psychotics. She still believes she found the baby in a basket. And there remains the question mark over the assault, as you know.'

'The basket is simply a projection of her own history –' Dr Deman began to explain but his words were brushed aside.

'Yes, I read the file, naturally. Very sad. Poor child. We'll see how things go and then consider ECT. It can brighten them up considerably, as you know.'

Dr Deman's pet hate was ECT, which, since no one had ever produced any real account of what it does to the brain, he regarded as a most pernicious form of witchcraft. He left Dr Nezat's office and the building in a state to find a parking notice on his car.

That night he did something he had done only once before. He got blind drunk in a bar and called up a prostitute to visit his hotel. The following morning found him full of self-loathing. He couldn't think what had led him to do this. Neither experience was satisfactory.

18

Chartres

For several days after their breakfast encounter Agnès heard nothing from Alain other than his early blackbird whistle from above. But the following Thursday, coming out of the door to the crypt, she met him again in person as she approached the North Door. He was standing at the foot of the steps, gazing up at the porch. 'I was thinking, I like this side best.'

'I do too.' It had provided her with her first sanctuary.

'You know all the cast of characters?'

'Some.'

'That's Job, up there.' He indicated the Old Testament exemplar of patience above the right door. 'Poor guy. What he had to suffer. And all because God wanted to win a bet with Satan. This here' – he pointed to the central portal – 'is Anne, Mary's mother. People imagine that it's Mary because she has a baby in her arms, but, look, see, she doesn't have a halo. I don't know why the Grandmother of God doesn't merit a halo but she doesn't.'

'And these?' Agnès indicated the two tall figures who had stood sentinel over her sleeping body that first night at Chartres.

'The one to the left is St Peter. The one on the right is the prophet Elijah. See that wheel he's apparently balancing on? It looks like a monocycle but in fact that's because the other wheel – look here – is broken. They're the wheels of his chariot of fire.'

Agnès examined them. 'They look so –'

'Yes, don't they? Domestic. And that behind you, there, is

the ark of the covenant.' She turned to look at a humble-looking medieval farm cart worked in stone.

'I like that.'

'Yes. I do. I like this too.' He walked across the porch to the base of another pillar. 'Look, David, here with his harp and there his sling, but look here – he's slaying Goliath but it's David who's lost his head, not Goliath! Ironic, isn't it? He lost it in the Revolution.'

'I don't know too much about the Old Testament,' Agnès said. 'I was brought up by nuns.' It was a remark more intimate than she had quite intended and she blushed.

If Alain noticed her slight discomfort he gave no acknowledgement. 'The stories in the Old are better, by and large.'

'There was one nun who liked some of those stories.' She was thinking of Sister Laurence. Sometimes she missed Sister Laurence. 'But mostly I heard about Jesus and the parables.'

'They're not bad either. A lot of wisdom in parables.'

They went inside. Alain pushed open the two heavy doors for her and she caught his distinctive male smell as she passed by his stretched arm.

'Have you breakfasted? I've some sausage left. And olives.'

Meaning to decline she said, 'That would be nice.'

'D'you want to come up?' He gestured at the scaffolding.

'Well . . .'

'It's only seven. Your aged admirer won't be here for at least an hour.'

Agnès, driven nearly to distraction by the Abbé Bernard's faltering demands, felt bound to defend him. 'He's only looking for someone to listen to him.'

'And who better than a pretty young girl? I don't blame him.'

'I'm forty in January!'

'That's a girl in his eyes. Anyway, forty's the fulcrum of life. I can't wait to get there.'

So, Agnès thought, he's younger than me. 'I don't think I –'

'Come on. You'll like it. God's-eye view. A god's eye, anyway.'

'All right.'

He unfolded a door in the fabric of the protective screen behind the altar. 'This is the secret entry to my kingdom.'

'I wondered how you got in.'

'Do you want go ahead so I can catch you or would you rather come behind?'

'I'll come behind you.'

Climbing up the ladder, trying to manage her full skirt, Agnès had a fleeting memory of another ladder – in the apple orchard at the convent.

When Madame Beck discovered that her new doll had gone missing, she was filled with a white panic, as if some demon had reached inside her and insolently tweaked her guts. Who could have perpetrated this crime? She had few visitors and fewer friends. Of those, only Madame Picot visited regularly.

Her mind ran rapidly through the list of visitors to her apartment since she had returned from Paris with the new doll. The air-conditioning man had walked around surveying possibilities for the conduits; but naturally she had accompanied him all the time. There was Jeanette of course. The only other suspect had to be Agnès.

Like many people whose energy is fuelled by malice, Madame Beck had a penetrating negative intuition; but in this instance it played her false. Perhaps she did not credit her old friend with sufficient guile to conceal such a monstrous disloyalty. She was inclined to underrate Madame Picot, who was more knowing, and more worldly-wise, than she appeared. Unlike Claude Beck, Auguste Picot had found his wife sexually attractive and had admired her amply rounded body to the end. On a visit to London once, he had sent her a postcard of a painting by Seurat, of a sexily plump woman sitting at her dressing-table applying a powder puff, together with a little amorous note on the back to the effect that the nights were lonely and the woman made him miss his 'Pretty Jeanette'.

Madame Picot still had the card tucked away with many lavender bags in a drawer of underwear that her husband had liked her to wear, for which, alas, she had only sentimental use now. Still, to have been attractive to the man one lives with is a blessing; it had conferred on Madame Picot the touch of indulgent benignity which Madame Beck scornfully regarded as weakness.

What Madame Beck had not reckoned correctly was the fear she inspired in her friend. Madame Picot had made no calculation when she gathered up the bits of the decapitated doll and hid them in her bag. She had acted on instinct without thought of what she would say when the matter came up – as it did that Thursday.

Had Madame Beck wanted to ascertain if Jeanette knew anything about the missing doll, she would have done better to tell her of it in person. She had made the discovery late the previous evening. The rage that had mounted in her overnight had led to a pressing need to vent her fury. She rang Madame Picot as early as seemed decent (unlike herself Jeanette was a late riser) with the news.

'My dear, I hope I didn't wake you but I've had such a shock. Lulu, my new little doll, is missing.'

Madame Picot had more command of her voice than her expression, and over the phone was able to sound properly concerned when Madame Beck had finished her tale.

'My dear, how very puzzling.'

'Puzzling? It's outright theft!'

'But my dear, who would want to steal a dolly? Was it valuable?'

'Indeed she was.' Madame Beck had actually beaten the price down by twenty euros at the shop, which, as a regular, she felt entitled to do. 'I shall have to speak to Mademoiselle Morel. She's been in since I bought Lulu. Do you remember seeing her when you were here last?'

Madame Picot did a rapid calculation. 'I don't recall, dear. As you know, I'm not the nosy sort.'

This was a mistake, since Madame Beck knew quite well that her friend snooped surreptitiously round her apartment when she supposed her hostess was not looking.

'She was quite distinctive, a little brown girl with a lace bonnet, on the round scallop-edged table, you know, the one Claude and I brought from Evreux, right by the sofa where you sit. I would have expected you to notice her.'

'I'm afraid I don't remember, dear,' said Madame Picot. She was aware that she was on dangerous ground and it seemed safest to stick to her story.

The suspicion that Agnès was to blame for the missing doll worked on Madame Beck's ill mood. Impossible to wait for her next cleaning day. It was ten minutes off 8.30 a.m., the time the cathedral officially opened. She dressed and without bothering even to take her usual coffee almost ran across the close to the Royal Portal.

She was just in time to meet the Abbé Bernard, slightly later than usual, who, deceived by the purposefulness of her expression, assumed it must be time for the public to be admitted and ushered her into the cathedral nave before him.

19

Rouen

It was only driving back from Le Mans, a town that by now he heartily loathed, smoking one of the Gitanes that, thanks to Dr Nezat's example, he had gone out and bought, that Dr Deman realized he had not delivered the turquoise earring. The recognition caused him such dismay that he took his eye off the road and narrowly missed another collision with a lorry. Swerving the car on to the hard shoulder in his effort to avoid the lorry's path, he felt the tell-tale bump, bump of a flat tyre.

The spare, he discovered on looking for it, was missing from the boot. Only then did he remember that he had taken it into the garage a few weeks earlier to fix a slow puncture.

Among the messages on his desk when, exhausted and demoralized, he got to his office the following morning, was a request to call the Mother Superior at the Sisters of Mercy. He had considered, during the time of Agnès' alleged assault on the nanny, whether or not to let the convent know what had happened to their charge. His disquiet over his own conduct had made him reluctant to discuss her case with anyone, let alone Mother Catherine. In the end, unsure what the right course was, he had let things drift.

So it was with reluctance that he took up the phone to return her call.

'Mother Catherine?'

'Yes, who is speaking, please?' The voice had lost none of its civil-service clip.

'Denis Deman. You called my office.'

'That was three days ago.'

'I regret,' said Dr Deman somewhat stiffly, 'that I have been away for a few days.'

'It was about Agnès that I called.' Dr Deman, who had had his fill of self-confident women, waited gloomily to hear what she had to say.

'We have only just had news of the awful tragedy.'

'Yes?'

'I must say this, Doctor, I think you should have informed us.'

Dr Deman summoned up his faltering moral courage. 'Mother Catherine. I had heard nothing from you or the convent for months. Had you been concerned about Agnès, you could have rung me.'

Mother Catherine's stock of moral courage was more than equal to Dr Deman's. 'I have rung you now.'

Dr Deman sighed inwardly and explained he had just come from Le Mans, where he had seen Agnès.

'And how was she?'

He was about to say 'fine' when he was overtaken by an impulse to be honest. 'The psychiatrist there seems happy enough with her progress. I felt concerned. She seemed to me to have deteriorated. Frankly, she looked terrible.'

Surprisingly, Mother Catherine's voice became more conciliatory. 'I was afraid of that when I heard about the move. The poor child was used to you and the clinic.'

'Yes.' But he had failed to protect her.

'The man who found her first informed us of what had happened,' Mother Catherine continued. 'In the circumstances I felt you should know. He would like to see you.'

'But of course. He can come to the clinic as before.'

'I gather he is unwell. He has asked me if I would ask you if you would consent to visit him at his home.'

'He might have rung me himself.'

'He believes he has lost your number,' said the Mother Superior. 'Or possibly he never had it.'

'I'll call him,' said Dr Deman. The weariness which had dragged him down since seeing Agnès again wrapped him round in another drear fold. 'Remind me of his number, if you wouldn't mind, Mother Catherine.'

Dr Deman postponed the call to Jean Dupère until the evening, when he could fortify himself with a large drink. His feelings of guilt about Agnès were now extending to Jean Dupère, whose trust in him seemingly had also been misplaced. He had the matchbox containing the turquoise earring by him when he finally nerved himself to ring.

The conversation was mercifully brief. Jean Dupère said he would be much obliged if the doctor would visit him as he wanted to hear about little Agnès. Unfortunately he was indisposed so could not go to the clinic himself. He was very sorry to inconvenience the doctor.

That Saturday, Dr Deman drove to Jean Dupère's farm. The year had just turned past the vernal equinox and the longer evenings were being lifted by stretches of yellowing light.

Driving through the dimming countryside, Denis Deman was reminded of his childhood. His father had been a country doctor, the old-fashioned sort, in a market town not so far from there. He had grown up near these wide, lush fields, cold rivers and solid white cattle. Perhaps he should return there and marry his adolescent sweetheart, Elise. According to his mother – who was not reliable – Elise still nursed a fondness for him.

Driving down the rough track to the Dupère farm, which he had found finally only by stopping to inquire at the local inn, the startlingly white form of a barn owl swept across the beam of his headlights. He pulled up at the black outline of a building.

No light was visible and it took him some time to find the door. He knocked and, getting no answer, was about to return, gratefully, to his car and drive quickly home when he heard a gruff call.

'Come in, please.'

Jean Dupère was lying, with a woollen muffler round his neck, in a bed in the kitchen, the kind of bed – wooden and built into the walls – he had occasionally seen when accompanying his father on his patient rounds. Over the bed was a patchwork cover of many-coloured, unevenly knitted squares.

'Please sit down, Doctor. As you see, I'm unable to get up. There is wine on the dresser. Please.'

Dr Deman helped himself to a glass of wine and sat down on a rocking chair and then started up again. 'I am so sorry, would you –'

'No, no. I have mine here beside me, thank you.'

The two men sat in silence. Dr Deman, rocking on the chair, found himself wondering how Jean Dupère managed on his own. But maybe he wasn't on his own?

'I heard about my little Agnès.'

'I am sorry.' It was the first time Dr Deman had had another soul to whom he could express his regret over Agnès and he felt some relief in expressing it now.

'My niece knows a nurse at your clinic. She told me. You think she committed this awful crime?'

Dr Deman rocked back and forth on his chair. In his early days as a psychiatrist, he had had a supervisor, a mentor, really, Dr Jacques Germaine, who was also a psychoanalyst. Jacques had never managed to persuade his young friend to undertake an analysis himself – Denis Deman lacked the necessary funds – but, none the less, he had imparted some of his insights.

One rather simple one, though easier said than put into practice, was that our deeper mind will tell us the truth of things, provided we don't impede it with controlling desires and thoughts. The drive through the twilit countryside of his childhood, the pearling sky, the hunting owl, the clean-tasting wine and the old man's hospitality – all acted as a balm on Dr Deman's ragged nerves. For the first time he allowed a mind free of guilt and doubt to contemplate the question.

'No, I don't,' he declared.

'I don't either,' the old man agreed.

Dr Deman didn't question Jean Dupère's credentials for making this judgement. The fact that he had seen Agnès precisely five times since the day he found her did nothing in Dr Deman's current mood to disqualify the old man from knowing Agnès as well, probably better, than he did himself. He had dreaded this encounter and yet it appeared that, far from furthering his guilt, it might do something to resolve it. Not quite meaning to, he got up and helped himself to more red wine.

'It is good,' Jean Dupère commented. 'It is from my brother-in-law in Saumur.'

'Yes, really it's excellent. Sorry, I shouldn't, I didn't mean to help myself.'

'Please take all you wish.'

'Thank you. You're not well?' Dr Deman suggested, aware that so far this subject had not been broached and that ordinary courtesy demanded it be raised.

'I have the cancer. It has moved into my spine. They wish me to go to hospital but I prefer to die here, where I was born. And where my grandmother and my father were also born.'

'And you have someone to care for you, I hope?'

'I have a good neighbour who comes in each day to fix me up a bit. It is enough. The pain at present is bad but it comes and goes and when it goes I manage.'

Dr Deman, rocking like a child in a crib, stayed for over two hours in Jean Dupère's congenial kitchen, which was hung about with baskets of herbs and hooks bearing thick sausages and dry hams. As they discussed the breeding of Charolais, the fiendish EEC farming policies and Jean's brother-in-law's seemingly insoluble problems with vine mould, the wood fire flickered on the stone flags and polished up the copper pans on the hearth, pans which had served the Dupère family for generations.

Dr Deman described a memorable meal he had once had in Brittany – a feast of nameless crustaceans which had lasted four hours – and Jean Dupère explained in turn his favourite way of cooking morel mushrooms (in a little bacon fat with a spoonful or two of thick local cream and plenty of ground black pepper).

At the old man's request the doctor warmed a saucepan of lentil soup over the fire and took a bowl himself, describing as he drank it his theories about the nourishing properties of milk and soup for his disturbed patients. By this time they were on Christian-name terms – Jean and Denis – and Jean volunteered that his grandmother, whose kitchen they were sitting in, had been of a like mind and would have roundly endorsed the doctor's nutritional theories.

When Denis Deman left to drive back up the uneven track, now lit by a sailing lemon-slice of a moon, his spirits were brighter than they had been for months. So upbeat was his mood that he quite forgot that he still had the matchbox in his pocket and that he had once again failed to deliver it to its intended recipient.

20

Chartres

At the top of the ladder that led to Alain's eyrie, Agnès came face to serious face with the Blue Virgin.

'I've never seen it, her, I mean, so close.'

'Ah, that's what I meant by God's-eye view. She's great, isn't she? Along with those three' – he gestured towards the three windows below the Western Rose – 'she's almost the oldest thing here. One of her own miracles.'

The blue-clad Madonna on her ground of ruby, with the solemn Christ child on her knee, stared grave-eyed into the eyes of Agnès, who involuntarily touched the silver chain at her neck. 'She's wonderful.'

'Yes. It almost makes you believe in her.'

'You don't believe in her?'

'I don't believe she was the Mother of God. But I don't believe Jesus Christ was God's son either. That is not to say I don't believe.'

'What, then?'

'Have some sausage.'

'Thank you.'

'Wine?'

'No, thank you.'

'Coffee?'

'Yes, please.' And 'What, then, do you believe?' she repeated when he had poured her out a cupful of dark coffee from a silver thermos.

'I don't believe in Christianity, or Judaism, or Islam, or Hinduism, or even Buddhism, though I'm quite drawn to that. But I think they all have something important to say. But so does paganism for that matter.'

'I don't really know what paganism means.'

'Well, the Greeks were pagans, for example. I wouldn't be without the Greeks. The Platonists, who taught here – there was a famous school in Chartres – claimed there were two doors to heaven: the door of winter, which let the light in, and the door of summer, which let it out. Plato claimed that the gods entered by the first door and left by the second.'

She thought about it. 'I like that.'

'It's good, isn't it?'

'But it's true,' she said. 'I remember at the convent being glad when the winter solstice was passed because it meant it would get lighter in the mornings and we didn't have to go to chapel in the dark.'

'You didn't like chapel.'

'No. Well, sometimes. I liked Christmas.'

'Christmas is all pagan. Jesus was probably born in September.'

'How do they know?'

'What?'

'About Jesus.'

'Oh, from the date of the census. They were in Bethlehem because people were required, for the census, to return to the place of their birth. Bethlehem was Joseph's hometown. Anyway, that dates the birth, but, you know, it doesn't matter for people who believe Jesus is the coming of light.'

Agnès tried to imagine what Sister Véronique would say to this. 'I don't think the nuns would agree with you.'

'No, they wouldn't. The think theirs is the one and only "truth" but the fact is that all religions are a hotchpotch. And they all have things in common. See these arches.' He pointed again down the nave. 'The pointed arch was one of *the* key marks of Gothic architecture – what they called the "new style". But if you look at them they're the spitting image of some of the Islamic arches. The Muslims didn't care for rounded arches. They thought they brought the spirit back to earth.' He made an arch in the air with his forefinger. 'The point rises upward to heaven' – he pointed his finger – 'and, the Muslims would say, towards new life. They felt that created a higher aura. The crusaders brought captive Muslim masons back to Europe and they had a hand in developing our building styles. Some became quite famous. People in the prejudiced West today forget that Islam was a very sophisticated culture long before ours, with a highly developed grasp of mathematics, particularly geometry, and philosophy – spiritually they were streets ahead of us. But you've got me going now. Sorry to be a bore.'

'No,' said Agnès, who had closed her eyes. She was imagining herself a captive infidel being brought back in chains to France. 'I'm not bored. Really.' She fingered again the silver chain round her neck.

'You're Catholic, you said?'

'No. I was just brought up by nuns. I don't know what I am.'

'You're Agnès. Which is all you need to be.'

'It would be nice to know where I came from.'

'You don't?'

'I was found,' Agnès said. 'In a basket in a wood.' How odd to be telling this stranger.

'Then you're a princess in disguise!'

'I can't say I've ever thought of it like that,' Agnès said, laughing.

She found herself laughing again as he described his various jobs and their many setbacks and the people he encountered through them. Despite his protestations of not wishing to bore her, he continued to instruct her about the cathedral. But he wasn't at all boring like Sister Véronique. Information bubbled out of him like champagne.

'But why is it so yellow?' she complained after he had explained the thirteenth-century process of making plaster – sand and powdered limestone. She didn't like the custard yellow.

'It always was that colour. We've simply cleaned it up. People imagine the cathedral was all dim and dark as it is now. But in its hey-day it was covered with paint. And if you think the ceiling's gaudy take a look up here at the keystones.'

But instead she looked down at her watch. It was close to 8.30 a.m. and she still had the ambulatory floor to sweep. 'I must go.'

'Sure.'

She started hurriedly back down the ladder. Towards the bottom, her left foot became trapped in her full skirt, so that she swivelled about and slid awkwardly down the last few rungs to the floor and fell against the screen door and on to the altar dais.

Alain, just behind her, jumped gallantly to help her up, just as Madame Beck, with Father Bernard trailing behind, stormed into the nave.

'It was quite obscene,' Madame Beck excitedly informed Madame Picot on the phone a mere half an hour later. 'There she was in the man's arms right by the altar, her skirt up showing her all to anyone who cared to look. No prizes for guessing what had been going on there.'

'Did you ask her about the little dolly, dear?' Madame Picot was suffering some nervousness on this score.

'I didn't have a chance. Father Bernard didn't know where to look. He was so upset I had to give him a cup of coffee. He's only just gone, in fact. I suggested he should talk to Father Paul.'

★

105

The Abbé Bernard did talk to the Abbé Paul but mostly because he too feared Madame Beck. He had been confused rather than upset by what he had seen, mainly because it seemed to cause such a to-do in Madame Beck to find Agnès being helped up from the floor by a young man. A nice young man, he had seemed to the Abbé Bernard. Still, he was grateful for the coffee, and the *éclairs*, which were quite delicious, and he promised to have a word with the Abbé Paul.

'But what is it she minded? I'm not sure that I quite . . .' the Abbé Paul asked, when, in answer to Bernard's request for 'a word', the dean had asked him round for a drink.

The Abbé Bernard was no longer sure. Not that he'd ever really grasped in the first place what it was that Madame Beck wanted of him. She talked so fast and seemed so very cross. It reminded him of the times his mother had scolded him and he had gone to bed in tears. Of course in his mother's case it was excusable. She had had a bad time and no doubt, as she had often told him, he was a very trying child.

'I think she was concerned about the scaffolding,' he decided. 'Something to do with its being dangerous for Agnès.'

The Abbé knew Madame Beck all too well. A concern for their cleaner did not strike him as probable. 'I don't see . . .'

'Agnès cleans for her too,' the Abbé Bernard explained. 'I expect she's worried for her. Nice girl,' he added mournfully. For all he had enjoyed the *éclairs* he would much rather have spent the morning chatting to Agnès.

The Abbé Paul offered Bernard more wine. Best to see Agnès himself, he decided. He was aware that Bernard was adrift over the matter and that generally his colleague was losing his grip. His heart bled for him. A dear man who should probably never have entered the priesthood.

But which of us should, wondered the Abbé Paul, pouring himself another glass of wine.

21

Le Mans

The visit to Jean Dupère's farm had acted as a tonic not only to Denis Deman's spirits but also to his resolution. His was a disposition to take things hard but also to take them high. A conscientious, if rather plodding, father and a frivolous, wilful mother had bred a contradiction in the son's nature. He cared – cared passionately – for the things he cared for but his conviction was liable to waver and be derailed. Jean Dupère's peaceful farmstead, the pleasing old-fashioned furniture and time-worn chattels, the old man's simple fortitude, his undramatic acceptance of his illness, had galvanized Denis Deman. And the warmth his host had expressed for the younger man rekindled his memory of his father's shy pride in his only child. He was aware that his father believed that he himself could have, maybe *should* have, done better in life and hoped that his son would do better than he had managed, hampered as he was by a slender ambition and a silly, vain wife.

It was the wife, Denis's mother, who had prompted him to flee his home and settle first in Paris, after medical school, then later in Rouen. He was aware that his mother's highest ambition for her son was for him to marry a local girl and settle down near her, to assure her, with the death of a much older husband, a well-tended old age. This had no doubt contributed to the fact that, despite an attractive appearance and, when it was convenient, his mother's easygoing way with the opposite sex, at forty-five Denis Deman remained unmarried. That it was rarely 'convenient' was a testament to Denis Deman's fundamental seriousness. He didn't 'put it on' – he had too high an opinion of women for that – but he had more than an inkling of how sexual charm could sometimes be useful.

If he had failed to employ it with Dr Nezat, it was because he had met the situation as nervous, to use a favourite phrase of Jacques Germaine's, as a kitten. He had been too much in fear of her professional judgement and his own bad conscience. But his conscience had now been awakened to a higher purpose. And there was a ready excuse to hand.

He had found the matchbox, which by now he associated with the array of smoking equipment he had observed in Jean Dupère's comforting kitchen, in his pocket when he undressed that same night. It was a testament to the benign effects of that evening that his first thought was not self-reproach but the idea that he might use it as another excuse to visit Le Mans. The matchbox containing its small turquoise treasure had become a kind of amulet.

He decided to ring rather than write. 'Dr Nezat?'

'Who is this?' Her tone was disconcertingly like that of Mother Catherine.

'Denis Deman. We met, you remember –'

'Yes, yes, of course. What can I do for you?'

Denis explained that he had something of Agnès' and would like to come to visit again to give it to her.

'Can it not be sent?'

'I'd rather not. It is a little relic found with her when she was abandoned – which has only just come to light.'

He detected a certain curiosity in Dr Nezat's response, which was that if he would like to name a date, she would make sure she would be available to meet him.

Easter was early that year. Denis Deman drove down to Le Mans on Good Friday, taking care to check that his spare tyre was securely in the boot. He had mentioned his previous difficulties over parking and Dr Nezat, having expressed surprise that he was able to take the day off, said that she would see to it that a parking space was reserved for him.

His new mood must already have had an impact, as she met him as an old friend, and once in her office offered him a cigarette over another cup of Nescafé.

'Thank you, I don't any more.'

'I shouldn't but otherwise I put on so much weight.' Dr Nezat patted her hips. 'So what is it you have brought for the girl? I told her you were coming.'

'Did she react?'

'As you know with her it's hard to say what is going on.'

Denis Deman decided it was time to take the bull by the horns. 'You asked me whether I thought it was likely she had committed the crime. To be frank with you, I think it most unlikely. Not a shred of concrete evidence was discovered to connect her with it. No weapon was ever found.'

'And the child was not hers.'

'Not at all,' said Denis decisively. Had she ever imagined so, the fault would be entirely his. 'Her child is, I imagine, quite elsewhere.'

'It is true that she never refers to the boy now.'

Denis took a calculated risk. 'If I may unburden myself to you, Dr Nezat, this is all my doing. I became alarmed. For some reason I connected her with the assault and questioned her about it. She seemed to admit to the crime but with hindsight . . .' Damnable hindsight.

'What I don't see,' said Dr Nezat, neatly tapping her ash into an ashtray bearing an image of the Mona Lisa, 'is why you connected her with the crime in the first place.'

In the split second before Denis answered her, the legacies of his father's honesty and his mother's guile hung in the balance.

The mother's legacy won. Outright admission of his sorry part in this story would not help him to solve the problem he had created. 'It was a foolish fancy born of fear.'

'Of course she's had a history with knives,' said Dr Nezat helpfully. 'And there was also the fact that the child in the case was the same age as the one she lost.'

'Exactly. Though I'm bound to say that the only person, as far as we know, she ever wounded was herself.'

'I wouldn't blame her if she wanted to take a stab at those dreadful nuns,' said Dr Nezat and smiled so broadly that Denis Deman began quite to like her. 'Come on. Let's take her your surprise.'

Perhaps because he was fearing worse this time, Agnès looked to him a little better. Her acne seemed less pronounced and her expression was more alert. She recognized him at once and smiled her winning smile. 'Doctor.'

'Agnès. Good to see you again.'

'It's nice to see you too, Doctor.'

'Agnès,' he said, sitting down next to her, 'I've brought you something.' He produced the matchbox from his jacket pocket. Over his shoulder, he could almost palpably feel Dr Nezat's curiosity rise. 'The man who found you found something in the basket where you were lying. He wanted you to have it for your sixteenth birthday. He gave it to me to give to you now.'

Agnès took the matchbox and held it as if she didn't plan to do more than look at it. Then very slowly she pushed it open.

Denis had considered whether to polish up the complex surround of tarnished silver in which the turquoise stone was mounted and decided against it. She should have the relic of her mother precisely as it was. 'The stone is turquoise. The silver will easily clean up.'

Agnès said nothing at all for some minutes. She sat staring at the little semi-precious gem in the palm of her hand. Then she looked up at Dr Nezat. 'May I have my ears pierced?'

'I don't see why not,' said Dr Nezat, who once more was smiling broadly.

Back in her office, after an hour during which Denis had managed a sustained conversation with Agnès, Dr Nezat pronounced that his visit had been a success. The visit had started a strand of hope in Dr Deman. Perhaps he might exert some influence over Agnès' treatment. But how to do it? Dr Nezat would not, he suspected, easily surrender any of her medical authority. The father and mother were weighed again and once more the balance came down on the mother's side. 'Dr Nezat, you have been enormously kind. May I have the pleasure of giving you dinner this evening?'

'How charming of you.' Dr Nezat consulted her diary and declared that by a stroke of good fortune she was free. She suggested a restaurant they might meet in – he having no local knowledge from which to choose one – and suggested he leave his car in the hospital car park; parking in the town was hell, she explained, and anyway most of their staff were off for the Easter holiday.

Denis Deman, who had brought nothing for an overnight stay, went out and bought a toothbrush, toothpaste and some razors from the nearby pharmacy and some socks and underpants from Monoprix. After checking into the expensive hotel, also recommended by Dr Nezat, he went back and bought a shirt and a tie.

22

Chartres

As it was Friday, the Abbé Paul found Agnès cleaning the labyrinth when he went in search of her at the cathedral. She was on her knees halfway round the left side.

'You follow the path when you clean?'

Agnès stopped what she was doing and got up. 'It feels right that way.'

The Abbé Paul nodded.

'What was it for, Father?'

'You know, I don't know. No one does, I think. People have said the cathedral clerics once played some sort of sacred game here. Who can tell what my colleagues will get up to but I have always supposed it provided some sort of aid to meditation. Walking frees the mind. The pattern is calming, don't you find?'

'Yes.'

'How are you finding us, cleaning here?'

'I like it, thank you, Father.'

'No problems?'

She guessed he had come to talk to her about yesterday. 'No.'

'It must be tough work.'

'I like it.'

'Good. You know the paving here slopes. In the Middle Ages the pilgrims slept here overnight. They set the paving on a slope so it could be washed down more easily each day.' He paused. 'Father Bernard mentioned something about a fall.'

'It was nothing, Father. An accident.'

'We're insured, of course. But we don't want you at risk.'

'Really, it was just a slip.'

'Father Bernard tells me that Madame Beck was concerned for you. You clean for her?'

'Yes, Father.' Though perhaps not, she thought, for much longer.

The Abbé Paul hesitated. He was not an interfering sort, having a pronounced dislike of being interfered with himself. But he was also intuitive. Despite Bernard's muddled report he sensed malice at work. 'I could do with a cleaner. Bernadette used to do for me but she sacked me along with the cathedral. If you needed more work –'

'Thank you, Father. I'd be glad to.'

'Only if you want to, mind. I can muddle along.' In fact, he had found that he enjoyed cleaning and was modestly proud to discover that he was rather better at it than Bernadette, who had once informed him that if the Good Lord intended us to see bacteria, He would have given us better eyes.

The Abbé Paul had gone when Alain climbed down the ladder. 'Was he telling you off for yesterday?'

'He wants me to clean for him.'

'What's with that old woman, then? You slipped out before I could get to you. She was looking at you like thunder.'

'Madame Beck? I clean for her.' For all their intimacy yesterday – or because of it – Agnès felt a return of reserve.

'It seems to me you clean for the whole town.'

'I don't expect she'll keep me on for long.'

'It's none of my business but if I were you I'd get out of there. I know that sort. Old woman alone gone sour – sexless and envious. Bad news.'

She shrugged. 'You were going to tell me the story of this.'

'The labyrinth? Oh, right. Yes. Yes, I was. I meant the original labyrinth. Built by Daedalus for Minos, King of Crete, to conceal the Minotaur. There was a bronze plaque at the centre of this here once – the Republicans took it to melt down for cannons along with the lead from the roof – but there was a drawing of it made before it was taken: the Minotaur with Theseus and Ariadne on either side. You know about the Minotaur?'

She shook her head. 'I only know Bible stories.'

'And why not? The Minotaur was the child of Pasiphaë, wife of Minos, the King of Crete. Poseidon sent a white bull from the sea to Crete and Minos refused to sacrifice it to the god.'

'Why?'

'Why the bull or why not sacrifice it?'

'Both, I suppose.'

'I don't remember. Anyway, Poseidon, who was a bit of a bastard, took revenge by having Pasiphaë fall for the bull. She got Daedalus, who was the palace inventor, to construct a hide shaped like a cow and she hid in it while the bull had his way with her.'

'Ugh!'

'Don't look like that. It's many women's sexual fantasy. Anyway, she gave birth to a monster, half man and half bull, called the Minotaur, though why he was named for the king who wasn't his father I don't know. Daedalus built a labyrinth to keep the creature in, and every year Athens was obliged to send a tribute of its prime youth to feed him – because of some peace treaty they'd agreed. Theseus persuaded his father, who was King of Athens, to let him sail to Crete among the tribute of youths and he found his way into the centre of the labyrinth and killed the Minotaur. Minos's daughter, Ariadne, helped him by giving him a clue of thread to help him find his way out again. They escaped together but he dumped her on an island while she was asleep and sailed off home.'

'Poor Ariadne.'

'Theseus got his come-uppance. Everyone does in Greek myths. He'd told his father he would change the sails from black, which they'd sailed out with – because of the coming deaths – to white if he had been successful and in his hurry to get away from Ariadne he forgot to make the change. So his father, seeing the black sails, assumed that the Minotaur had had his son for lunch and committed suicide.'

'Wasn't that a bit –'

'Rash? Yes. But that's the way they are in myths. Impulsive.'

'I suppose that –'

'Stop interrupting – there's a happy end. Dionysos, who's one of the sexier Greek gods, saw Ariadne while he was sailing past Naxos, turned himself into a dolphin and carried her off. If I were a woman, I'd a hundred times rather be Dionysos' lover than Theseus'. Theseus was a thug – strictly Alpha male.'

Agnès said, 'Poor Minotaur. How horrible to be killed by his own sister.'

'Half-sister. And she didn't actually kill him. She just helped his killer. There's not much sentiment in Greek myths.'

Agnès gazed down again at the labyrinth. 'Do you think –'

'I think it's interesting that the rose here' – he strode across the circling path to stand at the centre – 'which is a very old symbol for spiritual perfection, should have had at its heart a picture of this rather gory story. And most definitely not a Christian one. It makes me laugh out loud when I see them walking around it so solemnly, praying and crying and carrying on like I don't know what.'

'Perhaps,' Agnès said, looking at the iron bolts which once held the bronze plaque that had gone to make the new republic's cannons, 'everyone has a Minotaur hidden in their heart.'

Alain turned on her one of his long looks. 'You're a bit of a savant, aren't you, in your quiet way?'

'What's that?'

'A savant? A wise person. Someone with natural wisdom.'

'I was in the retards' class at school.'

'You shouldn't use that word.'

'Why not? It's what we were.'

'It's a horrible word. Don't use it.' Seeing she was blushing, he went on swiftly, 'Anyway that proves you are a savant. Savants are so clever they seem like fools to the foolish.'

'I must get on.'

'Or your elderly admirer will be upon you, I know. He didn't seem too bothered finding you yesterday in the arms of another. Very decent of him, I thought.'

'Oh, get away,' Agnès said. He had the strangest but most appealing gift of being able to make her laugh.

23

Le Mans

Dr Nezat, splendid in a figure-hugging dress, revealing an extensive cleavage, arrived at the hotel to collect Denis Deman. Her elegant calves were well set off by a pair of high-heeled, open-toed gold shoes. She seemed, Denis thought as she kissed him cordially on both cheeks, to have bathed rather liberally in what his sensitive nose suggested was Chanel 19.

He was to wonder in later life how Inès Nezat had coped with the smoking ban when, some years after their encounter, it was introduced into most of Europe. Perhaps by then she had given up cigarettes. But he always recalled her smoking like a navvy.

If his aim had been to charm his colleague, it appeared to have been achieved almost too easily. His only interest in her was Agnès, and the rescue plan he was devising. Not only Jean Dupère's conviction of the girl's innocence but the few conciliatory words of the unyielding Mother Catherine had restored his confidence that the girl would fare better under his care, even though that 'care' had been the unlucky cause of her incarceration. But as the evening went on he began to feel a touch of remorse that he had hooked this fish with so little bait beyond a clean white shirt from Monoprix and, he surmised, a thumping great bill to settle at the end of the evening.

He inquired about Dr Nezat's life as if he were truly interested and she described how she'd taken psychiatry as a second option. 'I really wanted to do surgery but I wasn't good enough.'

(Ah, yes, thought Denis Deman. So you hack about in people's minds instead.) He heard how she had married young, while still an unqualified medical student, and divorced her husband as soon as she got her first job. 'He was a drunk and a gambler. I knew this before I married him but I didn't realize the extent.'

Perhaps it had been drink, Denis Deman surmised, that had brought the Nezats together. Inès Nezat drank much as she smoked. An excellent claret disappeared before they had finished the first course and a second, slightly pricier – selected by her – vanished before he was halfway through his veal kidneys.

Denis Deman was fond of wine himself but he was not as a rule an immoderate drinker. Towards the end of his second course, he began to wonder if the usual amatory practices were being turned on their heads and that it was his guest who was attempting to get him drunk.

Happily, he had inherited his father's head for alcohol rather than that of his mother (who became more than usually embarrassing after one glass of cheap champagne). If that was Inès Nezat's game, he would sit her out. He was particularly anxious that there be no question arising of her sharing the expensive bed she had directed him towards, with, he now uncomfortably suspected, exactly that end in view. For one thing, it would be fatal to his plan to embarrass her by a refusal. For another he had not the slightest sexual interest in her.

It was tact as much as outright deceit that made him, not for the first time, produce what the English might refer to as his Bunbury, a fiancée whose existence he had called upon sufficiently often for her to have developed by now a distinctive, if necessarily ghostly, existence. A slender girl with pale, rather highly strung features and shoulder-length dark hair. Perhaps because of his mental connection with the famous alibi in the equally famous English play, this fiancée was English and based in London, which gave credence to his doing so much socially alone. For no reason he could explain – it merely came to him one day and he didn't especially care for it – her name was Anne, spelt in the French way with an *e*.

Anne's profession had careered somewhat wildly over the years of their long engagement. Having started life as another doctor (a cardiologist), Denis dropped that idea after one of the women he was trying to brush off suggested she get in touch with Anne when she was over doing a stint at Bart's (where he had currently located his imaginary fiancée). For some time now Anne had settled into being a vet. It seemed unlikely that anyone would wish to contact a foreign vet.

Inès Nezat, he suspected, would make short work of an absent fiancée, but she would be obliged to respect his principles. Principles had the merit of being admirable while at the same time acting as a useful deterrent.

He introduced Anne over the dessert via a discussion of the lowering standards required by medical schools.

'It always slightly surprises me,' Denis said, taking a cautious sip of the pricey Sauternes that his guest had ordered for them, 'that the requirements for a veterinary degree are so high. My fiancée studied at Cambridge and it was easily the hardest subject to get into.'

Inès Nezat raised two scimitar eyebrows. 'She's a vet?'

'Agricultural,' Denis said on a whim, mentally shifting the pliant Anne from a flat in Kensington to a draughty cottage in Norfolk. 'Very successful. Eventually she'll move here, of course; but there's plenty of farming work around Rouen.'

'How inconvenient to be apart.' Dr Nezat finished her wine and began to cast her eye about for the wine waiter. 'Shall we have another?'

'Let's,' said Denis, adding gallantly, 'it's really excellent.' The least he could do was to indulge her other tastes with a consolation prize.

After a lull in the conversation, Inès Nezat said she was going to powder her nose and returned with her war paint freshly applied. 'So how long have you two been engaged?'

Denis elected to say that he and 'his fiancée' had been together for some while but had only got engaged at Christmas. Happily for him, Inès did not pursue him for wedding details.

When the second glass of Sauternes arrived, he said, 'I was wondering if you felt it would help if I were to visit Agnès from time to time. I have a feeling that between us you and I could –'

'A kind of mother/father thing?' asked Inès Nezat, quite helpfully. Again, he found himself liking her.

'Exactly. I'm more and more convinced she didn't make that assault and if we can persuade her to recognize that –'

'Probably a displaced fantasy about murdering those nuns,' said Dr Nezat cheerfully. Her slight but noticeable aggression over the phantom Anne seemed to have been quickly dispelled.

She's not a bad sort, Denis reflected as he paid the monstrous bill. And would make quite a jolly friend.

He escorted her to her car, which, alarmingly, she revealed she proposed to drive home. 'Are you sure you wouldn't like me to get you a taxi?'

'Not in the least. I'm fine.'

He watched her skilfully manoeuvre the car out of its tight space and drive smartly off. She was the sort of woman his father should have married, he decided. Exuberant and probably good fun in bed, if 'fun' is what you wanted and she was the type you fancied.

Denis Deman called at the hospital the following morning. Inès Nezat had said she would not come in herself; as it was a Saturday, she was 'prescribing' herself 'a decent lie-in'. But when he arrived at Reception she had been as good as her word and had rung to say he had her permission to stay as long as he cared to with Agnès. Dr Nezat, he was informed, had also said he could use her office.

After about ten minutes, during which he examined Dr Nezat's sparsely filled bookshelf and leafed through an old copy of *Paris Match*, Agnès was ushered in by a nurse who said, 'Now be a good girl, Annie. Behave nicely with the doctor.'

Agnès stood looking blankly just behind his head until he said, 'Do sit down, please,' and then, 'What's with this "Annie"?'

'It's what they call me here.'

'Do you like it?'

'It's all right.'

' "All right" doesn't sound too all right to me. Would you like some coffee?'

'Don't mind.'

'Well, I'm having some.' He filled Dr Nezat's kettle at the small sink. It was, he observed, in need of a good clean.

'Sugar?'

'Yes, please.'

'How many lumps?'

'Two, please.'

Well, that was a start. He dropped two lumps of sugar from Dr Nezat's sugar bowl, which had Botticelli's naked Aphrodite printed on its side. 'Agnès, I wondered, I've been wondering what you remember . . .' Deliberately he let the sentence trail off.

'About what?'

'Anything. Anything at all.'

She thought. 'I remember your room. There was a map.'

'A map?'

'It looked like a map of something.' She made a spiral gesture with her forefinger.

'You mean the maze?'

Again she spiralled her finger and then, laying her other forefinger over it, made a cross.

'It's in a cathedral.'

'I liked the pattern.'

'Yes, I like it too. It's in the cathedral at Chartres.'

'Oh.'

'It's not far from here.'

She said nothing and he thought of how he had gone with his father to visit the cathedral just before his father died. He had been glad his mother had not accompanied them. She would have tarnished the whole experience.

Agnès said suddenly, 'I used to try to get to the middle with my eyes but I never could.'

'No, it would be difficult. I think you have to walk it.'

'How long do I have to stay here?'

'In this room?'

'No. In this place.'

'You don't like it here?'

She shrugged.

'If you, we, can persuade people that you won't do yourself or anyone else harm, we might be able to move you.'

'Will I be allowed to have my baby back?'

'No, I'm sorry.'

'I want my baby.'

'Agnès, I am so sorry.'

He sat there while she wept, and then, when he thought she must have wept her all, wept more, her eyes and nose running with the unchecked grief of the irreparable loss for which there was no comfort.

'Why didn't they let me keep him?'

'I suppose they thought you were too young.'

'I am not too young.' She turned her face shining with tears to him in an appeal he was powerless to grant.

'It's very terrible, I know.' There was no cure for the dreadful thing that had been done to this young life. And perhaps to her child's life. All he could do was to try to help her not fall further into the consequences. 'Agnès, I need your help.'

'What?'

'It's like this. I think I may have misunderstood you. I thought perhaps you had tried to get your baby back and' – he didn't want to speak words she might then put into her own mouth – 'and did not quite know what you were doing. A young woman, the nanny of a child, who wasn't yours –'

'He was mine.'

'No, Agnès. That child was not yours.'

'But I saw him,' Agnès said.

Denis Deman, who wanted to put his head in his hands and howl, instead said, 'Tell me what happened when you saw him.'

Agnès thought. 'He was in a pushchair. He had dark hair.'

'Was there anyone with him?'

She thought again. 'I don't remember.'

'So he was on his own, the child?'

'I saw him,' she said again, staring defiantly. 'Can I go now?'

24

Chartres

By the time Agnès' day of the week to clean came round again, Madame Beck's emotions had reached a pitch of excitement which she had seldom enjoyed since she uncovered Claude's first affair in Evreux. When the doorbell chimed, she opened the door to Agnès so swiftly that she gave her own ankle a nasty blow.

'Come into the salon, please.'

Agnès, who assumed there was to be some interrogation over the episode with Alain, wordlessly obeyed.

Madame Beck, limping slightly in her pale pink mules, pointed at the scallop-edged table. 'The doll.'

Agnès scanned the table, which was crowded with dolls in various states of fancy dress.

'Lulu, the little coloured doll' – Madame Beck paused for emphasis – 'is missing.'

For a moment, Agnès hadn't a clue what she was talking about and then she remembered. 'It was here last Tuesday.'

'You admit it?' Madame Beck was almost regretful to get such an easy admission.

'It was the day I washed the china. I noticed it was new.'

'And you notice it is not here now,' said Madame Beck grimly.

'If you say not, Madame.'

'I do,' said Madame Beck. Her ankle was beginning to throb. 'And you can either pay for it now or work the next three weeks for nothing.'

'I didn't take it,' said Agnès quite calmly, though she felt far from calm.

'I dare say you didn't. What I do say is that if you didn't take it, you broke it, and if you broke it, you concealed the damage from me. Had you come at once and owned up, I might have taken a different line,' said Madame Beck, quite untruthfully. 'But dishonesty is another matter.' She folded her arms over her high, well-bolstered bosom, the same bosom that long ago, when her world was young, her husband had liked to caress.

'I didn't take it or break it,' Agnès said. She had no expectation of being believed.

'No one but you has been here. No one else could have done it. Either you took it or you broke it. Or do you imagine that I broke it myself and it slipped my memory?' asked Madame Beck, smiling with a terrifying attempt at irony. Her teeth behind the thin lips were tombstones, large with gaps.

Agnès began, 'I do assure you, Madame –' but was interrupted.

'And I assure *you*, Mademoiselle, that I am neither forgetful nor demented.'

The scene brought to Agnès' mind another scene, when it also seemed she had done something she had no recollection of.

'If I'd broken it –' she began but once more was savagely interrupted.

'There is no "if". Either you broke it or you stole it. If the latter, then return it at once or I'll inform the police. If you own up to breaking it, I will allow you to pay for the breakage without informing the authorities.'

'I said I would pay for it.'

Robert Clément, trying once again to catch the faint shadow under Agnès' cheekbones that gave her face that hint of contemplative melancholy, dropped his pencil. 'Shit, the lead's broken. You can't do that. It's an admission of guilt.'

'I'd rather,' Agnès said. 'I'd rather pay her and leave.'

'Leave by all means. Leave you must. But neither must you pay for something you didn't do.'

'I'd rather,' Agnès said again. 'I don't want any trouble.'

'My dear girl, you are making trouble for yourself. How much is she rooking you for?'

'Sixty euros.'

'You're joking. A little china doll didn't cost sixty euros.'

'It was an antique.'

'She's mad. If you pay her I shan't let you work for me again.'

Agnès had never intended to sleep with Robert Clément. She did it for the simple and not uncommon reason that it seemed rude not to. He had, after all, set her up in Chartres, both helping to ensure that she stayed on at the café and giving her work as a model. But also it was through him that when she first arrived in Chartres she found her room with the Badons.

The Badons' large apartment was on the boulevard Charles Péguy close to the station, where the elderly Madame Badon lived more or less bedridden and from where her daughter, who worked in Paris, spent an unpredictable number of nights of each month away. Madame Badon the younger was looking for a reliable girl to help the elder Madame Badon to the commode and see to it that she took her sleeping pills or her laxative and didn't fall out of bed at night, or at least if she did to see to it that she was rescued from the floor. Also, someone to find her spectacles. Astonishing that in such a small space with such restricted movement she could lose them so often.

The room on offer was not large but it was the first real room Agnès had ever had to herself (you couldn't count the cell-like space at the convent). Once Agnès had established her credentials as reliable and clean, yet not averse to wiping her mother's bottom – a task that the younger Madame Badon found quite beyond her – the relief to the younger Madame Badon was such that she began to allow herself more and more latitude in time spent away. She had a lover in Paris on whom she found it necessary to keep an eye, so increasingly Agnès found she had only the elder Madame Badon to contend with.

The apartment had two bathrooms, but, as the elder Madame Badon never used hers, Agnès had a bathroom to herself. Apart from having no rent to pay, she saved money on food too, since the elder Madame still believed she had the appetite of her youth and had Agnès cook twice as much as – or more than – she could ever eat.

Agnès owed this stroke of good fortune to the fact that the younger Madame Badon had once been Robert Clément's mistress and indeed, though this was not widely known – or in fact known to anyone save Robert Clément and Madame Badon herself – she too had modelled for him in the days when her figure was firmer and both of them enjoyed seeing it naked. The affair had been one of mutual affection rather than passion, and, in the way of such arrangements, had drifted on until one or the other found a more desirable companion, or anyway one they were willing to own up to.

Madame Badon had met and fallen in love with her Parisian lover and had served notice on Robert but not without asking his aid in her search for someone to help with her mother. At the time, Robert had only recently met Agnès and she had agreed to model for him. He knew she was sleeping on Christelle's sofa and in need of more settled accommodation.

The introduction worked to everyone's advantage. It assured the younger Madame Badon that she and Robert would remain on good terms, it relieved Robert of Madame Badon (who was beginning to bore him), and it gave Agnès her first taste of secure freedom. So when, after a session sitting for Robert, he pressed her more ardently than usual and eased her, quite gently, down on to his studio couch it seemed only polite to let him proceed.

That this was a mistake she was to realize later. It gave Robert an appetite which she had no wish to continue to feed. She had endured a couple of sexual liaisons, both brief, unsatisfactory and, for various reasons, painful, arising more from a general difficulty in refusal and perhaps a faint hope of comfort than from any true desire. She didn't mind the modelling, though she preferred more active employment, but negotiating Robert's embraces was embarrassing. In the end, by way of explanation, she called upon the religion she had been brought up with. 'I'm Catholic.'

'It didn't stop you before.'

'I know but I can't again.'

'You can go to confession afterwards.'

'I'd rather not.'

Robert had been a handsome man in his youth and, having failed to take a realistic account of the inevitable erosions of time, he was still a little vain. He was disappointed that the lovely young creature whom he had felt sure he had satisfied had turned suddenly prudish on him. It was not the first time he'd met this feminine line of resistance but it never occurred to him that the reasons for these refusals might be more to do with the measure of his desirability than with piety or the exercise of moral scruples. In this case, however, it was more important to him that Agnès model for him.

Robert's was not at all a religious disposition except in one – for him – important matter: he had nursed for years an ambition to paint a nativity. Perhaps this was some sort of rebellion against his famous ancestor, whose paintings in the Impressionist style were secular in subject and mood. Whatever the reason for his passionate ambition, Robert felt that in Agnès he had found the perfect model for his Mary.

Because his bread-and-butter work was the production of versions of the stained-glass stories – sometimes simply a figure in one of the panels, sometimes the whole drama – the time he had for his own artistic interest was limited. But he was as dedicated as any religious devotee to his aim of accomplishing a representation of his ideal Madonna.

After twenty years, and many failed attempts, he was still struggling to pull off his dream. And Agnès, with her unusual capacity for stillness and her striking bone-structure, continued no less inspiring in his eyes.

Agnès for her part felt safe with him. She was fond of him, and in his debt. He was getting old, his peacock feathers were visibly moulting, and because she had a certain fellow feeling for all creatures on the run, or in decline, she allowed him, from time to time, to fondle her so as not to dent what she understood was a self-preserving vanity.

But, for all that, she was not about to follow his advice over how best to deal with Madame Beck.

25

Rouen

Almost the very moment that Denis Deman returned from Le Mans he rang Jean Dupère.

'Jean? Denis Deman here. I thought you might like to know I've seen Agnès again.'

'How does the little one do?'

'I wonder, if it's not inconvenient, may I visit you again?'

Spring had made bold strides since Denis had last driven out to the Dupère farm. The cows stood in solid white shapes beneath the dark green shadows of craggy apple trees, already crowned with flourishes of pink and white. The river flowed quicksilver in the clear evening light. There was no barn owl encounter; only a voluble gang of rooks, which rose in rowdy unison into the sheer sky as Denis Deman's old Renault rattled down the farm track, still deeply pitted with mud but thankfully now dry.

Jean Dupère was out of bed and sitting in the rocking chair by the fire. He did not get up but extended a veined brown hand.

'Good evening, Doctor. You'll take some Calva?'

The apple liquor burned Denis's throat and then spread agreeably across the lining of his stomach.

'That's quite something!'

'The apples are from my own orchards. We've had a still here since my grandmother's time, though the neighbour sees to it now. Sit, Doctor, please.'

Denis sat and for a few minutes simply sipped the heavenly scented Calvados from the stout green glass. Finally he said, 'I gave Agnès your earring.'

'Not mine.'

'The one you wanted me to give her. I never found the right moment before.'

The old man made a gesture with his two hands as if to say whatever the doctor did it would be right. The gesture irked Denis Deman, who knew that very little he had done for Agnès to date had been 'right'.

'I forgot about it,' he said coldly, and then felt remorse because the old man looked at him with bewilderment in his faded eyes. 'I didn't find a moment and then, you know, the fracas, and so, well, I took it to her in Le Mans last weekend. I told her you had planned to give it to her on her birthday. She was very pleased.'

'She is sixteen now?'

'Just gone.'

'January twenty-first. St Agnès' Day. I remember it like yesterday.'

He relived that moment often: the basket, the small baby wrapped in a white tablecloth; the little earring trapped in an unravelling weave of the basket. The basket which still hung on his wall.

'She seemed pleased,' Denis said again. He was feeling foolish. The conversations with Agnès had got nowhere.

'She is wearing it?'

'I don't know. She asked if she could have her ears pierced.'

'Please, Doctor, would you go to the dresser over there?'

Jean Dupère pointed at a dark oak dresser on which plates, cups and bowls of red-and-white china were ranged. 'The drawer on the left. There is a box.'

'This?'

'Yes. Bring it here if you would be so kind.'

Denis took the little green box to his host, who opened it and brought out a silver chain. 'I would like her to have this. The earring could be made to hang on it, I think.'

'I'm sure that's possible.'

'You will please give it to her as a birthday gift from me? It was my mother's. She had a crucifix on it but we buried that with her. Mother did not care for my niece. I have been puzzling whom I should leave it to.'

'Why didn't she like your niece?' Denis Deman ran the fine chain through his fingers.

'She felt she was greedy. My mother had good judgement. But she is all I have, my niece. Except the little Agnès.'

'I'll get a jeweller to fix the earring on this if you like.' It seemed all he was going to be able to do for his former charge.

But even in this he was foiled. 'I would like to pay for it. My wallet is also in the drawer, if you wouldn't mind.'

Denis found it and the old man took out a ten-franc note. 'This will be enough?'

'More than enough, I should imagine.'

'Buy her a little something with anything over. Some sweets. Or a little pastry. She is so thin.' He could cry aloud thinking of the child lying so still and gaunt in her white nightdress in her bed at the clinic.

'She's less so now,' said Denis. The physical change in Agnès was for him still very shocking, for one of his unfashionable beliefs was that appearances were an accurate reflection of the psyche.

'I would love to see her.'

'Yes,' Denis agreed, meaning that that was quite impossible.

But driving back up the track he thought, But why not? I could bring her here. She would be in my care. It might involve another sticky dinner with Inès Nezat but Paris was worth a mass.

Inès Nezat appeared to have digested the existence of the fictive Anne and elected to ignore her. Or that, anyway, was Denis Deman's conclusion when she arrived, splendidly attired, at the more modest hotel he had chosen for his next visit. 'Attired' seemed to him the correct term, as the excessive sheen on her satin suit and high-heeled silver shoes suggested some sort of fashionable armour. If previously she had bathed in scent, this time she might have washed her hair in it.

Denis Deman was prone to allergies, which were also affected by his emotional state. Assaulted by the emanations of his guest's pungent scent, his eyes began to run and he sneezed.

'You have a cold?'

'How are you, Inès? You look well.'

Inès Nezat took this compliment as if it were only to be expected. 'I am, thank you. You look tired.'

Denis, who had been feeling rather better, recognized that this was an opening gambit in a not-too-subtle game of power. Nevertheless, he felt dashed. 'I've been working hard.'

'All work and no play . . .' Inès wagged a playful forefinger at him, the nail expertly varnished a dark cerise.

'I agree,' said Denis, who didn't at all. He loved his work and as a rule couldn't wait to get back to it. It was holidays he disliked. Anne, of course, sensibly took her holidays alone – or with friends.

Inès said she had booked a new restaurant that they should try, which was conveniently located just round the corner from his hotel. The suggestion raised some alarm in Denis, since he suspected that the restaurant's proximity to his sleeping quarters might be part of a renewed plan of seduction on her part.

He inwardly vowed to keep the conversation solely focused on work.

'I'm afraid I didn't make much headway with Agnès last time I came here,' he offered, once they had been seated and an overly tall menu had been consulted. Inès had ordered an hors d'oeuvre of sweetbreads followed by lobster, while he, in an effort to control the cost of the evening – which, he predicted, would once again be considerable – had ordered a simple endive-and-Roquefort salad and, to follow, a rabbit ragoût.

Inès Nezat blew a cloud of considering smoke and stared hard at him. 'You seem very wrapped up in Agnès.'

Denis found himself blushing. 'I feel badly about her. '

'As I don't have to tell you, we must avoid an over-identification.'

No, you don't have to tell me, thought Denis Deman, who loathed psychological jargon. 'But I failed her. We must be prepared to acknowledge our mistakes, surely.'

'What was your mistake exactly?' She was still staring at him with her rather hard-boiled eyes.

Denis decided to volley a half-truth. 'I encouraged her to take long walks. She should have been supervised but there never seemed to be any question of her doing anyone other than herself any harm.'

'That was perhaps misguided,' said Inès, frowning slightly.

I've just said it was, haven't I? thought Denis Deman and outwardly continued in his smoothest tone, 'Somehow, having heard of the disaster, she developed the fantasy, as you know, that if she had not committed the crime at least that the child was hers. Had she been supervised better, this disaster could never have happened.'

'And we know she didn't do it?'

'We *know* next to nothing,' Denis Deman exclaimed, losing, for a moment, his self-command. 'She didn't mention the nanny at all when I was with her, then or now, but she insisted, and still maintains, the child was hers. But no evidence of her being there was ever discovered. And the girl was interrogated for days.'

'You weren't with her?'

'The psychiatrist appointed by the court saw her. Her answers were, he felt, ambiguous. In any case, enough for him to recommend tighter supervision. And so –'

'So she came to us. Well, she's coping fairly well. Shall we order the wine?'

Over the lobster, Inès Nezat, as he had feared, brought up his engagement. 'How often does Anne come over?'

'Oh, quite a bit,' Denis said, forking rabbit ineptly into his mouth so that some of the gravy juice ran down his tie. 'How's your lobster?'

'Very good. So you go to see her there? In the UK?'

'A little less. Animals you know are less likely to have nervous breakdowns and demand emergency treatment.'

The two scimitar eyebrows indicated that she found his attempt at humour slightly pathetic. 'So when are you two booked to marry?'

'Next year,' said Denis, in some desperation. 'In London.'

'But you said she lived in Norfolk.'

'Her parents live in London,' said Denis Deman stoutly. He'd better decide where. Maybe Kensington, where Anne herself had lived before he moved her east. Keen to get away from the subject of his fictive fiancée, he said, more bluntly than he had planned, 'I was wondering about Agnès. Would you have any objection if I took her to meet the old man who found her? He's got cancer and is probably not long for this world. It might help Agnès to meet him. She's become a bit of a fairytale child in his eyes.'

Inès Nezat's expression suggested that she had little truck with fairytales.

By the end of the meal, however, a bottle of Pouilly-Fumé,

a very good claret and a large Armagnac for Inès Nezat, the deal seemed to have somehow or other been clinched. And, thank God, Denis Deman reflected, sponging his stained tie in the bathroom of his modest hotel room, he had not had to clinch Inès Nezat in return. She was a woman, he decided, who liked to take a crack at things but was blessedly free of resentment when she didn't succeed. When she bade him good night, after a very matey kiss, she said, 'Give Anne my regards if you speak to her. Say any time she's over I'd love to meet her. You're very loyal to her. She must be quite a girl.'

He had wondered for a second if she was being arch but decided, giving the tie up as a bad job, it was simply that she was showing him that she was a good sport – or, at any rate, not a bad one.

26

Chartres

Philippe Nevers often encountered Agnès on her way to clean the cathedral as he made his own way down from his apartment in the place du Cygne, to catch the early Paris train. If he was not running late – which he mostly was – he usually stopped for a bit of friendly banter with his old babysitter. He had defended her once and those we defend will tend to occupy a tender spot in our loyalties.

Philippe managed a fashion boutique in Paris in the 16th arrondissement. For such an otherwise likeable young man he had made himself needlessly unpopular, as his friend Tan often told him, with women – especially the women of Chartres, who were cautious in their dress – with his bold sartorial suggestions. But he admired Agnès' indifference to fashion, an indifference, as he explained to Tan, which is the basis of true style.

However, that morning he had weightier things than fashion on his mind.

'Good morning, Agnès. Listen, my sister – you remember, Brigitte? – is coming to stay with her new baby. Things aren't going too well with her current man so she needs a place to hole up in while they decide what to do. I couldn't say no.'

Agnès, who remembered Brigitte, smiled.

'You couldn't do a couple of hours' cleaning for me? She's always been an obsessional, God knows, but with this kid she's become totally neurotic. Or maybe it's the break-up. Who can tell?'

'When do you need it done by?'

'Agnès, you're an angel. Look, take the spare key. You know where I am, by the flower stall, first floor, over the estate agent's. Any time before the weekend. I like that shade of red with the green, by the way.'

Agnès opened the inner door of the North Porch as quietly as the weight of the wood and the age of the hinges allowed. But Alain was there, apparently waiting for her on the altar dais.

'Breakfast?'

'Thanks, I've had some.' She went to the kitchenette but when she returned, bucket and mop in hand, he was there still.

'What's up?'

'Nothing.'

'In case you don't know, your face is an open book. What's up?' he asked again. He peered at her and then said, quite nastily, 'It's that bloody old bitch, isn't it?'

'Yes.'

'I'll go and see her. Tell her I was merely picking you up from the floor. No hanky-panky, though what in God's name it has to do with –'

'It isn't that,' Agnès interrupted.

'So what is it?'

'She thinks I took or broke something.'

'What?'

'A china doll.'

'What!'

'A little antique doll. She collects them. It's missing and she thinks I took it, or broke it.'

'So what if you did?'

'She said she'll report it to the police.'

At which he threw his head back, laughing. 'Don't be an idiot. She probably broke it herself in a fit of rage. My bones are good at clocking madness and they definitely dislike her. She's deranged.'

'That's what Robert said.'

'Who's Robert?'

'A painter. I sit for him.'

'The hell you do.'

'I've sat for him for years,' Agnès said. 'He's harmless. He comes in here quite often to paint the stained glass.'

'I've seen him. And his stuff. It's vile.'

'He has to make a living,' Agnès said. 'He's been very kind to me. He got me work when I came here. And a room.'

'Are you lovers?'

She blushed. 'Of course not.'

Alain treated her to a long look. 'It has been heard of. Anyway, Ma Beck can't report you to the police for a doll. Tell her to go and boil her head.'

But Agnès, having completed her work and chatted for five minutes with the Abbé Bernard, who was anxious to know if she believed in miracles – 'But the Holy tunic, Agnès, you think it really did effect cures?' – called by Madame Beck's apartment with an envelope in which she had placed three twenty-euro notes. She posted the envelope through the letterbox without ringing the chiming bell, which did not prevent Madame Beck from hastening to the window when she heard the letterbox to observe her former cleaner as she hurried away down the rue aux Herbes to the safety of Professor Jones's apartment.

The archiving at Professor Jones's was coming on apace. The faded and discoloured wallpaper in the study was now almost completely hidden by a collection of skilfully-mounted photographs of his past. Professor Jones had been so animated by the recovery of his own history that he had begun to write his recollections of his childhood in Wales. He discussed these from time to time with Agnès as she tried to sort his lectures and his lecture notes, a harder task for her than the letters or photos.

Seeing what she was doing, he said, 'May I have a look at the article on Rheims?'

Agnès stopped sorting. 'Which?'

Pointing vaguely he said, 'That one on the floor beside you.'

Agnès, who could recognize an *R*, passed him a paper.

'No, not Rome, Rheims.'

She looked up at him from her position on the floor and perhaps because of his recent plunge into childhood he understood that what he saw in her face was fear. 'Agnès, you can read?'

'No.'

'My God. And you've sorted all this for me. How?'

She shrugged, ashamed.

'One would almost say you didn't need to read with guesswork like that.'

'I wish I could, though.'

'Would you like me to teach you?'

'I can't. They tried.'

'Who tried?'

'Sister Véronique.'

'You have a sister?'

At which she laughed aloud. 'She was a nun. I was brought up by nuns.'

'You're Catholic, then?'

'I was an orphan,' Agnès said. 'I had no choice.'

It was many years since Professor Jones had felt any true concern about anyone but himself. Even his philanthropic interest in the beggars was, at heart, self-regarding. But the young woman with her brightly coloured clothes and her quiet presence had smoothed away some of the cares which had clogged his natural curiosity. The recovery of his childhood memories had restored something of the child's keener perception. He took her hand. 'How very horrid for you, my dear.'

And Agnès, on her knees, also felt a novel sensation. One she had not experienced for many years. She felt she was going to cry.

Two hours later she let herself into Philippe Nevers' apartment, as unlike Professor Jones's as it was possible to be. The salon, which looked over the tree-filled square, was full of light, the minimal furniture all in the latest contemporary taste down to the kitchen utensils, which that year were being sold in apple-green. Did Philippe renew them each time the fashion changed, or was it just a lucky coincidence?

There was a faint smell of cooking oil so she opened a kitchen window to air the place. Otherwise, it seemed spotless. The neurotic Brigitte could hardly find much to complain about.

Nevertheless, Agnès found a tidily arranged cupboard of cleaning materials and set to work. As she wiped the frames of the pictures on Philippe's walls, half wondering, but with no very burning curiosity, how his sister would react to these – for the most part they were images of naked men in startling erotic poses – she reflected on her strange morning with Professor Jones.

An unusually determined Professor had sat Agnès down at his kitchen table, which thanks to her was no longer covered in a patina of ancient grease, where he insisted on giving her tea, for, despite his many years of living in France, the professor clung to his native belief in the remedial powers of strong tea. Then he had begun her reading lesson.

Among the treasures of his past, revealed in the course of the 'archiving', were some of the professor's childhood books: *Treasure Island*, *Alice* both *In Wonderland* and *Through the Looking-Glass*, a child's version of Malory's *Le Morte d'Arthur*, *Doctor*

Dolittle, *Biggles* and the *Just So Stories*. None of these seemed to him quite the thing to engage a young, illiterate woman.

Searching through a cardboard suitcase, retrieved from under a sagging divan bed (now relieved of its cover of papers) and stuffed with a motley collection of books, the professor found a copy of *Little Black Sambo* which he concealed hastily in a paper bag. He did not himself see what was wrong with *Little Black Sambo* but he was aware that this, any more than *Doctor Dolittle* or *Biggles*, was not quite the thing for Agnès to learn to read from.

Further delvings into the suitcase revealed a paperback copy of *The Secret Garden*. Opening it, he read, on the title page in a round childish hand, 'If this book should dare to roam/ Box its ears and send it home to/ Gwen Williams, Church House, Broad Street, Presteigne, Radnorshire, Wales, Great Britain, Europe, the Northern Hemisphere, The World, The Milky Way.' Beneath these words was a picture of the sun, the moon, some planets and a shooting star. Each had a smiling face except the star, which was sticking out a contemptuous fiery tongue.

How did *The Secret Garden* come to have roamed so far afield? He remembered Church House, the home of his maternal uncle and aunt, with fondness: a square, redbrick family home with two tall chimneys, which stood by the grassy graveyard of St Andrew's Church, with its 'holy' spring and venerably twisted yew tree. He had had fine times there in the holidays, playing with his cousins in the roomy attic and immense cupboards, just made for games of Sardines and hide-and-seek.

The story of Mary Lennox, the orphaned girl sent from India to Yorkshire, he now suddenly remembered, he had read to his cousin Gwen, the summer she had chickenpox so badly that her face had swelled and she couldn't read. Was it merely one of those accidental thefts which had never been rectified or had he gone away with the book on purpose?

He had been a little in love with Gwen, who had wild dark red hair, which she tossed from her face like a mountain pony, and a white, white skin – skin like the slivers of bark from the birch trees that had fascinated him too, and which he had enjoyed peeling off for his cousin to make into fairy slippers and other magical artefacts. Once he had kissed her, while they were playing Sardines and hiding in one of the Church House cupboards, and she had seemed not to mind.

'I will translate this into French, simple French, and read you each chapter aloud first,' he announced to Agnès, 'so you will understand the story,' and commenced translating at once. After half an hour, he announced with unusual firmness, 'Now stop sorting and come here by me.'

It was the first time, since the days of Sister Laurence, that Agnès had listened to a story (other than those she heard on the radio) and, for all Professor Jones's odd accent and sonorous reading style, within three pages she was entranced.

27

Evreux

Agnès said very little on the drive with Denis Deman from the hospital in Le Mans to the outskirts of Evreux. She sat staring out of the passenger window, apparently absorbed in the sight of the passing countryside.

From time to time, he glanced at her to see if she was all right, but any question was met with an inevitable, 'Fine, thank you, Doctor.'

What a strange undertaking he had embarked on. Inès Nezat was right to be suspicious – it was untoward to take such an interest in the girl. But, more and more, he was convinced that it was he himself who had precipitated this further tragedy of hers, as if her circumstances had not been quite tragic enough without his clumsy interference.

The girl was illiterate. What in the world had induced him to suppose she had read her file? Sheer panic at his own foolhardiness in going to that address. And then he had compounded that idiotic error by writing the address in her file. And that error had led, by a ghastly chain of consequences, to the grosser error of his supposing that she had come to the conclusion at which he, so mistakenly, had arrived. What a complete and utter and ludicrous fool he had been.

His hope now was that meeting Jean Dupère might help the girl towards a better sense of her own reality. The past that she had really lived and not the fantasy in which he had haplessly encouraged her to believe. The real past, of course, was starkly painful. No parents, no known relatives, no knowledge of her background, no child, or any she could see or care for, only this one – rather decent – human being whose connection with her was probably too tangential to provide any true sense of being held in another's heart.

As the Renault bumped down the now familiar track to the Dupère farm, Denis Deman felt a clawing apprehension. It was very likely another of his mad ideas, bringing these two together again. Jean Dupère would not recognize in the lumpen, spotty girl with the lank and greasy hair the pale, sylphlike creature he had last seen, lying comatose in her bed in the clinic. Now the poor child was comatose again, in an alien waking world, muffled in her mind by the drugs in which he had no confidence.

The old man must have heard the car for he was waiting at an open door.

'Little Agnès.' Not a hint of surprise or disappointment in his face. Only an expression of eager welcome. 'Come in, come in.'

Jean Dupère's helpful neighbour had plainly been round, since lunch was on the kitchen table. He was anxious to tell them it was all home grown.

'Radishes and lettuce from the garden. Tomatoes. Our own cured ham and the Camembert is from our neighbour. Take some milk.'

Without waiting for Agnès to answer, he poured her a glass of milk from a pitcher from which he had removed a muslin cloth weighted with blue-glass beads.

Agnès sat and drank the milk obediently.

'Help yourself, sweetheart. Doctor?'

Denis Deman took several slices of ham. He found he was suddenly terrifically hungry. Jean Dupère helped Agnès to a mountain of food but took nothing except bread and cheese for himself. Silently, they all began to eat.

Suddenly Jean Dupère, wiping his moustache with a napkin,

said, 'See that basket hanging over there, left of the fire? That's what I found you in.'

Agnès stopped eating, fork poised in the air, and stared at the old straw basket.

'Go on. Take it down.'

She looked across at Denis Deman and he realized she was waiting for permission.

'It's OK, Agnès. You can get down from the table.'

She moved across the kitchen, reached up and detached the basket from the black hook.

'That's what I found you in,' the old man repeated. It was a moment he had envisaged often without ever quite believing in its realizable possibility. He was not, therefore, prepared for Agnès' reaction, which was to stand in the middle of the kitchen floor holding in her two hands what had stood in for her crib and shed solemn tears.

Jean Dupère was appalled.

Denis Deman tried to reassure him. 'Naturally, she is moved. It's catharsis.'

Which was Greek, of course, to the old man.

'I meant it for a nice surprise.' He had taken down the basket beforehand, in readiness for this moment, and shaken out the cobwebs, dead flies, moths and live earwigs, which had somehow negotiated a home there.

'It will be.' Denis Deman let Agnès cry. The old man's dismay also prevented his making any attempt at consoling the girl. Tearless now, she stood in a pool of summer light, trembling. She seemed to Denis Deman's imagination like the trapped leveret he had found as a boy in a meadow near his home.

'Really, you have done nothing wrong,' he assured the worried old man again much later, when Jean was conducting them round his farm and Agnès was picking field flowers. 'It is roughly what I expected – hoped for.'

'For her to take on so?'

'For her to begin to feel what she must so long have been feeling.'

'She will recover? She can come away from that – that place?'

'We can only hope so. You've done a good deal already with the earring, and now this. If she can recover the memory of her own life maybe she'll be able to give up the one she has created.'

'But she will never have her baby?'

The question, as they both knew, was rhetorical.

'She will have to learn to bear it. It is a wrong she has been done but we must be prepared to believe that the Sisters supposed they were doing what was best for her and the child.'

But if Denis Deman supposed he could get away with sanctimonious expressions, he was to be proved wrong.

'They did it because they believe in "good and evil",' Jean Dupère, with surprising heat, declared. 'I am to blame. I gave her to them. I did wrong but they, *they* have done her an evil in their wrong belief.' He turned candidly angry eyes on Denis.

'Maybe,' said Denis Deman, impressed by this vehemence. 'But the main thing is, what can we do now for her for the best?'

He was considering this further when the three had said goodbye, with a promise to meet again the next day, and he was driving Agnès to the clinic, where she was to spend one night.

Agnès was clutching the basket containing the already wilting poppies and cornflowers, some eggs, courtesy of Jean Dupère's neighbour, and an embroidered prayer card to St Agnès, which Jean Dupère had found in the pages of his mother's old receipt book. As they drove, she hummed a tune Denis Deman did not recognize.

'Did you enjoy the visit, Agnès?'

'Yes.'

'You would like to go again tomorrow?'

'Yes, please. I would like to.'

Well, that was a start.

She seemed pleased too when they arrived at the clinic and climbed eagerly out of the car, with the basket in hand.

'We've given you a room here. Come.' He led her to the private wing, where the rooms were single.

'I'm not sharing?'

'No. Unless you'd rather.'

'Maybe.'

'Would you rather, Agnès?'

'Yes, please, Doctor.'

This posed a problem. He could not in all conscience put her in with one of the fee-paying patients. It would have to be one of the others, who might disconcert her, and the visit must be as calm as possible if it were to be a success. Maybe, he thought, one of the nurses might be induced to spend the night with her.

Denis Deman had remained mildly attracted to the tall Australian nurse who had, quite unwittingly, set him off on his wild-goose hunt for Agnès' child. Inquiry revealed that she was about to come off her shift and he found her and explained the situation. 'Might you be willing to spend the night here with her?'

'Is she violent?'

'There's no evidence of it. She's only ever harmed herself. We, that is her current consultant and I, think now that this fixation she had on the other child is pure delusion.'

'Poor mite. Funny I should have known the family.'

To cover his embarrassment Denis Deman said, 'You might be able to help there. Talk to her about it. About him.'

'You mean the other boy?'

'Yes. What was his name?'

'Caspar.'

He remembered now the child's grotesque conjunction of names. 'The thing is, I feel if she can surrender this delusion that the boy is hers we can reasonably appeal to have her de-sectioned. She's no business in a secure hospital. She's quite harmless.'

'OK. But if I'm found knifed in the back it's on your head, mind. I want this in writing.'

Dr Deman spoke with some stiffness. 'Naturally, there will be someone on duty. I'm only asking you to sit with her and keep her company.'

'Don't get your knickers in a knot, Doctor. Of course I'll help out. What's she come here for, anyway?'

Denis explained. 'Ah, poor thing. It's like a story – a baby in a basket. So the old man wants to see her?'

'I wanted him to, in fact. I thought it might help establish her own history for her.'

'It would help. My dad never knew his dad. My grandma's indigenous – "abo" to you.' Denis Deman attempted to protest but she laughed and said, 'It's OK. We're used to it. No, as I was saying, my dad's dad was some white guy who had his way with my grandma and then relieved himself of any responsibility. Dad spent half his life trying to find him. Good riddance, Mum and I say, but blood's thicker than water, I guess.'

'But Jean Dupère isn't Agnès' "blood".'

'He might be the nearest thing. Of course I'll watch her. Nice little thing, she was.'

'She's rather a big thing now.'

'Rotten diet in those places. I wouldn't work in one myself.'

'Maddy, I forget, why did you leave?'

'It wasn't the boy. He was a pet. It was the father – couldn't keep his hands to himself. I can manage that but she, Miss

Moonshine, or whatever she called herself, guessed and there was an atmosphere. I hate atmospheres.'

Denis Deman took Maddy to introduce her to Agnès. 'So, then, Agnès, I'll leave you with Nurse Fisher –'

'Maddy, please.'

'Maddy will look after you this evening and I'll see you in my room tomorrow morning.'

When he had gone, Maddy said, 'Come to pay us a little visit?'

'Yes.'

'What's it like in Le Mans?'

'OK.'

'Nicer here, though.'

'Yes.'

'Well, I'm going to keep you company tonight. Anything you'd like to do?'

'I don't know.'

'OK. We'll just stay cool, then.'

Asked if she might like to walk in the garden, Agnès agreed that she might. They strolled for a while but she seemed ill at ease outside and said what she would really like was to watch the pop programme on TV.

'Sure. There's a TV in the common room. Supper now or after?'

They ate supper watching the pop programme. After about twenty minutes Maddy observed Agnès had kicked off her shoes. Later, as Agnès was getting ready for bed, Maddy said, 'You like it here, don't you?'

'Yes.'

'You know what, you might be able to come back.'

'How?'

'Well . . .' The doctor had told her to have a try at talking to her so why not have a go? Maddy sat down on the bed. 'The little boy you say was yours. He's not. I was his nanny so I know.'

Agnès stared at her.

'The thing is, the nanny with him was attacked, quite seriously, I hear, though she's OK now. Thank my lucky stars I was out of it or it might have been me. But they can't risk your maybe having done that. That's why they sent you off to Le Mans. If you can say he isn't yours, and you know that now and you didn't do anything and it's all been a terrible mistake, they'll maybe stop worrying about you going after someone with a knife. See?'

'Would it mean I could leave there?'

'Well, don't quote me but it's a possibility. They might send you back here for a while and then, you know, you could do what you wanted.'

'What would I have to say?'

'OK,' Maddy said. 'So this is how it goes. They'd have to believe you. So it has to sound like you mean it. Not like I've told you. Or anyone else told you. OK?'

She accompanied Agnès to Denis Deman's room the following morning.

'Everything go all right last night with you two?'

Denis Deman had passed a restless night. Much as he wanted to believe in Agnès' innocence, Maddy's quip about the knife in the back had unsettled him. Agnès was a dark horse. No one, he felt, least of all himself, had ever fully fathomed her. Perhaps after all his first impressions were correct and she had been the author of this violent deed.

'We had a great time, didn't we, Agnès?'

Agnès beamed. 'Yes, we did, Maddy.'

The reassurance from the strong Australian girl revived Denis Deman's spirits. 'Very good. Thank you, Maddy.'

'Not at all. We enjoyed ourselves, didn't we, Agnès? Remember what I told you, now?'

Agnès favoured her with a radiant smile.

'What was it that Nurse Fisher told you?' Denis Deman asked a little later. They were in his room. Above his desk, she saw again the maze on the wall. If she tried really hard she was sure she could follow the path with her eyes to the centre.

'Agnès?'

Oh, but she never could get past that first loop round to the right. 'She told me that she looked after the baby I said was mine and she told me he wasn't mine.'

'She did?'

'Yes.'

'And what do you think of that?'

'I think I made a mistake.'

'And you were never there?' It was a leading question but to hell with that.

'It was a mistake. I didn't do anything. Can I come back here now?'

28

Chartres

When, twenty years later, Agnès looked back on this period of her life, it seemed to her that she had descended into an intractable hellish nightmare and then everything had resolved into an improbably happy dream.

She only very dimly recalled the time of the first troubles, the hours and hours during which people had questioned her about the attack and her abiding feeling that all she had to cling to was that the baby was – must be – she knew he was – her own little Gabriel. She was assured of this again from the pictures she was shown – the little curly-haired boy with the pointed features and pale brown skin. Of course he was her baby. All she had done was try to take him back.

But this later time was different. He was not her baby. She knew this now. And to find her real child she had to get away. Maddy was her friend. Maddy had told her how.

'Stick to your guns, sweetie. Simple denial, repeated then repeated again, works wonders. My dad was accused of stealing once. He worked in a garage and some jerk was light-fingering the till. My dad said he just went on denying and denying and denying and they found who did it before he gave up. Tell them you made a mistake, you were upset, out of your mind, whatever helps. It's true after all.'

This time there were interviews she remembered in detail. Always holding on to the idea that the one fact Maddy had taught her would get her through. 'I know now he was not my baby. I made a mistake.'

'But you insisted he was yours at the time.'

'I imagined it.'

'And you were never at this address?'

A piece of paper was held out to her. 'I don't recognize it.'

'You never went there?'

She shrugged. 'I don't know where that is.'

But this was not enough to stop the questions. 'You have no recollection, then, of going to this address and attacking Michelle Boyet with a knife?'

Be firm, Maddy had said. Don't give up. Remember my dad. Stick to your guns.

'No.'

'No recollection at all?'

'It was a mistake. I was upset. I said things. I see that now. I say things that aren't true when I am upset.'

('Good girl,' Maddy had said when they were practising that night. 'Saying you were "upset" is just the ticket. They can't argue with that.')

Dr Nezat had of course become involved in the decision over the reconsideration of Agnès' psychiatric status. She gave it, at some length, as her opinion that Agnès had been suffering a psychotic delusion as a consequence of the trauma of losing her own child. Nothing remotely aggressive had ever been observed in her behaviour at the psychiatric hospital. On the contrary, she was passive and biddable, maybe even too much so, at all times. The girl's previous consultant, Dr Deman, had visited her, quite properly, as he was concerned that there had been a confusion in the diagnosis, and suggested they try this brief return to Agnès' past environment in the hope that it might jolt her into a better sense of reality. Clearly the experiment had worked. She, Dr Nezat, would certainly recommend that the girl be sent back to the clinic under Dr Deman's care for the rehabilitation, apparently so successfully started, to continue.

Maddy had been triumphant when, after many further discussions, it was agreed that the secure order be lifted and Agnès was, after some bureaucratic toing and froing, returned to St Francis's. 'Well done! See. It worked.'

'I want to stay here,' Agnès had said.

'You can't stay for ever. But the main thing is you've got that rubbish off your back. Real life's horrible but it's safer in the long run than make believe.'

But was it? Agnès wondered now, as she wiped over Philippe Nevers' perspex coffee table with the 'natural' orange spray, moving the glass sculpture of the couple, engaged in what looked like an act of sodomy, with especial care. The episode with Madame Beck, so reprehensible to Robert Clément, so laughable to Alain, was to her a source of renewed dread. Twenty years had passed safely in Chartres with nothing more troubling than the elder Madame Badon's lost spectacles to vex or perturb her. The scene over the missing doll brought back the fear she had lived with daily, hourly, through those dreadful years – the 'special' hospital in Le Mans, and before that the nursing home, and before all of that the day in the convent orchard.

She had told no one, not even herself, about that afternoon when, her duties all accomplished, she had climbed the slightly rickety wooden ladder she had found set against an apple tree. It must have been April, she supposed. The blossom was out, she remembered that, because that was why she had climbed up into the tree, to pick some sprays of bloom for the Mother's room. Mother Catherine had liked apple blossom.

Why the ladder was there she no longer knew, if she had ever known. Maybe the trees were being sprayed?

Pointless, oh, pointless such rememberings, brought back

now, and not a jot less painfully, by this fresh calamity with Madame Beck. And with it, like the long train of cosmic dirt of a slow, dangerously returning comet, the recollection of the other catastrophe.

The clinic and Le Mans. And kind Dr Deman, who had told her about the labyrinth. She had sat in his room so often while he had gently questioned her and she – she had to laugh a little at this now, polishing Philippe's bedside cabinet with the beeswax polish she had found in his neat cupboard – she had told him next to nothing, only answering as politely as he had questioned her, always staring up at the strange beguiling pattern he had behind him on the wall.

29

Chartres

'She would never have paid up so promptly if she hadn't broken it,' Madame Beck declared to Madame Picot at their next meeting.

Madame Beck's expression of satisfaction at Agnès' paying in full for the missing doll did not quite accurately reflect the true state of her feelings. Privately she was annoyed. She had been anticipating a longer period of resistance and the girl had seemingly got away from her. 'Add to that, there's the fact that she left without a word.'

Madame Picot, who felt uncomfortable at hearing of the incriminating envelope containing the sixty euros, hastened to voice strong agreement. 'It hardly suggests innocence.'

But her friend's reply was not what she might have expected. 'It's a nuisance. She wasn't a bad cleaner.'

'But, dear, you told me she was slow.'

'Slow but thorough,' said Madame Beck, adding, for the benefit of Jeanette's education, 'the two are not incompatible.'

'I know that, my dear, but you seemed so set against the girl.'

Many years ago Louise Beck had had an unhappy experience with an Algerian waitress whom she and her husband had employed at their restaurant in Evreux. She had caught Claude with the girl when he had assumed that his wife was occupied with their vintner ordering in the new stocks of wine. She had gone to the kitchen to check with Claude whether he wanted her to get in the '61 or the '66 Bordeaux – both good years – and had found him with their waitress in an amorous embrace. It was shortly after this that she had first found him out in another love affair.

With the discovery of the affair she had sacked the waitress to ensure nothing similar would happen under her own roof and had felt fully justified in doing so when she discovered that some of the restaurant's linen had gone missing. She was not aware that Agnès' colouring and demeanour had stirred a painful recollection and that she was once again paying one woman back for another woman's treachery.

If her husband's infidelity, the background to this episode, had conveniently perished in Madame Beck's pliant memory, the sense of a long-held grudge had not. She would have liked more time to effect a more substantial revenge on Agnès.

Agnès had not confided to Terry the reasons for her having left Madame Beck's, mainly because she did not want to hear Terry say she had told her so. When they met next for dinner at the jazz café, she simply said she had decided to leave.

'I told you so,' were Terry's first words. 'She drive you away? Bet she did. Foul old cow. She was round at Picot's when I picked up Piaf this morning. Yap, yap, yap, and I'm not talking about the doggie. Old Picot's hairstyle is looking more and more like Piaf's. It's true what they say about owners getting to look like their pets. But at least she has a head of hair even if it's a mess. Old Beck's going bald.'

'Poor thing,' Agnès couldn't help saying.

' "Poor thing" my arse. Just because she's going bald doesn't mean you have to feel sorry for her.'

Terry went on to say that Madame Picot had asked her to mind Piaf while she visited her daughter. 'It's the one she likes to say has "done well for herself and married a banker". She lives in Japan but her husband's coming to London on a business trip and they've asked old Picot to join them – worse luck.'

'It'll be good money, though,' Agnès suggested.

'To be fair, old Picot isn't mean. Beck strikes me as stingy as hell. Christ knows why Picot's so matey with her.'

'Maybe she's scared of her,' suggested Agnès.

'Well, I'm not scared of her,' Terry announced.

But Terry hadn't her reasons to be scared, Agnès reflected as she walked back down the hill to her room at Madame Badon's.

The elder Madame Badon had finally died and gone to pester her Maker over the whereabouts of her spectacles, if spectacles were required in the afterlife, which, Agnès supposed – quite enjoying her own small joke (though she had been fond of the elder Madame Badon) – was unlikely. The young Madame Badon had, since the loss of her mother, more or less decamped to Paris to oversee her unreliable man. But she was a generous woman, grateful to Agnès and had been happy to leave her as caretaker of the apartment. More than ever, therefore, Agnès had the place to herself, with the only expense being the greater amount of food she had to buy since the elder Madame Badon's rations were no longer available to her.

She made herself supper now, a fricassee of veal with beans and artichoke hearts, and ate it still immersed in thoughts of the past.

The unusually cold summer had given way to an unusually warm October and the whole of Europe was enjoying a fiery Indian summer. Groups of young people lounged on the south steps of the cathedral, drinking cans of lager, smoking, laughing, flirting, generally enjoying the good gifts of the weather and giving Madame Beck plenty to deplore.

Agnès, too hot to consider sleep, and disturbed by her recollections, felt the urge to walk. As she made her way back up the cobbled streets towards the lighted cathedral, she heard music. Eugène the organist was practising, as he liked to do of an evening in a cathedral free of visitors.

Reaching the cathedral close, Agnès stood in her sleeveless dress enjoying the mighty chords as they issued from the mighty edifice before her and enjoying, in a different way, the gentle currents of air on her bare arms. A skinny black-and-white cat, the crypt cat, René, slipped down the steps of the North Porch and slid under the railings. He had been named René because, as a kitten, he was found in the crypt among a stray's litter and, due to be put down with his siblings, had disappeared, only to reappear just as mysteriously two weeks later. Since then the reborn cat had been deemed to be under the special protection of Our Lady. Maybe it was through her influence that he had a secret inroad into the crypt that no one had ever found.

Agnès strolled round towards the flower-beds before the Royal Portal. In the warm night air, they were still exuding a heady summer scent.

'Good evening, Agnès.' It was the Abbé Paul, also out taking a stroll.

The two of them stood side by side listening to the music.

'Bach,' said the Abbé Paul after a particularly dramatic chord. 'Do you like Bach, Agnès?'

'I don't know. I like this.'

'Then you like Bach.' The grave sounds died away to be replaced by a less measured, more frantic sound. 'Ah, this now is Poulenc. By no means the genius that Bach was, but not a bad composer. Not bad at all. He was another who liked the organ.'

Agnès, feeling she should offer some response, said, 'I don't know much about music, I'm afraid.'

'You don't need to "know" anything. Listening is all that's required. Hear this bit . . .'

They stood, as the flowers cajoled by the warmth released their scent, the Abbé Paul with his hand behind his ear, for he feared he was growing a shade deaf and had recently purchased a hearing aid which he had not found the courage to try out. Feeling awkward at the priest's unusual proximity, Agnès said, 'I meant to say, if you still wanted someone to clean?'

The Abbé Paul, absorbed in the music, took a moment to grasp what she was talking about. 'By all means, if you were willing . . .'

'I've finished at Madame Beck's.' She wondered if Madame Beck had spoken about her to the Abbé. 'She believes I broke or took something.'

'So she dismissed you?'

'No, I left. I didn't take or break anything but she asked me to pay for it.'

'And you paid?'

'Yes.'

In the orange light, refracting from the beams trained on the famous Western Front, she saw his expression change. 'I understand. There is nothing to break at mine, or, I should say, nothing worth breaking and anyway I would never –'

But, from this mild man, who had not even inquired after the object of the supposed breakage, she could not take too much kindness.

'Thank you, Father. When would you like me to start?'

30

Evreux

It was Maddy's idea that Agnès should go to live with Jean Dupère. The return to the clinic had been beneficial: Agnès had lost all the weight she had gained and acquired a skill with make-up and, with it, a new confidence. Maddy had taken her in hand and was encouraging but brisk. While ignorant of the philosophy of Cognitive Therapy, Maddy was a natural exponent.

'No point in moaning on about the past. We have to look ahead,' was her maxim and constant refrain. But, in harmony with her philosophy, Maddy herself had decided to move on. She wanted to 'do' Europe, she said, before she grew elderly and staid.

'I can't see you ever "staid", Maddy,' said Denis Deman, who found himself a little in love with the tall, boldly spoken nurse. And then out of cowardice, because he did not want to let on that he would, just a little, miss her himself, he inquired how she felt Agnès would react to her departure.

'I would say she's well enough now to go back into the world.'

'But where?' Denis Deman twirled his pen between his long fingers. He was surprisingly aroused by the sight of Maddy's hands and strong forearms with her sleeves rolled back and found himself involuntarily envisaging them caressing his naked body.

'Not back to those terrible nuns, for sure. How about the old man?'

'Jean?'

'Why not? By all accounts he needs help and she's ace at housework. You have to hand it to the nuns: at least they gave her that. And from what you say he dotes on her.'

It was not at all a bad plan, Denis Deman reflected, as he drove the Renault once again down the rutted track towards the Dupère farm.

Jean Dupère, though decidedly frail, was proving resilient. His constitution, hardened through years of working outside at all hours and in all weathers, with only a couple of hands to help, seemed for the time being to be keeping death waiting.

Denis Deman had several times taken Agnès to see him since her return to the clinic in Rouen. The affection the old man felt for the girl was patent. And, as Maddy implied, she in turn seemed to take real pleasure in washing up for him and preparing tasty meals to tempt his flagging appetite. But whether he would want the responsibility of taking on a girl whose mental health was potentially as fragile as his physical health was another matter.

Denis Deman put the idea to the old man as they were enjoying their customary shot of Calva.

'Have Agnès here?' Jean looked perplexed.

'To stay. To help you out. She's so much better and really there is nowhere for her to go except the nuns.'

Denis Deman had in fact inquired about that possibility and the response had not been promising. Mother Catherine, he was brusquely informed, had left the convent. (Months later, during a conversation with Sister Laurence, he learned more: during Holy Week in Rome the Mother had re-encountered Father Ignatius, with whom a *tendresse* had sprung up when they had met, also in Rome, many years earlier at a summer school on Johannine theology. Their greater maturity, or maybe the well-documented inflammatory effects of the Eternal City, had reignited a passion which, they revealed to each other, neither had fully forsworn. A few glasses of Valpolicella, followed by a stroll on the Palatine, and the pair had forsaken their vows with the zeal of an elderly Romeo and Juliet. The sheer pleasure of that experience encouraged them to give in to the doubts that each had secretly harboured about their vocations. Within a fortnight, they had declared their intention of leaving the Church and marrying.)

The convent had taken the news of Mother Catherine's dereliction badly. A new Mother had to be appointed, and fast. For reasons of seniority, the choice had fallen on Sister Véronique, never too popular on account of her sharp intellect and still sharper tongue. Under Sister Véronique's inexpert management, the Sisters of Mercy had become more than usually subject to a seething discontent. Communal maladjustment, kept firmly in check by Mother Catherine's authoritative hand, had set in.

When Denis Deman rang, asking for the Mother, he had been startled to hear, rather than clipped civil-service tones, the tense, high-pitched voice of Sister Véronique. Her reply, when he tentatively raised the possibility of Agnès' return, was shrill. They really could not take on serious mental cases, she had enough on her plate already, God knew they had tried their best for the girl, but it was clear she was unstable if not, Mother Véronique dared to hope, actually the host of evil.

So he was grateful that when he broached the subject to Jean Dupère the robust retort was, 'Send her back to those damned nuns? Over my dead body.'

Agnès, with her few modest belongings, including a new make-up bag, a gift from Maddy, moved into the Dupère farm on January 20th, the eve of her seventeenth birthday. Denis Deman and Maddy came for supper the following day. Agnès cooked a chicken, really more of a fowl, she explained, as it was an old bird, but with carrots, swede, turnip and potatoes, simmered in Jean Dupère's brother's wine, it made for their modest needs a feast. For pudding she made a *tarte aux pommes* from the apples in the Dupère store-room, followed by the Dupère Calva.

Agnès wore the little turquoise earring, now hanging securely on the silver chain. Maddy gave her some blusher and eyeshadow in several shades of mauve and Dr Deman gave her a photograph.

'What's that?' Maddy asked.

Agnès looking at it said, 'It's in a church. A cathedral, I mean, isn't it, Doctor?'

'That's right. Chartres. I remembered you liked it.'

Maddy said, 'It looks more like something my grandma's people might draw back home. Nice, though.'

Denis Deman drove Maddy to the clinic, where, with a hand made unsteady from overindulgence with the Calva, he helped her from the Renault – quite needlessly, as she was a good deal steadier than he was – and, with a head giddy not merely with alcohol but also with relief at the success of their joint enterprise, asked her to marry him.

Maddy, however, refused him. She was determined not to make that mistake again, she explained. But she said she was very flattered and thanked him for the offer.

31

Chartres

Madame Picot had had no thought of consequences when she swept the broken parts of the china doll into her handbag. But she could never, she wordlessly complained to her reflection in the bathroom mirror, have expected the episode to be fanned into such a fuss. Her first instinct was to pretend that nothing had happened – to herself as much as with her furious friend. But in the corner of her heart there shone a glimmer of decency which made her want to repair the situation.

Chartres is one of the few towns in the world that still boasts a dolls' hospital. It stands on a corner of the rue au Lait, opposite the rue aux Herbes and too dangerously close to Madame Beck's watchtower for Madame Picot to want to venture in there. Madame Beck, however, had announced her intention to go to Paris. So on that same day Madame Picot, the doll and its severed head, guiltily swaddled in tissue, set off to see Albert, the doll doctor.

Albert if not quite a midget was not much bigger than one. He was perhaps no taller than a nine-year-old but with a face as pitted and weather-beaten as the hills and spectacles on the end of his nose, giving him the appearance of a cartoon character. When it came to human beings, Albert was bad-tempered almost to a pathological degree, though with his dolls he exercised a singular patience. Unlike the other local doctor, Albert Boulez, the GP, who had once misdiagnosed a broken arm as a boil and urged the sufferer, a steel worker, to get back to work,

Albert the Doll Doctor hated his patients to leave his care. The little girls who sent their toys for repair had to beg and wheedle them out of him with sworn assurances of treating their charges better in the future.

Madame Picot knew Albert by sight, and a little by reputation. Her main anxiety was that any transaction be kept secret from Madame Beck, who had the knack of seeing round corners when it came to underhand dealings of any kind – far more so when anything shady touched her own person. Madame Picot therefore approached Albert with a bright smile and a carefully composed story.

'My daughter's old doll,' she explained. It did not seem quite safe to invent a granddaughter – her daughter was *bona fide* at least. 'She treasured it as a child and has asked me if anyone can repair it.'

Albert pushed his spectacles up his nose and examined the head. 'Recent breakage?'

'Yes,' agreed Madame Picot. 'In a move. My daughter lives in Japan and I suppose the movers were careless.'

'She back here, then?'

An inquisition was not what Madame Picot wanted. 'Just at present she's in London. I'm visiting her there next week and hoped to take the mended doll with me. Might that be possible?'

While unable to blame Madame Picot directly for the accident, Albert was not visibly softened by this story but offered to do his best. He surveyed the doll's head and then its neck and gently placed the two together and examined the join.

'Can you mend it?' asked Madame Picot anxiously.

Albert glanced over his spectacles. 'Her.'

'Pardon?'

'*Her*. Not it. Her head will mend up well. Doubt you'll see the join. I'll paint over if anything shows.'

'Thank you, thank you so much,' said Madame Picot, quite wanting, in her relief, to kiss the ugly little man. 'My daughter will be thrilled.'

She considered asking him to say nothing about the doll but thought better of it. He was unlikely to meet Madame Beck, and if he did he was even less likely to make any connection.

Madame Beck had gone to Paris partly with the intention of replacing the lost Lulu but also to try on a wig. The trichologist, on her last demoralizing visit, had hinted that in certain circumstances a well-fashioned wig might provide better results than further treatments. Madame Beck had rejected this suggestion as an impertinence, but repeated examinations of the parting at the top of her head had led her to reconsider the proposal.

She was annoyed when Philippe Nevers came bounding up the station stairs and tumbled into the same carriage as hers; more so when, on seeing her, he took a seat beside her. The nature of her trip made her irritably nervous of any local attention.

Philippe was chattily polite. 'I usually get an earlier train but my sister's arriving today and I had to leave a key with the shop downstairs and they don't open till ten.'

'Ah, yes. Your sister.' Madame Beck recalled her. An obnoxious child with fat glossy brown ringlets. 'Bernadette?'

'Brigitte. She's coming with her little baby.'

'And her husband?' asked Madame Beck, hoping for scandal. Scandal would be a pleasant distraction.

'Just her. She needs a rest.'

'How old is the baby?'

'Only a couple of months.'

'She won't be getting much rest, then.'

'I suppose not. Nor will I,' Philippe said cheerfully. 'You off to Paris?'

'Yes.'

'A shopping spree?'

'I'm going to replace a doll. One of my antique dolls. It was taken by my cleaner.'

'How horrid of her. Who is or was she?'

Madame Beck pursed her lips. She did not welcome this interrogation. If there was interrogating to be done she liked to be the one to do it. 'Her name is Morel.'

'Not Agnès?'

'Yes.'

'Oh, I'm sure there's a mistake. Agnès would never take anything.'

'I'm afraid she did,' said Madame Beck. 'I am not in the habit of telling lies.'

'No but –'

'If you wouldn't mind,' Madame Beck said, getting out her magazine, 'I'd like to read.'

As they disembarked at the Gare Montparnasse, Philippe, coming up beside her, said quietly, 'Agnès cleans for me and for Father Paul. I feel sure you've made a mistake, Madame.'

Madame Beck's trip to Paris went badly. The shop which specialized in antique dolls had a notice on the door saying it was temporarily closed, the card machine at the salon which specialized in wigs was out of order, and when she tried to get cash from the machine her credit card was refused twice and she dared not try it again. She returned to Chartres doll-less and wig-less and in a black mood.

32

Chartres

If there had been a time in her life of unalloyed happiness, Agnès thought, as she walked by the river from Robert Clément's studio, where she had been sitting for him, it was the two years she had spent living with Jean Dupère. In her memory, the days and nights were hallowed by an aura of deepest peace.

The farmhouse possessed only one bedroom so she slept in the kitchen, in the box bed where Denis Deman on his first visit had found Jean Dupère. She rose early, often before dawn, and lit the fire during the cold months, prepared breakfast, woke the old man, bathed and shaved him and then, increasingly, as the months passed and his strength declined, helped him to dress.

Their days were spent in domestic routine, she performing household tasks, sweeping, dusting, washing, as he sat, less and less mobile in his rocking chair, chatting with her sometimes, sometimes simply co-existing in companionable silence. She was never bored. Boredom is a luxury of a life lived without fear.

Although the milking was now done by machine, Agnès, under the instruction of Yvette, Jean Dupère's helpful neighbour, learned how to milk by hand. 'If you've the hands for it, it's very agreeable,' Yvette told her. 'They catch your mood – mind you, the times I've been in a temper and they wouldn't yield. But you catch their mood too, which is mostly good. We couldn't manage without machines now but I still like to keep my hand in with a few of the old girls.'

Sitting with her cheek against Maribelle's or Josette's warm flank, the regular sound of the milk squirting into the pail as the cow's hooves shifted with a peaceable restlessness on the concrete floor, was indeed, Agnès found, soothing.

Yvette also taught her how to make quince preserve and to bottle fruit in *eau-de-vie*; she especially loved to see the results of the latter in the larder, the coloured fruits gleaming in their glass jars, plums, cherries, greengages, all from the Dupères' old orchards.

Dr Deman came to visit them, bringing, on one occasion, an excitable Sister Laurence. Maddy, Dr Deman told Agnès, was now in Vienna. She didn't like the Austrians much, she had written, but the pastries were fabulous. She had apparently gained four kilos and was learning ballroom dancing.

For two years and a month Agnès had lived a life in rhythm with the seasons, with the time of day, or night, with the weather – a lull, in her so-far stormy life, of kindly, uneventful calm. Without either of them discussing it, she took to calling Jean 'Papa' – he was, after all, her foster father, for without him – though this they never discussed either – she might not have been alive.

And then one morning, a couple of weeks after she turned nineteen (an event they celebrated, quite contentedly, alone, just the two of them), she found him in his bed distraught.

'There's pipi on the sheets, and worse. I'm sorry, sweet-heart.'

Agnès, recalling this, stopped by the banks of the Eure to look at a green canoe on which a mallard duck had alighted. Horrible and humiliating for her 'father', but she was grateful for it now. It had given her a chance to demonstrate the depth of her love for him. (And what could be worse – she half thought – than to have loved and been given no chance to make it known?) Tenderly, she had washed her father's withered bottom and balls and sponged his veined old penis and pow-dered him with baby talc and put him to sit, in clean vest and warm pyjamas, by the fire before stripping the mattress of its soiled sheets and sprinkling it with Yvette's remedy for bad smells, bicarbonate of soda and dried lavender.

That night, after a glass of warm milk followed by his cus-tomary Calva in the little green shot glass, she had put him to sleep in her bed, the box bed in the kitchen, while she sat watch by the fire.

It was a night of freezing February fog. Even with the fire stoked up the room had grown chilly. Checking him around midnight, she felt his feet were far too cold, and to warm him got into bed beside him. She fell asleep with one arm across his thin shoulders.

In the morning, she had climbed from the bed into the chill darkness and made up the fire to a blaze to warm the room. Even the inner windowpanes were bleared with frost.

Outside, in the occluding fog, the blurred shapes of trees and bushes loomed thick with rime. She had gone out to hang ham fat from the apple trees and scatter cake crumbs for the birds; and also, she recalled now – how odd the small things that lie waiting to be uncovered in memory – to put out a saucepan of warm water, because birds die as much from lack of water as from cold when the frost is severe.

Crossing the bridge over the Eure to take her up the hill towards the cathedral, Agnès remembered how glad she had been that morning that her 'father' was sleeping later than usual, and how when she checked him she had found him cold, colder than any fire could ever warm.

33

Chartres

Madame Picot had put off the usual meeting with her friend Madame Beck. She was preparing for her London trip, she explained over the phone, and up to her eyes with things to do.

'Whatever are you taking with you?' asked Madame Beck. 'I thought you were only gone a week.' Although Madame Picot was irksome, Madame Beck did not care to feel abandoned.

'It's not that, dear. It's Piaf. Terry has agreed she can stay with her and I want to get her used to the idea. She's never spent a night away before.'

'How will staying in help her get used to your absence?'

'I can't explain, dear.' Madame Picot became flustered. 'You're not a dog person. I can't explain.'

Madame Beck rang off with none of her customary expressions of affection.

The day before her departure, Madame Picot nervously pressed the bell of the doll clinic and slid furtively through the door. The ugly little man disappeared into his workroom and returned, doll in hand.

'Can you see the join?'

The doll looked as good as new. Or as good as new as a nineteenth-century china doll could look. 'My goodness. That's a miracle. Albert, you are a genius.'

This was not news to Albert, who gave an imperious nod and asked for thirty euros.

Madame Picot, who would gladly have given twice the

amount, retrieved her wallet from her capacious bag, in which she then stowed the recovered doll.

'Careful with her now. She's rare enough, that one. There's not so many from that period that's dark.'

'Oh, I know. Thank you. My daughter will be thrilled.' She was anxious to be off before there was any chance of being spotted from the Beck watchtower.

Madame Picot sidled out of the shop, walked slowly up the rue aux Herbes and up the stairs to her friend's apartment, trying to master her breath.

Madame Beck took a little longer than usual to open the door. 'You're all packed, then?'

Madame Picot peered. Louise had had something radical done to her hair. 'All packed, yes. I'm taking Piaf round to Terry's this evening. And her tins of chicken and her chews and her sleep cushion, of course.'

'How long are you gone for?'

'Just over a week, dear, as I told you.' Surely it was a wig. 'Julie is coming back to Paris with me. We're spending a night there before I return home.'

'So Julie doesn't care to visit her old home town?' It was Madame Beck's decided belief that Jeanette had spoiled that girl.

'It's not that, dear.' It must be a wig. My goodness. Whatever next? 'Her husband is very busy, you know he's moved to a very big job in a top finance company, and they can't spare the time. Besides, you know, it's nice for me to get away.'

While Madame Beck was in the kitchen making an angry clatter with the kettle, Madame Picot was calculating. Where might she conceal the doll so that a discovery would seem credible?

'Just popping to the little girls' room, dear.'

The door to Madame Beck's bedroom was ajar. Madame Picot stealthily opened it, moved, quick as a cat, to the bed and slid the doll deftly down in the narrow gap between the mattress and the bed's foot. She returned to the salon to find Madame Beck standing there impassively, tea tray in hand.

'Just powdering my nose, dear.' Good God, but her heart was pounding.

Madame Beck's pale face beneath the hennaed wig looked to her friend more forbidding than usual. Should she mention the change to her hair, Madame Picot wondered. Tentatively, she volunteered, 'You're looking very well, dear.'

Madame Beck sat down and poured a cup of tea. 'I hear the Abbé Paul has taken on the Morel girl as a cleaner.'

'Really, dear?'

'It is my duty to warn him of her character.'

But Madame Picot's flabby conscience was pricked at last. 'Louise, I do think before you blacken the girl's name you should be quite sure of your facts. Have you made a really thorough search of the apartment?'

'I beg your pardon?' Madame Beck's face looked thunder and lightning.

'She has a good reputation in the town and I hardly think that the Abbé Paul would –'

'Do you suppose, Jeanette, I have lost my mind?'

'Well, dear. We all grow forgetful with age.' What a tyrant Louise had become. She was glad to be getting away.

'There is nothing wrong with my mental processes, thank you.'

Madame Picot left as soon as she judged it safe to do so without arousing comment, with the excuse that she had 'a few last things' to buy for her daughter.

'What can she want that she can't buy in London?' asked Madame Beck suspiciously.

'Nougat,' said Madame Picot, with happy inspiration. 'She can't get the good soft nougat we have here.' She made a mental note to buy some to add verity to the story.

Hurrying out of the sweet shop on the rue des Changes, with a bag containing four bars of nougat, it was a shock to almost run into Agnès carrying a sponge mop.

'Good morning – Agnès, isn't it?'

Agnès stopped. Madame Picot, she knew from Terry, was a crony of Madame Beck's. 'Yes, Madame.'

'The sunny weather is holding up well,' Madame Picot said, smiling at Agnès. 'That's a pretty dress. I can't wear red myself, strawberry-blondes can't, but it's a lovely colour on you.'

'Thank you, Madame,' Agnès said. She shifted the mop into her other hand.

Madame Picot nodded civilly at the mop as if it too were an old friend. 'I hear you are cleaning for our dear Father Paul? He must be a pleasure to clean for. Such a saintly man.'

'Yes, Madame.'

'Well, I mustn't stand here all day chatting. I'm off to see my daughter in London tomorrow and I still have so much to do.' She smiled again, effusively. 'Goodbye, my dear.'

Hurrying along the rue Saint-Pierre, congratulating herself on her democratic civility to her friend's former cleaner, Madame Picot suddenly realized who it was that Agnès reminded her of. The picture of a young woman asleep, painted by – oh, what was the artist's name? – on a postcard that her husband had brought back from the Courtauld Gallery on his London trip – the same trip, she smiled to herself, when he had sent her the postcard of the woman at her dressing-table, the woman he had so sweetly likened to herself.

Agnès was on her way to the Abbé Paul's house when she encountered Madame Picot. She had found it poorly equipped with proper cleaning materials and had already renewed the dusters and replaced his cheap all-purpose spray with a decent wax polish.

The Deanery was old and bare, the dark oak furniture simple

and sparse but to her eyes beautiful. It was the furniture of the Dupère farm. The china, likewise, was an old-fashioned country make. Washing it, Agnès was reminded again of Jean Dupère. It was the very same china as his, down to the white coffee bowls with the three thin dark red stripes around the rim.

She had prepared just such a bowl for his coffee on the morning she put her hand to his cheek and found it so cold. Not knowing what to do, she had run up the track to find Yvette, who had called the doctor and after him the undertaker. But it was she and Yvette who had laid her 'father' out. Yvette had done this more than once before, she said.

Together they had washed him, cleaned away the faeces and urine which, Yvette explained, was always the death's first legacy, and put him into a clean white shirt, which she'd ironed again specially, and his dark blue serge trousers. As an afterthought, she put woollen socks on the corpse, because the sight of the swollen cracked feet and yellowed toenails was more than she could bear. No matter that there was no longer any way for them to feel the cold.

The niece came grudgingly from Dreux, with her even more grudging husband, and made a business of organizing a chilly little funeral service at which she countermanded any flowers. Her uncle, whom she had visited maybe once a year, she declared would 'not have wanted them'. (After the funeral, Agnès put on the raw-earth grave a jam jar of wild snowdrops, white with delicate green tracings, from the wood where her 'father' had discovered her.)

No will was ever found. Perhaps the old man had not made one? Or perhaps it was a part of the large bonfire that the niece had her husband make the morning after the funeral? After the fire, and before Agnès left the house for the last time, the niece said, 'Do take something that you might like to remember Uncle by. Something small, naturally.'

Agnès had taken the basket she had been found in and Jean Dupère's old army coat, which still smelled of wood smoke, rescued from the pile the niece had set aside for 'the poor'. It was only when Agnès got to Evreux late that same evening that she realized with dismay that she had left Dr Deman's maze tacked on the head of the bed on which her 'father' had died. When she rang the following day to ask about it, the niece's husband said, 'I'm afraid we burned it today with the rest of the junk. Sorry. We didn't know it was yours.'

'Wasn't she the girl involved in that stabbing incident?' he asked his wife when he put down the phone. 'Amazing that your uncle risked having her here, with her reputation.'

His wife was engaged in looking under a loose floorboard in the hope of hidden valuables. 'I think he was a little touched in the head, to be honest,' she said, dusting down her dress. 'That creature couldn't even keep the place clean. This floor is quite disgusting.'

34

Chartres

'Not a maze, a labyrinth,' Agnès said aloud to herself. The air of the Deanery was redolent of the peculiar smell of old books from the Abbé Paul's extensive library. She paused in her dusting to inspect the titles.

Agnès' reading lessons with Professor Jones were progressing. Perhaps because the professor had no expectation of failure she found that she was able to take in his lessons quite naturally. Her new teacher had no time for phonics: indeed, he would have had no clue as to what phonics were. He proceeded with Agnès in the old way he had learned to read himself: by reading to her aloud and then asking her to repeat the words after him, line by line.

That the system was working was apparent because Agnès found she was able to make sense of most of the titles on the Abbé Paul's bookshelves. She could see, for instance, a whole shelf on the history of the cathedral and several volumes on the labyrinth.

The Abbé Paul found her with one of these open on the library table.

'Oh, excuse me, Father . . .'

'Not at all, Agnès. Books are there to be read.'

'I can't read, really. That is to say, I am learning with Professor Jones.'

If the Abbé Paul was surprised to hear that his cleaner was not literate, he gave no sign. 'You're welcome to read anything you like here. You are interested in the labyrinth?'

'When I was a young girl I had a picture of it. I didn't know then what it was.'

'And you do now?'

'No, no. I mean –'

'I'm teasing you. But since no one knows what it quite was there's no reason why you shouldn't be the one to uncover the mystery.'

'Maybe it is better left uncovered.'

The Abbé Paul looked at Agnès rather as Alain had, with respect. 'How sensible. People are desperate to probe mysteries which for the most part are best left unprobed. It is the modern curse: this demented drive to explain every blessed thing. Not everything can be explained. Nor should be, I think.'

'Some things should be, though.' She was thinking of the riddle of her own birth.

'To be sure. I often wonder if happiness isn't knowing what should and what should not be explained.'

'But how can we tell which is which?'

'Hmmm,' said the Abbé Paul. 'That, I suppose, is wisdom.'

'The nuns who brought me up used to say that happiness was self-control. But they were not very good at it themselves, or I didn't think so anyway.' The image of Sister Véronique, her face boiling with anger, still frightened her.

'No,' said the Abbé Paul, and he sounded sad. 'That, I fear, is too often the way with we religious. Full of fine precepts but none too fine at putting them into practice. I include myself in this bad habit.'

Agnès, looking at the old black-and-white photograph in the open book, said, 'Someone told me there was once a plaque in the middle here with a picture of – is it the Minotaur? You can see the bolts there still.'

'Minotaur is right. And the Minotaur's slayer, Theseus – and Ariadne, who became a spider in some tellings.'

'Do you have the story?'

'Many versions of it. Would you like to borrow one?'

'They'd be way too hard for me.'

The Abbé Paul went across to a modest pine bookshelf that stood on its own under the window and took out a slender book. 'These here are my old books from childhood. And this one was my introduction to Greek myths when I first came to France from Scotland. My mother was French so I spoke it well, but I was behind in my reading. You're very welcome to borrow it, or any of the others on the shelf, and if there are words I can help you with, please . . .'

That evening the Abbé Paul had poured himself a glass of Chinon when the doorbell rang twice, and ferociously. He had learned to interpret his callers from the manner in which the bell was rung, so it was with the anticipation of trouble that he put down his wine.

'Good evening, Father.'

Madame Beck. In what could only be a wig. 'Madame, what a splendid evening, is it not?'

'I'm sorry to trouble you, Father.'

You're not sorry at all, thought the Abbé Paul, ushering his unwelcome guest into his receiving room.

'Only I heard,' said Madame Beck, ignoring the visitor's chair and placing herself instead in the dead centre of the blue chaise-longue, the better to fix him with her disturbingly pale eyes, 'that you had taken on my ex-cleaner.' Her throat in pronouncing the 'ex' made a slight but sinister click.

The Abbé Paul thought very longingly of his wine. 'Oh?'

'Mademoiselle Morel.'

'Yes, Agnès.'

'I felt that I should warn you, Father. She is a thief and a liar.'

Under duress, the Abbé Paul thought effectively and fast. It was a quality he had perhaps inherited from his father's military ancestor, and indeed had his conscious inclinations not been of an opposite bent he might have made a successful general himself. 'I am so sorry, Madame Beck. My hearing is not what it was. Would you be so kind as to wait while I go and put in my hearing aid?'

He left the room and almost ran to his study, where he dashed down most of the glass of wine before removing the untried hearing aid first from his bureau drawer and then from its irritating packaging. How in God's name did one get the damn thing to function?

Returning, with the aid lodged uncomfortably in his ear, to the room where Madame Beck sat marmoreally on his chaise-longue, the Abbé Paul began to talk at high speed.

'I'm so grateful to you, Madame, for sending me Agnès. It was extremely generous, as she's such a marvellous cleaner – well, of course you know that from your own experience. I was going to ring you myself to thank you but you've beaten me to it, so let me go and cut you some of my roses instead, as a thank-you, you know. With this weather we're having they're blooming again and it seems too selfish of me to keep them all to myself. My goodness, but you are looking well. I do think a spot of sun does us good, don't you . . .' And keeping up a relentless flow of conversation, he steered an astonished Madame Beck into his garden, where, donning gardening gloves and taking up his secateurs, he cut a bouquet of his sweetest-smelling roses, while still maintaining the flow.

And really, he thought, removing the aid after his unwelcome caller had left holding the flowers, too overwhelmed and out-talked to say what she had clearly come to say, the poor creature has probably not been given flowers by a man for years, so it was the right and proper Christian thing to do.

And the Abbé Paul, after examining the little hearing aid, which had done nothing but make his ear hurt, threw the annoying device into the waste-paper basket and poured himself another glass of wine.

35

Chartres

Philippe had invited his sister to stay – or, more precisely, had acceded without protest to her inviting herself – because, as his friend Tan said, he was easy-going. But Philippe was also good-natured and sorry for his sister. She was one of those people who seemed always to be in trouble, and on this occasion it seemed she was in trouble with her man. Philippe was too delicate to ask the precise circumstances. But he knew that she had had a newborn baby.

Philippe had never met this partner, or any of Brigitte's men, but he had come to a point where, he confided to Tan, he had nothing but sympathy for the current unfortunate and could not imagine how he had stood the course with Brigitte long enough to spawn a child. It was not so much that he minded how she had taken over his clean, uncluttered apartment – though he minded that greatly – but that nothing satisfied her. Nothing, he could see now, was ever going to satisfy her.

She had always been one of nature's complainers. What was new now was her attitude to her child. She left him to cry. This was more disturbing at night, as it woke Philippe so that he was unable to get back to sleep; but he minded less for himself than for the baby.

He rang Tan in some distress. 'The silly creature has read some book which says you can "train" babies by leaving them to cry.'

'Train them for what?' Tan had asked.

'To sleep, I suppose. But it doesn't work.'

That it didn't work was evident. On the first night of their stay, little Max howled and howled and then, which was more dismaying, was left to sob uncomforted. Finally, unable to endure it a moment longer, Philippe had got up and gone himself to the shaking little body, whereupon Brigitte had flown at him screaming reproof.

Philippe had had to relinquish the tearful creature to his mother but he could hardly bear doing so. During the day, he was told, the baby was subjected to a regime of black cloths placed over his buggy to ensure that he slept at the correct hour.

'But he's missing all the sunlight and the vitamin D,' he'd suggested, exasperated. But his sister had angrily told him he knew nothing about it, to shut his face and keep his opinions to himself.

Walking to the station, wondering how this situation had come to pass, he considered his sister's history. That he had always been the favoured child he was guiltily aware. His mother was fair-minded and even-handed; but children can sniff out a preference more accurately than a truffle hound a truffle. Brigitte had been neither clever nor good-looking. She was the one who whined, who wet the bed, who had had few friends at school. In short, as he was ashamed now to recognize, she had been rather obviously despised by her family. When he had left for art school, his sister had quarrelled with both her parents. Their parents had retired since and moved to the south-west, where, he gathered from his mother, his sister had never visited them. Indeed, it was the first time since she had left to become a secretary that Brigitte had been back to her home town of Chartres.

Meeting Agnès on his way to the station, he answered her

polite inquiry with, 'Since you ask about Brigitte, she's driving me insane.'

'She doesn't like the apartment?'

'Oh, she likes the apartment all right. It's her child she doesn't like. Poor scrap. I'd adopt him if I weren't single.'

'How old is he?' Agnès asked.

'Just gone two months.'

'Perhaps she needs some help. A baby can be overwhelming.'

'Rather you than me!'

'I expect she's just tired.'

That evening Philippe tackled his sister. 'You should take a night off sometime. We could get in a babysitter.'

'Who?'

'Our old babysitter Agnès.'

Brigitte made a face.

'What's that supposed to mean? She was good enough for us. Maman thought so.'

'Maman! What did she know?'

'Quite a lot, as it happens. You were very horrid to Agnès then. She may not want to help you.'

'So? I don't particularly want her type –'

'Stop,' said Philippe, holding up a warning hand. 'Just stop before I have to kick you out. OK?'

'Pardon me for living!'

'Jesus!' said Philippe under his breath and left for the jazz café.

It was Wednesday, so Agnès and Terry were at the café too. Terry was telling Agnès about a man she had met, maybe a potential boyfriend. 'He's cute. Younger than me but quite mature. And not stingy. I hate stingy.'

'How much younger?'

'Five years. He's thirty-three.'

'What does he do?'

'He's a patents lawyer. Brainy.'

'He sounds OK,' said Agnès. 'Don't mess it up.' Terry's impossible standards had wrecked many relationships.

'I'm not going to. And I'm going to sleep with him right away. If all that's not going to work, it's better to find out soon.'

'What is?' asked Philippe, joining their table suddenly.

'Nothing you need to know about, big ears,' said Terry rudely.

'It'll be sex, then. Listen, Agnès. I'm going crazy with my sister staying and I can't go out every night. I'm not exactly paternal but it's completely awful the way she treats that little kid. I know she was a pig to you when we were small but for me might you –'

'Yes,' said Agnès. 'For you I would.' She did not add 'and for the baby'.

When Philippe got home, his sister was lying on the sofa with a copy of *Marie Claire*, apparently indifferent to the sound of desperate sobbing from the room next door. Philippe walked into the spare bedroom and picked up his nephew.

Cradling the squalling Max, Philippe spoke in a voice of low anger. 'He's sleeping with me tonight, and tomorrow night, or soon after, you are going out. I need a break. You need a break and your baby needs you to take a break. I've asked Agnès and she'll come over and I'm paying. And that's final.'

He left the room, shutting the door firmly but quietly, so as not to further distress the child.

The following evening Agnès rang the bell at Philippe's apartment. Philippe appeared at the door with Max over his shoulder. 'Thank goodness you're here. He's been sick.'

'All babies are sick.'

'He's been sick all down me.'

'It'll wash off. Babies' sick is harmless. Here.'

Agnès took the tiny soft person from Philippe.

'I'm glad you're here, Agnès.'

'He's adorable.'

Agnès sat on the sofa with Max in her arms and Philippe made coffee. 'Have you eaten? Because there's masses in the fridge.'

'Don't worry. I'll make something. Where's Brigitte?'

'I threw her out. Told her to go to the pictures, or whatever.'

Agnès said, 'Why don't you go out too? I'll be fine.'

'To be honest I wouldn't mind an early night. He slept in my room last night. I was so nervous I didn't sleep a wink. His feeding stuff's all here. You have to sterilize everything.'

'It's OK. I know.'

Philippe opened the fridge door. 'There's soup.'

'Thank you, no.'

'Eggs, you could do an omelette. Or finish the rillettes, they won't keep, and there's some Roquefort that needs eating. And fruit. I've red and white currants, the white are specially good. And there're fresh walnuts in the bowl on the side.'

'I'm fine. I'll have something when he's asleep.'

'He looks very comfortable with you. By the way, I met Old Ma Beck on the train. I gather you've fallen out.'

'Yes.' Agnès' face became instant stone.

Guessing he had blundered, Philippe said, 'Hey, don't take what she says to heart. She's a batty old woman. No one listens to her.'

Philippe had gone for his shower. Max, after drinking half a bottle of milk and then much jiggling by Agnès, had finally burped and fallen asleep on her shoulder. As always it was the feeling she loved and dreaded most. The soft, relaxed, utterly trusting weight and the faint moth's breath against her cheek.

Try as she might, she could never recall the exact moment

when they took him from her, her own baby with the crumpled tangerine-coloured face, the snubby nose bearing a trace of her blood, the marvellously curled hands, which had held her finger in the firm clutch of exquisite rosy fingers – a grip so instinctively sure of belonging, an instinct so brutally denied. Her baby. Her own Gabriel, of whom she had not a single clipping of his mother-of-pearl nails nor a black curl of his squashed little head.

Little Max with his soft black hair was very like Gabriel. He stirred and sighed in his sleep, and she began again to walk him up and down, flexing her knees from time to time to make a slow soothing bounce.

She had 'sat' for many children since she came to Chartres, but it was the babies she loved to be with most. She was 'good' with them. People said so – and she knew it was true. She had the knack of calming, of lulling them when they were fretful. Odd that someone as frightened as she was could be such a source of calm. But it was so – even poor old Bernard felt it, for he was well on the way to being a child again.

The fracas with Madame Beck had churned up the terrible memories – of that other child who wasn't Gabriel, and the dreadful time in Le Mans. A lifetime ago and yet always there, like a dangerous old wreck under the sea ready to rise up and hole her fragile raft.

She buried her face in the child's soft neck and breathed in the milky smell of innocence. She was afraid, always afraid. Since those two blessed years with her 'father', only when holding a child had she been quite free of fear.

The baby stirred again and she resumed her walking. What had happened to Dr Deman? Did she try to contact him after she left the farm? And Maddy? What happened to Maddy? She owed her escape from Le Mans to Maddy. She couldn't recall at all.

Those few months before she came to Chartres were also a

white blur. She had found work here and there, washing dishes, waiting, living in hostels with some rough people, though some kind ones too, always short of food, hungry, never sleeping, always afraid. And then, one day, thinking of the picture that Dr Deman had given her, and she had so carelessly abandoned, she had come to Chartres.

Philippe put his head round the door in his bathrobe. 'I'm done in. If it's really OK by you I'm going to put my head down. But call me if you need me.' He came across to look at the baby. 'Good night, Maxling. He's sweet, isn't he? I wouldn't mind one myself.'

'He's very sweet.'

'His crib's next door. D'you want to put him down?'

'In a minute,' Agnès said. 'I'll make sure he's really off first.'

When Brigitte came home, Agnès was on the sofa reading.

'Baby asleep?'

'Yes.'

'He go down all right?'

'He was fine.'

'Really? Thanks.'

'Any time.'

'I might take you up on that. What you reading?'

'A book about Greek myths.'

'I hate that old stuff.'

'I'd better be off, Brigitte. Good night.'

'Night, then. Thanks.'

For all that the days were still unseasonably warm, an autumnal nip was sharpening the air. In the light of the street lamps, the sky glowed a vivid indigo. Agnès turned right to walk through the close, passing the cathedral, its stone facets palely pleated into the darkness. Walking down to the Boulevard, under the spangling stars, she heard an owl hoot and shivered.

There had been both tawny and barn owls at the farm. There, from her box bed in the kitchen, the long, low calls of the tawny owls had sounded homely.

Thinking of little Max, heavy in his lightness on her shoulder, she thought, as she always thought, of her own son. Gabriel would be twenty-five in January. He might be married. He might even have a child, or children of his own.

36

Chartres

In November, it was Sister Laurence's fiftieth birthday. There was a tradition at the convent that on significant birthdays the Sisters were permitted to choose a treat, or 'jaunt', as Sister Camille called it. After much wavering and changing of her mind, Sister Laurence decided that what she would like best was to make a visit to Chartres.

'I've never seen the cathedral. People say it's most remarkable.'

'It is the very apex of the Gothic style,' pronounced Mother Véronique. 'I should like to see it again myself. And of course the Holy veil.'

She booked two rooms at the Hôtellerie Saint-Yves by the cathedral, deciding that it was as well it was Laurence's birthday since this was sufficient excuse for them not to have to share.

There was a good deal of excitement, and not a little envy, at the idea of the visit and a certain amount of muttering among the Sisters that Laurence had got lucky with the Chartres trip only because the Mother fancied going too. The pair set off in a coach with their stout but modest cases, Mother Véronique's heavily packed with historical guides.

During the journey, Mother Véronique lectured Laurence on the history of the cathedral. 'The first known cathedral was in 876 and we know that it was dedicated to Mary because . . .'

Sister Laurence, gazing out of the window at the long avenues of yellowing poplars, let the Mother's words drift past her ears. Every so often she nodded, affecting agreement, or made feeble stabs at seeming to comprehend.

Mother Véronique's voluble sighting of the twin spires roused her colleague from a doze. 'The farther spire,' Mother Véronique gestured magisterially, 'was built by Bishop Fulbert, who founded the famous Platonic School of Chartres. It was part of the cathedral saved by the Blessed Virgin from the great fire of 1194. The nineteenth-century architect Viollet-le-Duc considered it the most perfect spire in Europe. The other spire, nearer to us, do you see it? – quite ornamental in what is called the flamboyant style – is of a much later date. Sixteenth century. The roof, as you can tell from the green colouring, is copper . . .'

'Jesus,' said a man behind them. 'We haven't even got there yet.'

Mother Véronique's face darkened and Sister Laurence suppressed a giggle.

The coach disgorged its passengers and the two Sisters trudged up the hill towards the cathedral, dragging their cases over the cobbles. Mother Véronique, released from the restraints of impertinent fellow travellers, resumed teaching mode.

'The north side of the cathedral, as you will be seeing, Sister, represents the Old Testament. The significant figures King David, the Blessed Virgin's Mother, the prophet Isaiah are there. The south side celebrates the second coming . . .'

Before them the great Western Front, pale honey in the afternoon sun, faced her down, mildly reproaching anyone who sought to reduce it to a lecture. Sister Laurence, who was not without poetry in her soul, stood and stared. 'It's wonderful.'

'The statuary is known for –'

But here Sister Laurence rebelled. 'I'd like to just look at it for the moment if you wouldn't mind, Mother.'

★

The Hôtellerie Saint-Yves, now a commercial enterprise, had been the old lodging house of the pilgrims. 'We are still pilgrims,' said Mother Véronique on being imparted this information.

'But of course,' the polite girl with the green specs who was showing them around agreed. 'It was only to explain that the association with pilgrims in the house is a historic one.'

Sister Véronique said she was quite aware of this and asked if her room was en-suite.

'All our rooms are en-suite, Mother. Yours, I think, also has a TV and Wi-Fi. The other Sister, I'm not sure . . .'

Sister Laurence hurriedly interjected that she needed neither a TV nor Wi-Fi.

'I must have the Wi-Fi for my emails,' said Mother Véronique, though no one had challenged her right to this privilege.

It was maybe fortunate for Sister Laurence that among the emails that Mother Véronique had to attend to was an especially irksome one – a long-running dispute on a matter concerning a land drain – which brought on one of her headaches, for which she had forgotten her homoeopathic remedy. Unable to blame Sister Laurence for this omission, she nevertheless dispatched the sister to find Nux. Vom. for her at one of the local pharmacies.

'The powder, mind, Sister, not the pills.'

The clement weather was generously spilling over into November. Sister Laurence succumbed to a stifled gaiety as, choosing the further afield of the pharmacies recommended by the green-bespectacled girl, she walked down cobbled streets which had retained an air of their medieval past.

The purchase of the Nux. Vom. powders was almost too easily accomplished and Sister Laurence dawdled back – in a quite unchristian spirit, given the severity of the Mother's 'head'. Coming up from the place de la Poissonnerie via the rue de la Petite Cordonnerie, where one of the nine great gates to the close had once stood, she passed a dolls' clinic and stopped to read the article about it posted in the window.

Above and before her, framed by the houses which lined a narrow alleyway, she saw the imposing pattern of the South Rose window, the surrounding stone, in the glow of the midday sun, appearing the palest chalky pink. Walking up the alley, charmingly called the rue aux Herbes, Sister Laurence's eye was caught by a tall, dark-skinned woman standing – as Mother Véronique, had she been present, would surely have explained – beneath the tall figure of Christ as Teacher, sentinel on the trumeau of the Central Door of the South Porch.

The woman was wearing a distinctive skirt of tawny orange beneath a jacket of chrysanthemum yellow. Caught in the sunlight as she descended the wide stone steps, it seemed to Sister Laurence's heightened sensibility as if the woman were surrounded by an aura of shimmering gold.

The woman walked towards her as if to make her way down the alley from which Sister Laurence was now emerging into the cathedral close. To her left the spire so much admired by Viollet-le-Duc was calmly piercing a cerulean sky.

The woman approached, now in the shadow of the buildings and out of the sanctifying light of the sun, and Sister Laurence, with a shock, recognized her. 'Agnès?'

Agnès stopped still, her expression as frozen as that of the stone figure of Christ behind her.

'Sister Laurence, remember me? Agnès, child. Little Agnès. What a miracle to find you here.' Excited beyond measure, Sister Laurence seized Agnès' reluctant hand. 'What in the world are you doing here?'

'I live here, Sister.'

'But this is marvellous. Quite marvellous. Mother Véronique will be thrilled.'

'Sister Véronique is the Mother now?'

'Mother Catherine left us. It's quite a story. She met an old flame and they fell in love, all over again it seems, and now they're married.'

'Heavens,' said Agnès, though she was not in fact so very surprised. She remembered the former Mother's underwear drawer.

'Such a shock when we heard, but I think it's very romantic. And we hear now that Father Ignatius, as was, of course, has secured a position teaching theology at the university in Tours. I shouldn't say this but Mother Véronique was livid when she heard. We – she and I – are here for my fiftieth birthday. What a piece of luck. To find you is the best present of all.'

(Madame Beck, above in her watchtower, observed Agnès talking to a gesticulating nun and felt an animating curiosity.)

Mother Véronique if anything felt annoyance rather than pleasure at the news brought back by an excited Sister Laurence. If Agnès was to be rediscovered, it was more fitting that she, and not Sister Laurence, should have found her. She covered her irritation with a forensic foray of curiosity. 'How did she come here? What does she do? Is she married? Children?'

'I don't know, Mother. I was anxious to get back here with your powders.'

'You took her number, I suppose.'

Agnès, who was on her way to Professor Jones's, had given Sister Laurence her number most unwillingly. The sudden appearance of the nun had more than startled her. It seemed to give substance to a superstitious feeling that to recall her past was in some sinister way to summon it up and cause it to rematerialize. The news of Sister, now Mother, Véronique's presence alarmed her. She had happy memories of the stories Sister Laurence had told her and the bon-bons she used to slip her from her habit pockets. Her memories of Sister Véronique's unpredictable rages were of another order.

Preoccupied with these forebodings, she hardly listened to the chapter of *The Secret Garden*, which until then she had found unexpectedly absorbing. She had been drawn to the querulous, lonely Mary Lennox with her fiery temper. But today, when it came to her turn, she read badly, stumbling over words she had already mastered.

'Not feeling too good today?' the professor asked.

'I'm sorry, Professor.'

'Tell you what. I'll read on. The secret of reading well is being well read to.'

He read on in the droning voice and funny accent she had grown to enjoy – associated as it was with so much good will – about the robin, which had shown Mary the key to the hidden garden which belonged to the cold house in England.

There had been robins nesting at the Dupère farm, she remembered. She had watched one summer as the fledglings grew into round balls of freckled rust-coloured fluff with droll, down-turned mouths, and had finally seen them fly tentatively off, only to return as smart red-breasted adults with black, beady eyes. She had pointed the young birds out to her 'father', who had sat outside in his old cane chair delighting in watching them grow.

Mother Véronique had some criticisms of the hôtellerie to air when she and Sister Laurence met for breakfast the next morning. Her room was, she complained, too near the lift, which apparently had been going up and down all night.

'Like a whore's drawers,' suggested Sister Laurence under her breath.

'What was that, Sister?'

'Nothing, Mother. An old joke.'

'It's no laughing matter, Sister. I slept very badly.'

For all that, Mother Véronique's fund of knowledge seemed undiminished as she strode up the stone steps to the cathedral, almost elbowing aside a beggar, who, abject with her scallop shell, requested alms before the door.

On gaining entry the Mother released a cascade of information. 'The blue of the West Rose derives from a special variety of cobalt oxide. The same blue can be found in the window of the Virgin on the Seat of Wisdom, which unfortunately' – Mother Véronique admonished the boarded scaffolding behind them – 'appears to be hidden behind this.'

Entranced by the great dim bejewelled space, Sister Laurence gazed about her in silence.

'The North Rose' – the Mother turned now to face the amazing harmony of peacock tails and lozenges of coloured light – 'was donated by Blanche of Castile, then Queen of France and granddaughter of Eleanor of Aquitaine.'

She continued, as they moved along the south aisle of the nave, to expound on the themes of the windows.

'This here, Sister, is the parable of the Good Samaritan. It illustrates the well-known exegesis by the Venerable Bede.'

Sister Laurence did not perhaps feel the shame that she might that she had neither read nor heard of this 'well-known' commentary. Nor was she too sure, when she considered it, about the dates or even the identity of the Venerable Bede.

'The Good Samaritan, as you will be aware, Sister, is a symbol of Christ rescuing our sick and wayward souls from the desolations of the wayside.'

Some part of Sister Laurence began to wonder if there might be a latter-day Samaritan to rescue her from tedious explanations.

'Observe, Sister, up there in the central section of the window, the Lord creating the world and Adam, and there' – stabbing the air with a stocky forefinger – 'see, no, no, not there, *there*, the Good Lord is pulling our grandmother Eve out of Adam's rib. And there, you see Adam choking on the apple – we get the term "Adam's apple" from this. The fruit in Eden was quite other than an apple, naturally.'

Sister Laurence nodded her head to express enthusiastic agreement.

'You know the origins of this misconception, Sister?'

Sister Laurence shook her head energetically.

'A wordplay on the Latin for apple and *malus* – "evil".' She afforded her colleague a rare and, to Sister Laurence's eye, slightly terrifying smile.

They moved up the aisle to examine the two windows celebrating the death and assumption of the Virgin Mary and the many miracles she had wrought at Chartres. These, Mother Véronique pronounced, were her favourite windows. If she was familiar with the butcher donors' slaughtered pig in the bottom corner, favoured by Robert Clément, she made no comment on it.

They moved back down towards the South Transept to inspect the Holy Nail. 'You see, Sister, at the summer solstice the sun strikes the spot right here. Of course we are not at the right time of year to witness the miracle but if you bend down . . .'

But here a welcome distraction for Sister Laurence occurred. A party of English visitors were being shown around by a learned English authority who had lived and discoursed on the cathedral for over sixty years. His audience milled about him, distracting Mother Véronique from her examination of the Holy Nail.

In a low voice he described the history of the cathedral and the story of the Holy birthing gown. Mother Véronique heaved herself up to listen. Describing the ravages of the terrible fire of 1194, the authority made a small joke. 'After three days the priests emerged from the crypt with the gown intact. They called it a miracle; we might call it marketing.'

'Impertinent nonsense!' exploded Mother Véronique.

Sister Laurence had taken the opportunity to escape to the north aisle of the nave. When Mother Véronique tracked her down, Sister Laurence declared that she had decided that her favourite window was Noah and the flood. She particularly liked, she said, the pink elephants and striped pigs.

'Boars,' corrected Mother Véronique.

'Oh yes, of course, "boars",' repeated Sister Laurence with seeming meekness but with enough of a treasonous glint in her voice for Mother Véronique to embark on a lengthy account of the life of St Lubin.

St Lubin's window had been donated by the vintners, whose trade was advertised on panels depicting scenes of merriment connected with wine. Sister Laurence, trying to absorb the details of the life of the saint, wondered if, given that it was her birthday, she dared suggest to the Mother that they too might enjoy that evening a convivial glass of wine.

For the moment, however, she confined herself to wondering if they might maybe ascend the tower, from which vantage point, a notice advertised, a magnificent view of Chartres could be seen. But her request was refused. Mother Véronique had had, she said, since adolescence a horror of heights and always feared she might succumb to the temptation to throw herself off, a temptation she went on to compare with that of Jesus, similarly tempted by Satan in the wilderness.

37

Chartres

Although she didn't always understand the words, Agnès tried each evening to read as much as she could manage of the Abbé Paul's schoolboy book. It had grown to be a ritual: supper (she always cooked herself something) and then her reading.

She had started with Theseus and the Minotaur. It was slow work but from what she could make out numbers were important. Seven Athenian children of each sex were sent every nine years to Crete to feed the Minotaur. It was, she reflected, what Alain had been telling her about.

'It's all number here,' he had said only that morning. She had followed him up to his eyrie again for an early breakfast of sausage and coffee and had noticed a sleeping bag.

'You do sleep here, then? I thought that was a joke.'

'The rooms in the hôtellerie have thin walls. There's someone snoring like a herd of swine in the room next to mine so I thought tonight I'd stay here and get a better night's sleep.'

'Is it allowed?'

He shrugged. 'Who's to notice?'

'What about washing?' she wondered.

He laughed, showing his pointed eye-teeth. 'You mean where do I pee? Plenty of buckets around. I don't pee in the font if that's what you're imagining.'

'No, I –'

'Are you more interested in my ablutions or what I was telling you?'

'What you were telling me, of course.'

'OK, so, this place is all number. Three is the number of the spirit, the Trinity to Christians, but it's a holy number in many faiths. Four is the physical number – four elements, earth, water, fire, air, four corners of the earth –'

'But –'

'Yes, I know it doesn't have any – but it did – the four winds and so on. And if you add them together, spiritual plus physical, you get the number seven, which is wholeness. The medieval –'

'Stop, stop.' She was laughing again. 'I'm only a poor uneducated cleaner.'

'That's rubbish and you know it.'

'I don't.'

He gave her one of his long looks. His eyes, she noticed, moved very slightly slower than those of most people. 'I'm sorry. I'm an arrogant beast. I'm dreadful when I get into lecture mode.'

'No, no, I like it.' She did like it. She liked his airy confidence. 'Go on.'

'OK. But stop me when you're bored. So, what was I saying? Seven. Well, the medieval curriculum was divided into two parts, the Trivium – grammar, rhetoric and logic – and the Quadrivium – geometry, arithmetic, astronomy and music. This is where the seven liberal arts come from – you can see them over the right door of the Western Front. Seven is a magic number: the days of the week, the seven deadly sins, and virtues, seven last trumpets at the end of time. Three times four is twelve, three times three is nine, and twelve and nine are also important here.'

'The signs of the zodiac?'

'Exactly – they're on the North Porch.'

'And the window.'

'There too. Twelve months of the year, twelve apostles, twelve branches to the tree in the Jesse window. Nine is the triple trinity – there are nine doors to the cathedral, nine porches to the close, or were, and ditto to the town. The nine orders of angels on the South Porch are in three choirs of three: Seraphim, Cherubim, Thrones –'

'Dominions,' she joined in. 'Virtues, Powers –'

'Principalities, Archangels, Angels,' they concluded in noisy unison.

'Well, I never,' he said. 'I've won bets reciting those.'

'There's some good in a convent education.' She laughed.

'What?'

'I was remembering you said you weren't "chatty".'

'This isn't chat, lady.'

When she clambered back down, it was reluctantly. But the Abbé Bernard was about to arrive and she needed to get on with the ambulatory without his trailing round after her.

When, later that same day, Agnès put down the book of myth in order to put on the kettle, she realized that the Abbé Bernard was still on her mind. His decline seemed to be hastening daily. Twice lately, he had asked her if she had noticed the Satan behind the screen covering the scaffolding, where, he assured her, the Prince of Darkness had his rebel troops concealed. Only that morning he had taken her down the south steps, his freckled hand gripping the flesh of her arm, and round to stand before the donkey with the hurdy-gurdy on the south-western end of the cathedral.

'See there, see there,' the Abbé Bernard had said, stabbing the air with an agitated finger at the odd stone figure. 'His works are everywhere.' And, as the white train which transports the gullible tourists around Chartres rattled past, he turned angry eyes upon it and denounced that too as 'under the devil's spell'.

She tried to stop thinking about the old abbé and to think about the tale she had read. Seven boys and seven girls were sent to Crete every nine years. Maybe that was why the story had found a place in the cathedral?

The phone rang. 'Agnès?' From the prickle down her breast-bone she knew before the recognition became conscious whose the overloud voice was. 'Mother Véronique speaking.'

'Good evening, Mother.'

'Sister Laurence told me she had bumped into you. When can we see you?'

'Well, I . . .'

'Tonight isn't possible, I'm afraid. But tomorrow would suit us very well.'

'I work, you see, Sister.'

' "Mother", it is, now. Where do you work, Agnès?'

Unable to resist that commanding voice from her past, Agnès said, 'First thing, I start in the cathedral, Mother.'

'What time is "first thing"?'

'Six. But the cathedral doesn't open to visitors until eight thirty.'

'Sister Laurence and I will come to find you tomorrow morning at eight thirty sharp,' said Sister Véronique. 'Good evening.' She rang off.

38

Chartres

'You can always take flight,' said Alain, when she told him that two of the nuns who had brought her up were arriving that morning. 'Say "Hi", tell them you've another appointment and then skedaddle.'

'I would. But Sister Véronique – "Mother" she is now – will be sure to find me.'

'Terrier or bloodhound?'

'A bit of both.'

'Well, remember I'm up aloft, your guardian angel, if not archangel. If you get into trouble, give me a sign and I'll drop in on you. I'd quite like to meet these Holy Terrors.'

Agnès was so relieved it was not the Sisters entering at eight thirty sharp that she almost welcomed the Abbé Bernard. He had had another dream about his mother. This time, 'She was walking along a wall, quite narrow, and when I looked up it was on the cathedral roof. But the roof was not green as ours is green but like the scales of a great dragon. It is the Leviathan, Agnès.'

'It was a dream, Father.'

'But the Leviathan . . . "Canst thou draw out leviathan with an hook? or his tongue with a cord thou lettest down?" '

'I know, Father. But we must hope your mother is with Our Lord in heaven.'

'I fear she is with Beelzebub, Agnès.'

'Let us hope not, Father.'

He went off muttering just as Agnès became aware of two figures in grey bearing down on her.

Mother Véronique gave her a bristly kiss and Sister Laurence hugged her close. She smelled, Agnès noticed, of one of the Mediterranean scents which could be sampled free in the pharmacy on rue du Soleil d'Or.

'So you work here, Agnès.'

'Yes, Mother. And for other people in Chartres.'

'I am anxious to hear all about your life since we saw you last. We know about the incident, of course.'

Sister Laurence said, 'Dear Agnès, this is such a marvellous environment. I'm so happy for you to be here.'

'Yes, I am lucky, Sister. Father Paul has been most kind.'

'And Father Paul is . . .' asked Mother Véronique, keen to get everyone into their proper place in her mind.

'The Dean here, Mother. I clean for him too.'

'Very good. Very good, Agnès.'

They walked round the cathedral, with Mother Véronique issuing bulletins of information. 'This here, the Prodigal Son window, is the only one that is not signed by a donor.'

'It is very beautiful towards the evening,' Agnès suggested. 'With the sunset behind it.' She herself liked the Miracle window donated by the blacksmiths just round the corner, with its image of the sturdy white horse being shod.

'Notice up there, the young man consorting with harlots,' instructed Mother Véronique. Sister Laurence narrowed her eyes the better to see. The eponymous Son appeared to have a firm grip on the buttocks of one of the 'harlots'.

Mother Véronique felt compelled to pause before the choir and complain about the white masonry 'grouting' painted on the ceiling. 'How vulgar. Why are they painting the joins like that?'

'We're taking it back to the original.'

Mother Véronique turned to the young man addressing her. 'I beg your pardon.'

'What you see – the ceiling colour and the painted mortar joins – is the way the original was – *is*, in fact.'

Mother Véronique's expression became severe. 'I'm afraid you are mistaken. The original was as we see here.' She gestured at the grey vaulting above the altar.

'Sorry, Sister, but you've been misinformed.' The young man was smiling but his pointed eye-teeth gave the smile a faintly sinister aspect. Mother Véronique moved very slightly backwards.

'This here,' he continued, indicating the ambulatory ceiling, 'the yellow with the painted mortar lines, has all been taken back to its thirteenth-century state. Eighty per cent of it is the original intact.'

Mother Véronique became mulish. ' "Mother", actually. I am sorry to contradict you but –'

Anxious to save the Mother from further humiliation, Agnès said hurriedly, 'Mother, this is Alain Fleury. He works here as one of the cathedral restorers. Alain, Mother Véronique.'

'I see. Very interesting. Is there somewhere we can take some refreshment?' Mother Véronique turned from the impertinent restorer, who winked at Agnès.

Outside, at a table belonging to the restaurant café that was once 'Beck's', Mother Véronique ordered coffee for Sister Laurence and Agnès and a chamomile tea for herself. 'I have these dreadful "heads", you may remember, Agnès.'

Agnès, who remembered all too well how they had affected Sister Véronique's temper, nodded.

Sister Laurence said, 'Please tell us how you've been, Agnès. We so often talk about you at home and wonder.'

'I've been well, Sister. I came here twenty years ago and, as you see, I stayed.'

'And the good man who found you? He must have passed away long since.'

'Yes.'

'And your doctor? Such an agreeable man.' And Sister Laurence wistfully recalled her entertaining drive down to the farm to see Agnès with the attractive doctor. 'What has happened to him?'

'Dr Deman and I spoke quite regularly on the phone,' interjected Mother Véronique. 'Naturally, he kept me well informed.'

'I don't know. We lost touch after my – after Jean died.'

'I shall make inquiries about him on my return,' Mother Véronique declared.

Agnès explained she had to leave now to go to her next job and Sister Laurence asked if she might accompany her. Mother Véronique said she preferred to stay put. Her "head" had quite drained her. She would wait there for Sister Laurence, study her guide and perhaps take another tisane.

Sister Laurence accompanied Agnès to the place de la Poissonnerie. 'My employer lives up there.' She pointed out the professor's apartment.

'You clean for her?'

'Him. Professor Jones. I've been sorting out his work. He is, was, an English professor, though he writes in French. He has a lot of papers.'

'You *have* done well, Agnès.' Sister Laurence beamed. She was happy to see her little girl transformed into this competent, elegant young woman.

'I am learning to read at last,' Agnès said, the expression in Sister Laurence's brown eyes encouraging her to confide. 'Professor Jones is teaching me.'

'How lovely. So you can read stories to yourself now.'

'I'm beginning to, yes.'

'You did like stories. Rapt, you were as a little girl. I did love to tell you stories, Agnès.'

'I liked you telling them to me too, Sister.'

Sister Laurence kissed her protégée goodbye and made her way, rather circuitously, back to the café, where she found Mother Véronique deep in conversation.

'Sister, this is Madame Beck.' The elderly woman extended a beringed hand. She appeared to have a head of unusually luxuriant hennaed hair. 'Madame, this is Sister Laurence. Madame Beck was asking me about Agnès, Sister. Agnès cleans for her.'

'Not any more.'

The woman turned two accusing eyes on Sister Laurence, who blinked. 'Oh, I hope there was nothing –'

'I have been explaining to Madame Beck, Sister, about poor Agnès' "episode". She was really very ill, you know, Madame. She had to be hospitalized. And then there was that other unfortunate incident with the child.'

'Mother,' said Sister Laurence. 'I wonder if –'

'Incident?' asked Madame Beck, and her eyes appeared to Sister Laurence to hover momentarily in her face like pale blue flies.

'Agnès had a child while she was only a child herself. We were all very distressed. It was adopted of course. A young woman in the vicinity caring for another child was later attacked and it was thought that maybe Agnès –'

'Mother,' Sister Laurence interrupted again with unusual vigour, 'I would really like to show you the Maison du Saumon –'

'All in good time, Sister. Anyway, poor Agnès was thought to be involved in the assault. Praise God, I believe later it was found not to be the case.'

'It was indeed,' said Sister Laurence firmly. 'She was discovered to be quite innocent. Poor girl. On top of everything else that she'd been through it was very bad luck indeed.' She almost glared at Mother Véronique.

Almost the first thing Mother Véronique did when she returned to the convent was to telephone St Francis's to inquire about Dr Deman.

'We have no Dr Deman here,' the switchboard operator announced.

'I assure you he used to work at St Francis's.'

'When was this, please?'

Mother Véronique consulted her memory. 'I would say 1987. Yes, he was certainly there then. A consultant psychiatrist.'

'Madame, that was twenty-four years ago. He's probably moved on or maybe even retired.'

'May I speak to someone in authority?'

The receptionist, well schooled in handling difficult callers, put her through to a line on which a long queue of callers was already waiting to make complaints.

Two hours later Mother Véronique rang again and this time got through to the 'Administration Department' without too much of a wait. Perseverance with a bored-sounding clerk finally brought a result.

'According to our records Dr Deman left the clinic in 1991.'

'Do you have a record of where he went?'

'I'm afraid we cannot give out personal information, Madame.'

'I am the Mother Superior of the Convent of Our Lady of Mercy,' said Mother Véronique, with lofty irrelevance.

The irrelevant sometimes succeeds where honest reason fails. An amused voice came back down the line. 'A colleague here tells me he moved to England.'

'Do you have an address?'

The amused voice made a muffled inquiry. 'He moved to a hospital in London.' After a further muffled exchange the voice named a well-known psychiatric hospital. 'It's famous, I gather.'

'Thank you,' said Mother Veronique. 'I have of course heard of it.'

39

Rouen

It was some weeks before Denis Deman came to hear of the death of Jean Dupère. His contact with Agnès had not ceased; but over the two years of her stay at the farm it had diminished. She was so at home, so patently happy there, that by and by her former doctor ceased to trouble about her. They had both survived his panicky error and the outcome had maybe been more favourable to her than if he had never been so foolish as to make it in the first place.

Or so he consoled himself.

So it was with alarm he heard the news, via one of the nursing staff, a friend of Maddy and aware of his interest, that the old man had died and Agnès had been more or less thrown out by the niece.

Denis Deman remembered this niece: the one whom Jean Dupère's mother had not cared for; the one to whom the old man had not wished to leave the silver chain. Reproving himself for not keeping a closer eye on Agnès, Denis Deman sat down at his desk and wrote to this unpopular niece care of the farm, marking the envelope for forwarding. Hearing nothing, he wrote again. His letters were not returned but if they were forwarded to Dreux, where the niece, he recalled, had come from, then he must assume she had elected not to reply.

Finally, in the absence of any other source of information, Dr Deman drove down the familiar track, where a sign advertising the sale of the farmstead stood at the junction with the road. He stopped not at the Dupère place but before it, at the neighbouring farm where Jean's neighbour Yvette lived.

Yvette was pleased to see him and invited him in for a glass of Calva.

'What happened to the little one I have no idea,' she told him. 'She left so quietly we didn't hardly know she was gone and none of us have seen her since.'

'But you'll let me know if you hear anything?'

'Such a nice girl and so fond of Jean. Between you and me I don't like the niece.' Yvette made a graphic gesture with her hand. 'Greedy as sin and not so much as a tear squeezed out for her uncle, who left her everything, bless him. Poor little Agnès wept her blessed heart out at the funeral. Not that that was much to write home about. Very cheap, we thought.'

Denis Deman left asking again that she would kindly let him know if she heard news and leaving his card.

Unsure whom else he could turn to, he rang Inès Nezat in Le Mans.

'I can't help you, Denis, I'm afraid. I've heard nothing since Agnès went back to you. I'm sorry the old boy has passed on. How is Anne?'

Denis Deman, who had not had to have recourse to Anne for a while, was momentarily puzzled. 'Anne?'

'Your fiancée. Or is she not any more?'

'Oh *Anne*. Sorry, I thought you were thinking of Maddy, the nurse here at the clinic whom Agnès liked. Anne's very well, thank you.'

'Have you seen each other lately?'

'I'm off to England for Easter, since you ask.'

'Which part?'

'The Lake District. It's supposed to be very pretty in the spring.'

And whether to salve his conscience (for he retained an

affection for Inès Nezat), or because the fib, as can happen, had kindled his imagination, or for the want of anything better to do, Denis Deman did in fact go that Easter to England for a walking holiday in the Lakes.

At his hotel, he met a young woman who had suffered a sprain to her ankle while descending Scafell Pike. As a doctor, he offered his services. The young woman bore a startling likeness to his image of Anne, the fiancée whose powerful non-existence had brought him there in the first place. So much did the girl resemble his long-standing ideal that he proposed to her almost immediately and, shortly after, to his mother's disgust, he moved to England in order to marry her.

40

Chartres

That Sunday, just before lunch, as Agnès was preparing *lardons* for a salad, Terry rang.

'Sorry to be a pest but I'm in deep shit.'

'Oh dear.'

'That horrible little pooch has gone missing. I should never have taken her in. Never trust Pekes.'

'What happened, Terry?'

It transpired that what had 'happened' was that Terry had gone to spend a night with the patents lawyer and had taken Piaf with her.

'I couldn't leave her overnight at mine, could I, so I asked if I could bring the pooch over to his. He said, yeah, fine, but then, when I get there it's "Oh I don't want a dog in the house", so in the end I put her in the shed in his backyard. I left the shed door open so she could do pipi in the night and in the morning she's only gone and done a runner.'

'When does Madame get back?'

'That's just it, she's home tomorrow. God alone knows what'll happen if the pooch isn't there to slobber all over her fat face. Shit!'

'You want me to help look?'

'Too right I do!'

But after three hours of fruitless searching Agnès said, 'We should put up notices.'

'That'll advertise the fact she's gone.'

'Terry, you'll have to tell her tomorrow anyway.'

'Why did I take her, for Christ's sake?'

'For three hundred and fifty euros?'

'Don't remind me. That's going to be history for sure.'

'So, you will have to face the music.'

'Just my luck and all for that wanker too.'

Madame Picot, arriving home, and bearing the extensive London purchases with which she hoped to arouse the envy of Madame Beck, was greeted by an uncharacteristically nervous Terry, who broke the news of Piaf's disappearance. Madame Picot reacted as a tragic operatic *prima donna* might when faced with the news of the death of the love of her life.

'She literally screamed,' Terry recounted to Agnès. 'Never heard anything like it in my life. Not even my little brothers screeched so loud. Yelled and cried and called me a murderess. I tell you, I'm done with dogs.'

They were at the jazz café, which, it being Monday, was not playing jazz. Agnès, who had felt that Terry needed something if not to cheer her up at least to distract her, had suggested they meet there for a bite.

Monique, the owner, who had been made aware of the loss, said, 'You know, Pekes are intelligent. Piaf will find her way home.'

'If she's not dead,' said Terry, who had reached the point in her drama where people refuse to be comforted.

She cheered up later when Philippe turned up. 'I dare say Piaf is in someone's hamburger.'

'Oh, thanks a bunch, Philippe. Yours, let's hope.'

'I never touch the stuff. It's ruinous to the skin.'

Philippe bought them all a carafe of wine to give him the licence to complain about his sister. 'She and her man have decided to split so I'm stuck with her till she finds somewhere else to live.'

'How is little Max?' Agnès asked.

'Maxling is great. I adore Maxling. But I can't stand the way she treats him.'

'The black cloth?'

'What's that?' asked Terry, curiosity finally prising her from private grief.

'It's a dire method of training little children that my mad sister has adopted. You leave the kid to cry to "teach" them to sleep. Except it doesn't work.'

'No,' Agnès said with unusual firmness. 'It wouldn't. Nature gave babies a special cry in order for women to respond to them.'

'Men too,' said Philippe, not wanting to be outdone. 'I can't stand hearing him cry.'

'You're a girl,' said Terry. 'You don't count.'

Philippe blew her a kiss and said, 'Any time you feel like taking young Maxling off our hands, Agnès, you're welcome. I'll pay you to have him for a weekend. My sister's got to go back to Auxerre to get some of her stuff and she doesn't want to take him with her.'

By the time Mother Véronique left Chartres, she and Madame Beck had become fast friends. Madame Beck had accepted an invitation to visit the Convent of Our Lady of Mercy, which, Mother Véronique explained, had recently opened a 'Retreat' wing to offer rest and respite to weary souls in need of refreshment.

All this, Madame Beck was eagerly waiting to impart to her friend, with the added pleasurable prospect that she might induce a little jealousy at the news of the acquaintance, made in Madame Picot's absence, with a Mother Superior. Especially one as intellectually distinguished as Mother Véronique.

But the first part of the afternoon, when the friends were reunited after Madame Picot's return, was taken up with the drama of the missing Piaf.

'My dear,' said Madame Beck, who, pushing out the boat in honour of her friend's return, had bought some raspberry tartlets at the *pâtisserie*. 'I know how you feel. I went through this over Lulu.'

'I hardly think a china doll is the equivalent of a live dog, Louise.'

'Well, you know, I'm not a dog person, dear.'

'It's the most terrible thing that has happened to me since Auguste died. And Terry . . . I trusted that girl and she has betrayed me.'

'How did it happen, dear?'

'I can't get the story clear. She was visiting a friend and somehow Piaf got out through the fence.'

'How very careless of her.'

Madame Picot was too taken up with Piaf to be as excited as her friend was by the news of Agnès' past.

'So she had an illegitimate child?'

'Apparently she was only fifteen. They never got out of her who the father was. But then, she herself was someone's unwanted "love child".' Madame Beck's voice took on its most conspiratorial tone. 'You see, I was right about her. There's bad blood there. I knew it. Blood will out, Claude always said.'

'But you say another child was involved. I don't quite –'

'A nanny for an adopted baby whose parents lived near the psychiatric hospital where Agnès had been sent –'

'A psychiatric hospital?'

'Yes, Jeanette. Have you not been listening? She attacked the then Mother, a Mother Catherine, Mother Véronique told me, with a knife. Appeared stark naked knife in hand by the Mother's bedside. Mother Véronique, Sister as she was then, of course, had to rescue Mother Catherine. They had to have her sectioned.'

'The Mother?'

'Don't be a fool, Jeanette. Agnès.'

'Oh dear.'

'She's a little exhibitionist, all right. You can see that. She was showing us everything, cool as a cucumber, that day Father Bernard and I caught her in the cathedral with that man.'

'But I don't quite understand, dear,' Madame Picot was confused by the torrent of information gushing from her friend's busily working mouth, 'where the nanny –'

'I told you, Jeanette. Do listen. *A nanny with a baby*, the same age as Agnès' adopted one, was attacked with a knife.'

'How dreadful. And it was Agnès?'

'Well,' Madame Beck retreated into vagueness. 'I gather from Mother Véronique that they never discovered who did it for sure. But the finger pointed at Agnès and the evidence must have been strong. She was sent to a secure hospital for the mentally deranged.' Had someone presented Madame Beck with a whole showcase of antique china dolls she could not have looked more satisfied.

'Oh dear,' said Madame Picot again. She had had a happy week with her daughter shopping in the King's Road and her love of scandal had been temporarily ousted by her love of acquisition. 'How very unfortunate.'

'I shall have to tell the Abbé Paul, of course. It's my Christian duty. The girl has quite bamboozled him, you can see. I did try to tell him about her taking Lulu but he couldn't hear me. Poor man, he has gone quite deaf. He was quite convinced that I had recommended her to him.'

'So you said nothing?' Madame Picot's bad conscience over Lulu was renewed.

'I left him in his fools' paradise,' said Madame Beck. It was her plain opinion that this was where most men preferred to live. 'But I shall have to make sure he grasps the danger now. With all I have learned they can *not* keep her on at the cathedral. I shall refer the matter to the Chapter. If necessary the Bishop must be informed.'

41

Chartres

Philippe's sister, Brigitte, had planned to visit Auxerre the following weekend and it was agreed that baby Max would be brought to Agnès' apartment on the Friday evening.

Agnès, who had heard nothing from Madame Badon for weeks, months even, was dismayed to arrive home early, in order to get things ready for Max, to a message on the answerphone announcing that she would be coming down to Chartres that weekend and she would be bringing her 'friend'.

'Too bad,' Philippe said when Agnès rang with this news. 'That's so like life. People you never see turn up just exactly the moment you don't want them.'

He called back a little later. 'Listen. I was having a friend over this weekend but he says I can go to his. So why not come and look after Max here? All his gear's here anyway.'

On Friday night, Agnès rocked Max to sleep in her arms and then laid him down beside her in Philippe's king-sized bed. The little bundle wriggled and squirmed, but he woke fully only twice for feeds and then snuggled down again against Agnès' neck, where he spent the rest of the night behaving like a miniature merry-go-round.

They breakfasted together, Max on Agnès' lap, while he ate his baby cereal and she drank her coffee listening to France Culture.

'That's Bach,' she told him. She recognized the unique chords from listening to the Abbé Paul's CDs as she dusted.

The morning was fine and, though a November chill had now set in, the twin spires were still sharply defined against a canopy of the clearest blue. Agnès joggled Max in his buggy over the cobbles on the north side of the cathedral close towards the jazz café.

Monique, seeing them, called out, 'What a beautiful baby,' and as she came closer to greet them bent her knees to look. 'Bless him. I could eat him. May I?'

Max, who was not yet asleep, gravely consented to be thoroughly kissed by Monique and volubly admired by several of the regulars who were taking coffee and beers in the sun.

'Where are you taking him, Agnès?'

'I'm going to show him Notre-Dame.'

Inside the cathedral, a wedding was taking place. Side by side at the crossing of the transepts, before the silver altar – which so resembled a blacksmith's anvil that it added its own fairytale dimension to the scene – the bride and groom stood, she glorious in a meringue and whipped-cream lace frock, he in a stiff suit, brand new. Hand in hand, they glanced at each other, smiling shyly.

Behind them their families were ranged, the women resplendent in hats bought specially for the occasion, the men in their best suits, their shoulders braced to witness the plighting of the troths of the two young hopefuls who had no idea what a pack of troubles lay ahead of them.

Agnès, standing below the window of the Prodigal Son, watched the drama of present and projected bliss. Max in his buggy was making the quiet animal snuffles of a baby lost in sleep. The sun, shifting in its westward path, was already lighting the South Rose window and smudges of colour, refracted through the glass, were blessing the grey stone of the walls by the scaffolding that concealed the benign Blue Virgin.

As the wedding party started on the hymn 'All the Saints and

All the Angels', Agnès, looking up and over towards the South Transept and the covered scaffolding, saw something . . .

When Agnès came to, a crowd was round her and the air seemed to be full of incense. Little Max was sobbing in the arms of an unknown woman. Struggling to sit up, Agnès cried aloud, 'Give me my baby!'

'Agnès.' It was the Abbé Paul. 'You fainted, my dear. Here.' He offered his arm and she sat up while he helped her to rest her back against a column.

'Please, give me the baby.'

Max was handed down to her and, holding him fast, she rocked him, feeling the stone base of the column reassuringly solid against her spine. 'It's all right, sweetie. There, there, lamb. I'm here.'

'I'm sorry, Madame.' It was the woman who had been holding him, looking anxious. 'He was crying so much I thought –'

'No, please, it is fine. Thank you.'

The Abbé Paul said, 'Would you like us to call a doctor, Agnès?'

'No, no. Please. I am fine.'

'Why not come over to the house?'

The wedding party had stayed, it seemed, to ensure that this episode was no symbol of bad luck and they clapped and cheered Agnès as, holding little Max, she crossed the transept to the South Door.

Madame Beck, standing at her watchtower, was put into a veritable ecstasy of rage at the sight of the Abbé Paul carrying a buggy and following Agnès down the south steps. She rang Madame Picot, brimming over with the news.

'That girl has positively bewitched him. I shall have to go round again.'

'There is still no news,' said Madame Picot mournfully at the other end of the phone.

Three people had rung in answer to the notices placed by Terry and Agnès advertising the missing Piaf. One man had seen a terrier somewhere, one had offered his own unwanted dog, and yet another woman had tried to sell her a puppy. 'They weren't even Pekes,' Madame Picot complained.

Madame Beck made not the slightest attempt to pretend to care about the bogus Pekes.

'She had a baby with her. With her reputation. It is my bounden duty to report this. After all, I have it on the Mother Superior's authority that there was violence towards a child.'

The Abbé Paul followed a peculiar branch of Christian practice that meant he tried always to put himself in the shoes of others and to do to them as he would wish them to do to him. He therefore made no inquiry about what might have caused Agnès' fainting spell but when the three of them were settled in his receiving room, he offered Agnès a glass of wine.

'And maybe a little something to eat,' he suggested. 'I have some good Brie, some bread or a sweet biscuit, maybe?'

Agnès accepted the wine and a biscuit. The Abbé Paul poured them each a large glass of one of his better Chinons. Max, nuzzled close into Agnès' breast, had fallen into a contented doze. Through the window, the Abbé Paul could see the pale mauve of the late Michaelmas daisies still in flower.

When in doubt the Abbé Paul tended to say nothing. He was unafraid of silence. Indeed, he welcomed it. And Agnès did not look as if she were ill. On the contrary, she looked unusually well as she sat, with the child in her arms, on his dark blue silk chaise-longue. The Abbé Paul, who was susceptible to all things beautiful, drank in the face and form opposite him even as he drank in his good wine.

After a while Agnès said, 'I am sorry to be a nuisance, Father.'

'You're not a nuisance, Agnès.'

'I feel fine. I ought to get going.'

'Please stay as long as you wish.'

But Agnès, aware that baby Max's next feed was almost due, finished the wine and got up to go.

'How are you getting on with the Greek myths?' Possibly the Abbé Paul wanted to detain her a little.

'I like them, Father. I like –' She paused. What was it she liked? 'I like that they are, maybe, a bit wild?'

'To be sure the Olympians are not your Christian God of love and mercy.'

The Sisters of Our Lady of Mercy had not always been so merciful. 'No, Father. But –'

'Yes?'

'They can't –' She didn't have the words, though she had the glimmer of a sense of the feeling of them. 'They can't be so *used*,' was the best she could come up with.

'Ah,' said the Abbé Paul, for he understood her. 'That is true. The Olympic pantheon is not pliant. Those pagan gods were less easy to press into the wrong sort of service. It is a fault, no doubt, of our own religion that it can be.'

And the Abbé Paul sighed.

When, only a few minutes after Agnès had left, the bell rang twice, and loudly, the Abbé Paul was in no doubt about the owner of the face that he would meet when he went to the door. He thought of ignoring the insistent ringing, but he had learned from experience how the devil pitches his tent in the spaces of procrastination. Nevertheless, he hastily poured himself another glass of wine and got most of it down before opening the door.

'Madame Beck?'

'Good day. Father, I must speak urgently with you.'

42

Chartres

Agnès had returned baby Max on the Sunday evening. Brigitte, who was due back by the six o'clock train, had not arrived.

Philippe, who had had a wildly erotic weekend with his friend Tan and was feeling on top of the world, said, 'Stay for supper, do, you're most welcome.' But Agnès did not like to think of parting with Max in front of his mother.

She made her way home via the close and encountered the cat René sitting on the north steps beneath the long statue of St Modeste.

A cat is not a baby with soft black hair but in its way it can be soothing. Agnès, approaching quietly, scooped a reluctant René up in her arms. After a while he submitted to her attentions and began to purr. When she put him down, he made towards the railing by the crypt door.

She had tried before to see where René got in and out of the crypt. But this time she was able to follow him with her eye as he vanished. Peering round, she saw a very small gap, invisible to a superficial glance, by the lower lintel of the door.

So that was his route. Clever creature. She was about to move on when something stayed her.

A distant wailing. Another cat? She listened again. No, that was a human note. Someone was in the crypt and it sounded as if they were in some distress. The cathedral keys were on her key-ring in her handbag. She unlocked the door and switched on the lights.

'Excuse me. Is anyone there?'

The faint sound stopped. She walked downwards, towards the chapel where the venerated figure of the Virgin had once presided before it was burned in the zealous revolutionaries' fire.

On one of the benches the Abbé Bernard was slumped, his head held in his crumpled hands. 'Father?'

'Lost, lost. All lost.'

'What is "lost", Father?'

'Are you lost too, child?'

'What is it, Father?'

'It is the Satan come for me.'

'Where, Father?'

He turned a stricken tear-wet face to her and she was shocked at how old and mad his features had become. 'You want to see him?'

'If you'd like to show me, Father.'

The Abbé Bernard struggled to stand, swayed slightly and clutched for support at Agnès' shoulder. 'He hides in the pagan well.'

The Well of the Strong, into which the Vikings allegedly once tossed their victims, was widely – if wildly – reputed to have been originally of druid making. The Abbé Bernard, shuffling and swaying erratically, and Agnès, supporting him, made their way through the chapel towards it.

'There. There. I cannot look. His face, oh, his face is terrible.'

Agnès peered down through the grille, which for reasons of health and safety had long been lodged beneath the mouth of the well to prevent any Viking-like activity. Impossible to see anything in there; it was far too deep.

'I think maybe he has gone, Father.'

'He never goes, child.'

'Well, for the time being I think he may have done. Shall we go now?'

It was easier to continue round the long path of the crypt and out by the South Door. Passing the entrance to the ninth-century St Lubin Chapel, which leads to the very lowest and oldest part of the crypt, the Abbé Bernard halted. 'Hear. Hear. He has retreated there.'

Agnès, about to reassure him, also heard something.

'He has assumed the likeness of a dog. The head of a dog is one of his guises.'

'No, Father. I think that really *is* a dog.'

It was maybe not the best plan to have the Abbé Bernard follow her. But he was unwilling to let go of her hand. He rattled off a string of incoherent forebodings as they descended into the most ill-lit and ill-smelling part of the cathedral.

Coming to the remains of the bases of some Roman columns, Agnès stopped and called out, 'Piaf. Good girl. Piaf.'

'Not Piaf, child. No. She is a singer, I believe. Beelzebub, Beelzebub.'

'No, Father. Listen for a minute. I think a dog has got trapped here. A lost Pekinese.'

She held his hand while he muttered phrases, some of which she recognized as coming from the books of Jonah and Job. There issued from the enigmatic ancient Gallic darkness another disembodied yap.

'Father, please, wait here. I am going to try to get along that passage.'

'The Lord of Darkness will consume me for I have sinned.'

In the diminished light she felt rather than saw the anguish in his face.

'Listen. Hold this, Father. It will save you from him. It is' – she had taken off her silver chain – 'a charm.'

'A charm?' She felt him shudder.

'A relic, then. A very powerful relic. I'm putting it in your hand now, Father. I'll be as quick as I can.'

Agnès, inching her way along the abandoned Carolingian passageway, called, 'Piaf, Piaf.'

She heard another 'yap'. Around a corner, there was a ledge and reaching out, trying to banish any thought of rats, she felt a bundle of damp fur.

'God, what a relief.'

Terry was bathing Piaf, who, after a tin of chicken and much water, seemed remarkably chirpy.

Agnès, experiencing the strange affection of a saviour for the saved, said, 'I wonder how the poor scrap survived?'

'She's a tough cookie, this one. Mice, maybe. Or rats? I wouldn't put it past her to have a go at a rat.'

'And there's enough water down there anyway. I was dripping when I got out.'

'The main thing is she's here. I'll ring old Picot and take her round and eat truck-loads of humble pie. Then we can go out and celebrate. On me this time.'

'I'm going to talk to Father Paul about Father Bernard first.'

'What now?'

'He's dementing. I'm afraid he will harm himself. I don't even know where he has gone tonight.'

'You and your old guys!'

The Abbé Paul's feelings, when he answered the door to Agnès, were less straightforward than usual. As always, he was glad to see her but the interview with Madame Beck was sticking in his craw.

Madame Beck had gone into Agnès' 'history', as she seemed to wish to call it, with a monstrous superfluity of detail – detail that made him flinch even at his studied non-recollection of it. At every turn, to the Abbé Paul's mind, his unwelcome caller appeared to put the worst possible complexion on matters: the unknown circumstances of Agnès' birth, the underage pregnancy, the subsequent adoption, the attack on the Mother Superior, naked and armed with a knife, the psychiatric clinic and last but not least the murderous assault on the nanny and the subsequent sectioning of Agnès in the secure hospital in Le Mans. About this assault, he had pressed Madame Beck, sensing some haziness in her account, which in all other details had the triumphalist ring of truth. Madame Beck had responded with a vehement vow to pass on to the Abbé Paul the newspaper cuttings that Mother Véronique had promised to send. Mother Véronique had, he was told, been careful to keep the file on Agnès that she had found in the former Mother's bureau.

The Abbé Paul cared not so much for what this distasteful account revealed about Agnès, for an aspect of his peculiarity was an insistence on judging everyone solely from his own experience and never by repute. But he felt distress that Agnès had been stripped before him by Madame Beck's gleeful cataloguing of her past.

And now he was in a quandary. He did not care to have knowledge (if that is what it was) of another without their also being aware of it. On the other hand, he would find it impossible to raise with Agnès any hint of her most painful-sounding history.

His dilemma was deferred, however, as Agnès was too anxious to convey her concern about the Abbé Bernard to speak of anything else.

'How long has he been like this in your view, Agnès?'

'For some time, Father. Since his mother died, I would say. But lately it has got worse. He's terrified that Satan has come for him.'

'Oh dear,' said the Abbé Paul, who believed that the only

true Satan was the idea of Satan. 'I'm afraid Bernard was always overly religious.'

'I think maybe he should see someone.'

It crossed the Abbé Paul's discreet mind that if any part of Madame Beck's account were true, Agnès would be a judge of dangerous mental states. 'I am grateful for this advice, Agnès. I shall look into it tomorrow, first thing.'

'I think it might be best, Father.'

'Thank you again, Agnès. Good night.'

43

Chartres

Robert Clément's studio on the rue du Frou backed on to the River Eure. He was in the habit each morning of viewing the river from his landing stage, where the shifting early-morning light and the enigmatic movements of the mallard ducks held for him the promise of artistic inspiration.

On that particular morning, Robert spotted something untoward bobbing against the bridges of the old watermill of the Abbaye Saint-Père just up river from his landing stage. Hastily he summoned both ambulance and the police, and was present when the latter hauled a sodden form out of the water and laid it on the cobbled ramp which led down to the water beside Robert's house.

The barely recognizable water-swollen face, on which strands of straggling waterweed had pathetically stuck, upset Robert more than he could have predicted. And not simply because the sight was a horrible one. It seemed like some ghastly presage not so much of his own death – still, in theory at least, many years off – but of the encroaching despair that he knew, if not in his conscious mind, that old age often brings on.

Robert was not a sentimental man. He was aware, a little better than most maybe, that humankind is mortal, that he was a man and that being so he must, in time, die. He was aware too that the Abbé Bernard had been in decline for some while. Agnès had spoken of it, lightly, as was her way, but enough for him to have taken note that she was concerned about the old man, and he had even felt, God help him, some jealousy at her concern.

Robert was not unacquainted with despair but mostly he kept the acquaintance at bay by the usual methods: drink, daydreaming and outright fantasy. But that quiet morning he saw in the face of the drowned priest a reflection of his own condition. He was a failure, a failure as a lover but more crucially as an artist. He would never paint his Madonna, or not one he could ever rightly worship.

Robert Clément's life at that moment took a strange turn. Atheist as he was, and remained till the end of his life, he determined there and then to enter the Church, not as a priest but as a monk. In some quiet abbey, out of the world, he might lose his false hopes and find another source of meaning.

But his present action was to go to find Agnès.

He found her, as he had expected to, in the cathedral. Or more properly coming out of it.

The Abbé Bernard had not made his usual appearance that morning and Agnès was already worried. When they had emerged, with the draggled Piaf, from the cathedral, he had not wanted to surrender the silver chain and, with some reluctance, she had allowed him to keep it. That the chain had not done the work she had attributed to it, by protecting the benighted man from his diabolical fears, she now learned from Robert Clément.

'I thought there was some danger. I lent him my chain. I hoped . . .'

'I'm sorry, Agnès. It looks like suicide. I know you were fond of him.'

'I don't know that I was fond of him,' said Agnès, who had a peculiarity almost as odd as that of the Abbé Paul's: she tried always to tell the truth, if not to others then to herself. 'But I worried about him. Poor soul.'

'You need worry no more. He's gone wherever believers go.'

'He wasn't a believer. That was the trouble.'

(And indeed a perfectly rational-seeming note was later found affirming that the Abbé Bernard had left his estate to an association for the promotion of humanism.)

Agnès repeated the essence of her comment when she went to tell the Abbé Paul.

'I wonder. It seems to me he believed too much. Wasn't it Satan he was afraid of? The Church has much to answer for, Agnès. Not least in the fright it can implant in a child's mind.'

'Yes,' said Agnès, who knew all about this phenomenon. 'Maybe he's better off dead.'

'We are all better off dead, in a way, I suppose,' said the Abbé Paul. 'But I do believe that we have a duty to try to keep on living.'

That evening he conducted a solitary conversation with his old teacher and colleague over a bottle of Chinon. 'You see, Bernard. The devil does exist but only in people's minds. That is his power.'

The Abbé Paul was less sure of his ground when three days later he again opened the door to a triumphant-looking Madame Beck. She is the devil incarnate, he thought grimly to himself, and his voice and tone were uncharacteristically abrupt.

'Yes, Madame?'

For answer, Madame Beck thrust a manila envelope into his unwilling hand and pushed roughly past him into the hall.

'Do come in, please,' said the Abbé Paul, who was a natural ironist but only rarely indulged himself with a parishioner.

'The Mother has sent me all the evidence.'

'Evidence? We are not in a court of law, surely, Madame?'

'That girl should have been by all accounts if she hadn't persuaded them she was soft in the head. Got a psychiatrist to back her.'

'I don't know that –'

'She should *not* be cleaning Our Lady's cathedral with a past like that. Never mind minding little children.'

'Madame Beck,' said Abbé Paul. 'Have you perhaps forgotten what Jesus' mission on earth was? Was it not the forgiveness of sins?'

He had never actually seen anyone sniff with disapproval but that was precisely what Madame Beck did in answer. 'He also said "Render unto Caesar those things which are Caesar's." The cathedral belongs to the state.'

'Madame Beck, Agnès also cleans for me. For what it's worth I would trust my life to her.'

But if he hoped to impress his guest with emotional appeals he was to be disappointed. She sat on the chaise-longue as if she were a queen on her rightful throne about to command a beheading.

'As to that, Father, all I can say is I hope you have better luck with your "life" than that poor young woman in the newspaper report. From what I've read there she nearly lost it. I've warned you. I shall take my own action.'

'Perhaps, then, you would be so kind as to take this with you as well.'

But even here he was foiled. She merely looked at him and made a mysterious and sinister movement with her chin. 'I've made copies. You can keep them. I'll see myself out.'

Pouring himself a glass of remedial wine, the Abbé Paul addressed his old friend. 'You may have been right after all, Bernard. He taken human form these days. But I suppose he always did.'

While Brigitte was in Auxerre collecting her things, she had met an 'old boyfriend' who had apparently invited her back to stay with him.

Philippe was all for it. 'Of course you must go. A new start.' As he confided to Tan, he couldn't wait to be rid of her.

'Agnès can mind Max for me.'

'You're not taking little Maxling with you?'

'You're joking. Take a baby with me on a first date? He'd be yelling just at the moment –'

'I thought he was an old boyfriend,' said Philippe, who had no wish to have his imagination invaded by images of his sister's sex life.

'That was ages ago. We need to reconnect.'

'I don't think you should leave a two-month-old baby again so soon, Brigitte. Max needs to "connect" with you too.'

'Three months, nearly. Anyway, she likes having him.'

The avenue of stately limes that graces the grounds beside the Musée des Beaux-Arts at the east end of the cathedral is a common parade ground for the babies of Chartres. Agnès was walking Max there and had nodded and smiled to many parents out showing off their offspring in the sunshine.

At the end of the avenue, she came face to face with Alain.

'So who's this?'

Max had woken without protest, opened a pair of deep blue eyes and, with the steady, unwavering gaze of the still truly innocent, was taking in the stranger.

'This is Max.'

'Hi, Max. May I join you?'

'If you like. We're just walking.'

' "Just walking" is exactly what I was planning on doing.'

They walked down the rue des Acacias to the gates of the hôtellerie. Alain said, 'Would you mind if I nipped up to my room? I shan't be a moment.'

He was back in less than five minutes, with his wallet in his back pocket. 'I forgot to tell you. The snorer. It was your old nun. Talk about a farmer taking his pigs to market.'

'Not Sister Laurence?'

'No, no. The bulky one, the know-all with whiskers. I'll tell you another thing. She had the TV on first thing really loud. And Paulette, the nice maid, told me she had a bottle of whisky in the room. Not that I begrudge the old girl her tipple. Except it probably increased the volume of the snoring.'

'I was terrified of her when I was a girl.'

'You didn't look too jolly when I saw you with her in the cathedral.'

Agnès laughed. 'She was livid when you put her right about the paintwork. Sister Laurence was thrilled. But Sister Laurence is OK.'

'Sister Laurence is quite attractive. If my heart weren't committed elsewhere I'd have seduced her.'

They had reached the bottom of the hill which led down to the river and Agnès was turning the buggy to walk alongside it, so he couldn't see the expression on her face. She began to walk a little faster so that Alain had to quicken his pace to catch up with her.

'How about lunch?'

'Thank you but I –'

'My treat. I deliberately put myself on short rations during the week so I can feast at weekends. And I've no one to share my extravagances with. Come on. Max would like it, wouldn't you, Max?'

And Max, with the divine timing of a baby, turned his grave blue gaze on Alain and broke into a wide and gummy smile.

They ate in a restaurant on the rue du Frou, where according to Alain the roast partridge was excellent. Agnès chose cassoulet and Max, contented on her lap, ate a jar of banana cereal.

'Isn't he a bit young for solids?'

234

'She thinks it will help him sleep. But they start them early nowadays.'

'But you don't approve? Don't answer. I see you don't. My big sister breastfed her brood till they were eighteen months at least. Two in one case.'

'You have a sister?'

'Three. I'm the baby of my family. And my dad died when I was a tiddler so I was brought up entirely by women. I was like Stendhal. I used to lie on the floor and look up their skirts.'

'Stendhal did that?'

'One of his earliest memories was lying on his back looking up his mother's skirt. In those days they didn't wear drawers.'

She laughed, embarrassed. 'Max, cover your ears.'

'Max looks to me as if he'll enjoy looking up a woman's skirt when the time comes.'

A slight awkwardness arose when Robert Clément, whose local restaurant it was, came over to their table.

'Agnès. How are you?'

'Fine, thank you, Robert. This is Alain. He works on the restoration.'

'Yes, yes, I know.'

Alain smiled, apparently to himself, and Robert, almost turning his back on him, said to Agnès, 'I hope they find your chain.'

'What are you smiling for?' Agnès asked when Robert had made his way back to his own table.

'Oh, just life. Can I have a turn with that baby?'

After lunch, they walked, Alain still carrying Max, over to the old watermill where the body of the Abbé Bernard had been found.

'My guess is,' Alain said, tipping Max over his shoulder, 'there you go, Max, that's a good burp – my guess is the old boy threw himself in for unrequited love of you.'

'That's not nice.'

'I'm sorry. I didn't mean it nastily. But don't you think all suicide in the end is a love matter? A failure of love somewhere?'

'Maybe.'

'Poor old chap. He can't have felt loved. Certainly not by his God.'

'He'd stopped believing in God. And he'd lost his mother, who was very important to him.'

'Mothers are. I'd be nowhere without mine.'

'Yes?'

'Christ. I'm sorry. I'm putting my big feet into it fair and square today, aren't I? You never had any clue about yours?'

Involuntarily she touched the nook between her collarbones where the turquoise earring on its silver chain usually lay.

'The man who found me, whom I called my "father", also found a turquoise earring. I've always worn it, on a silver chain, which my "father" gave me. I gave them to the Abbé Bernard the evening before he died.'

'Why?'

'He was scared. He thought Satan was after him. And I told him that the chain would protect him.'

'He didn't believe in God but he still believed in Satan. That says plenty about the Catholic faith.'

'It's not important now.'

'He didn't return it?'

'I forgot to ask him.' This was not the case. She had wanted him to have its protection a little longer: a 'protection' her relic could not, after all, provide.

'Agnès, this is serious. You must ask the police. He may have had it on him.'

'I did ask. I asked the Abbé Paul to ask and he asked the police and then he went to look himself in Father Bernard's house and neither he nor his housekeeper found anything. It doesn't matter.'

'It does matter. It matters most extremely.'

'Oh well.' She shrugged.

'Agnès, that shrug of yours is a bad sign.'

'It's only a –'

'Stop it. Listen to me.'

Max, still in Alain's arms, disturbed by the deep raised voice, began to whimper and she took the baby back, putting him into the buggy and rocking it on the cobbles. 'It's gone. It doesn't matter.'

'Agnès, if your mother's earring wasn't found in the Abbé's house or on his body, then it's probably in the river. And that can be searched.'

In answer, she looked down to the river, purling grey below them. 'How?'

'Listen. This isn't a promise because I may not be able to keep it, but if it's in the river I will find it for you.'

44

Chartres

Philippe was staying over at Tan's till Monday, so it was to Brigitte alone that Agnès handed over Max that Sunday evening. Brigitte returned later than agreed, apparently having had a good time.

'Sorry to keep you. They cancelled the earlier train.'

Agnès inwardly reflected that she found that unlikely and outwardly explained that Max was fast asleep, having had a good feed at 7 p.m.

'Great. I'm knackered. I didn't get much sleep to be honest.' Brigitte wiped over the perfectly clean draining board with a disinfectant wipe and poured herself a whisky.

'Do you want anything?'

'Thank you but I should get home.'

Anxious to be off, Agnès did not notice immediately that Brigitte had forgotten to pay her but she assumed that Philippe would see to it on his return. So she was not surprised to answer the door to Philippe the following evening.

'Hi, Philippe. Did you have a good weekend?'

'Agnès.'

He looked tired. Even ill. 'Come in. I'm about to eat. It's chicken curry and there's plenty if you would –'

'Agnès. Max is in hospital.'

'My God. Why?'

'Apparently, he was crying all day and when I got home I said we must take him to hospital.'

Philippe sat down and stared at his hands.

'Is it serious?'

'They took an X-ray and it seems he has a broken wrist.'

'How did that happen?'

'Agnès, it must have happened on your watch.'

Agnès stared at him. Then she too sat down. 'What are you saying?'

'He's very bruised. They want to see you.'

'They?'

'The hospital.'

The doctor who invited Agnès into her consulting room was scrupulously polite. 'Thank you for coming to see us, Mademoiselle Morel.'

'I wanted to. How is poor little Max?'

'He has a fractured wrist and is very badly bruised. He may have a head injury. But he'll survive. Of course we're trying to establish how the accident occurred.'

'He was fine when I put him to bed last night.'

'And that was when?'

'About eight. His mother was due home at seven but there was a problem with her train.'

'A problem?'

'It was cancelled.'

'I see. And your day with Max, how did that go?'

'He was with me for two days.'

The doctor raised well-groomed eyebrows. 'I see. You've looked after him before?'

'I've babysat for him once for an evening and twice for a weekend.'

'So, could you run past me the events of last evening?'

'I gave him some puréed sweet potato about five, then a bath about six. Then we played a little.'

'Played?'

'With a toy rabbit his uncle gave him. We played peep-bo with it. I gave him his bottle about seven, it took about half an hour for his feed, and then I walked him, with him on my shoulder, until he fell asleep. I put him down in his crib on his side, as usual. His mother got home around nine and I left then and went back to my own house.'

'And at no time was there any accident that you noticed? He didn't fall from your shoulder, roll off the bed, or the sideboard while you were changing him, for instance?'

'I would have noticed that.'

'No collisions with the pushchair?'

'No.'

'No bumps, knocks to yourself while carrying him when he could have been jolted?'

'No.'

'Nothing you can think of that might account for his injuries? Was he fretful at all with you?'

'No.'

'Would you say Max was a difficult baby?'

Agnès paused. 'Not with me.'

'So who would you say he might be difficult with?'

'I didn't say he was difficult with anyone.'

'Does he cry much?'

She paused again. 'He can do.'

'And does that, or did that, anger you at all?'

'No.'

'Crying babies can be very frustrating.'

'I didn't do anything to Max.' She was trying not to cry herself now. 'I love him.'

'But he's not your child, is he, Mademoiselle Morel?'

'No, but I love him. May I see him, Doctor?'

'I'm afraid not, Mademoiselle Morel.'

★

Agnès did not go to work the following morning. When she came back from the interview at the hospital, she had vomited till her stomach hurt; she retched again the following morning. She had been told that 'someone from Social Services' would be coming to see her. By eleven, she had drunk three pots of strong coffee.

The social worker, who introduced herself as Isabelle, refused coffee when she arrived but said if there was 'something herbal' she 'wouldn't say no'.

Agnès, who since her convent days had had a repugnance for herbal teas, dug out an ancient mint teabag, left over from the days of old Madame Badon's chronic dyspepsia. While making the drink, she poured boiling water over her hand.

'Careful, now. That can turn nasty and blister. Pop it under the cold tap, I would.'

Isabelle had come, she explained, to try to 'straighten out' the facts of Max's accident.

'Now, you've babysat for Max before, Agnès?'

'Yes. I told the doctor. I've stayed with him as well.'

'Here?'

'No. I stayed at his uncle's apartment while his mother was away. His uncle too.'

Isabelle consulted her notes. 'That would be Philippe. He's a friend of yours, Agnès?'

'I was his babysitter when he was small. Brigitte's too, in fact.'

'I see. So an old family friend?'

'I suppose so.'

'And tell me what you did with Max this last weekend, Agnès.'

'On Saturday we did a bit of shopping. Nothing much. On Sunday, I walked him in the buggy. And we had lunch.'

'Just you and Max?'

'No. With a friend.'

'Girlfriend? Boyfriend?'

'A male friend. He's not a boyfriend.'

'And Max was OK at the lunch? He was with you?'

'He was on my lap all the time.'

'And no tumbles there?'

'No.'

'What did your friend think about Max being there?'

'He liked him. He likes children.'

'I see. And what did you and your "friend" do after lunch, Agnès?'

'We went to the river.'

'Did you two do anything special there?'

'We went to the old watermill.'

'And . . .'

'It was where the Abbé Bernard was found drowned.'

'I see. Sort of spot the scene of death?'

'I was with Father Bernard the night before he died.'

'Right.' Isabelle wrote something in her notes. 'So did this "friend" come back with you to the apartment?'

'No. Max and I went back to the apartment alone.'

'So there was no one with you yesterday from when would you say . . .'

'I suppose about 4 p.m.'

'Long lunch?'

'I don't know. Yes. Maybe.'

'Now, Agnès, I'll have to speak to your friend but is there anything else you'd like to tell me?'

Mother Véronique had not intended any outright malice when she sent off the envelope with copies of the press clippings to Madame Beck. She had revealed Agnès' story partly as a consequence of her pique over Alain's corrective account of the cathedral decoration, a pique which bit the harder for the correction having taken place in front of Agnès and Laurence. But a further, more potent reason was to demonstrate that she was 'in the know'.

Madame Beck had expressed such interest in Agnès that it seemed impossible not to confide her own superior knowledge. That the knowledge was second- or even third-hand was no longer something Mother Véronique herself perhaps fully grasped. She had found a file on Agnès in Mother Catherine's bureau after her predecessor's departure. It contained details of Agnès' vaccinations, a number of disappointing school reports, some receipts for shoes and, inexplicably, her first bra, a letter from the adoption society which had taken the baby boy and a letter from Dr Deman at the St Francis Clinic, explaining that they would be keeping Agnès there for observation and if necessary treatment.

But there were also cuttings from the press describing how a 'female minor who could not be named' was being questioned by the police over the assault on Michelle Boyet and then a further article saying that the 'assault suspect' had been sent to a secure hospital but that no hard evidence had been found to convict her.

Knowledge is power. And for Mother Véronique the demonstration of power was crucial to her self-esteem.

And in this Mother Véronique was somewhat in accord with her new friend and confidante, Madame Beck. The news about Agnès spread fast and Madame Beck was in her element when she reconvened with her old friend, Madame Picot.

'Well, they can't say I didn't do my best to warn them. I passed on all the Mother's information to Father Paul and he refused to take me seriously. I've written to the Bishop already, as I said I would, but I think these' – brandishing the press cuttings – 'must be shown to the police.'

'Oh dear, Louise, should you?'

'Naturally, I should, Jeanette. One young woman nearly died and now a baby is attacked in her care. Of course the police must be informed.'

45

Rouen

'Now, Agnès, we need to ask you what you were doing on October 28th. Do you understand?'

'Yes.'

'So, tell us what you were doing that day.'

'Walking.'

'Do you remember where?'

'No.'

'Why were you walking, Agnès?'

'Dr Deman told me to.'

'Were you going to see anyone in particular?'

'My baby. I was going to see my baby.'

46

Chartres

'Thank you for coming in, Mademoiselle Morel. Do sit down. We're making some inquiries into the accident that occurred to Baby Max Nevers. I wonder if you could clarify for us exactly what happened while he was in your care? This is just an informal inquiry but you are entitled to call a lawyer if you prefer.'

47

Chartres

Professor Jones had not known what to think when Agnès failed to turn up at his apartment. Her arrival was such a dependable event in his week that for half an hour he thought that maybe he had got the day, or the time, wrong. So much so, that he went out to check with Nicole at the tourist office to see if his watch and diary were correct.

Although assured that he had muddled neither the time nor the date, he was no less at a loss. He wandered up the rue aux Herbes towards the cathedral to see if maybe Agnès had been detained there.

It was years since the professor had visited the cathedral and he had forgotten how its grave and graceful loveliness could smite the heart. As usual, there were many people moving quietly about, either absorbed in the cathedral or going about its business.

Professor Jones stood at the crossing point of the transepts while his eyes adjusted to the reduced light. He began to stroll round the cathedral, half looking for Agnès, half looking again at the sights he had not visited since the departure of Marion. As he strolled he ruminated. If there could be such a thing as time-no-longer, then it followed that time itself might be created. It was a novel idea and he was strangely elated by it.

The Abbé Paul had also gone in search of Agnès. Like Professor Jones, he had gone to the cathedral and, not finding Agnès there, had walked down the hill to her house. But, while he had both knocked and rung the bell, he had raised no answer.

The Abbé Paul was not a man to panic but he felt seriously alarmed. Until the age of nine he had lived with his family in a village outside Edinburgh, where his father held a university appointment. One summer, a series of anonymous letters had been circulated, in which malicious rumours were spread about several of the villagers. The young Paul, without knowing how, had instinctively guessed the identity of the perpetrator of this poison, a highly respectable woman whose only obvious crime was that she patted him on his head in a manner he found, though he lacked the word for it at the time, aggressive. After some nights of agonizing, he had tried to share his suspicions with his mother but had been strongly reproved for his scandalous suggestion. Mrs whatever her name was – the Abbé Paul no longer remembered – his mother had scolded, was a woman whose life was 'beyond reproach'.

The letters led to some serious unhappiness. An elderly homosexual had been forced to flee the community; a shaky marriage was broken by the suggestion of adultery; an old man had died believing his daughter had left home because she did not love him. Since that time, the Abbé Paul had come to trust his nose for malice.

As he walked back up the hill from his fruitless mission to the Badon apartment, he observed the tops of the two cathedral spires almost effaced by the November mist. Not a day, nor a change of weather, passed, he reflected, without those two ancient co-habitees taking on a fresh aspect. Sunday was the first day of Advent and he had promised to speak with Emile, the choirmaster, about the setting of the William Byrd mass. And there was the Christmas crib and the Advent candles to see to. Whatever had prompted him to take on this profession? Suddenly, the Abbé Paul felt excruciatingly tired.

Entering the cathedral through the North Door, he stopped to look at the window of the Prodigal Son. It was his favourite of the windows, perhaps because of all his mentor's famed parables it was the story that the Abbé Paul most turned to in his mind. But even that source of reassurance did not answer his needs that day.

The Abbé Paul's favourite image of the presiding spirit of the cathedral was the window of the Blue Virgin and many times over the years he had stood and contemplated her image. But he also had a soft spot for the story worked in the glass beneath her feet: the story of the wedding at Cana, where the supply of wine had threatened to run out and Mary's son, at her request, had changed the plain water into a plenitude of wine.

Over the years, the Abbé Paul had come to believe that this gift, of this most remarkable of men, was maybe the most telling of all the gifts in the peculiar story it had been the ruling aim of the Abbé's life to follow and to serve. The other miracles, as he put it in the strict privacy of his own inner dialogues, were all well and good. But this one seemed to have been born out of a simple celebration of life and a desire to increase for others its quota of joy. It was an attitude which the Abbé could wish more of his fellow Christians shared.

Because of the restorations the Blue Virgin window was out of sight. Nevertheless the Abbé Paul stood by the scaffolding, summoning, to his imagination, the grave contemplative gaze of the mother and child. As he stood there, a young man came through a door in the screen behind the altar, a good-looking man with a sardonic, tanned face. In his hyper-alert state, something told the Abbé Paul that this was the young man that the Abbé Bernard had seen with Agnès on the occasion which had somehow involved the egregious Madame Beck.

The man walked towards him as if to leave by the South Door and instinctively the Abbé Paul put out a hand to touch the young man's arm.

'Excuse me,' said the Abbé Paul. 'But you don't happen to know where Agnès Morel might be?'

The young man stopped and looked quizzically at the Abbé Paul. Then his expression relaxed. 'I've been asked to talk to some social worker about her. Is she in trouble?'

The Abbé Paul sighed. 'I'm afraid she may be. There have been some ugly rumours in which Agnès' name, I feel sure falsely, has been implicated.'

'She didn't come in here today or yesterday or, come to think of it, the day before. I thought she might be ill. I was going to go round to her house this evening to see.'

'If she's there she's not answering.'

The young man frowned. 'Shit. Sorry, Father.'

'Not at all. It's a dirty business. When do you see the social worker?'

'Right now, as it happens. She's coming to the hôtellerie where I room.'

'Might I walk there with you?'

'Of course.'

Together the two men walked in silence down the hill. Approaching the hôtellerie, the young man said, 'I'm Alain Fleury, by the way.'

'And I'm Paul. I'm very fond of Agnès. She cleans for me.'

'I'm very fond of her too.'

'She needs friends. Might you feel able to come and tell me how things go with the social worker?'

'I'd be glad to.'

'Thank you. You know my house?'

'One of the finest in Chartres. I'll come after six, if that's OK, when I finish at the cathedral.'

Just after six the Abbé Paul welcomed Alain and took his visitor into his study, where a fire was filling the room with a pleasing smell of chestnut wood. He showed Alain to a worn leather armchair and offered him wine.

'Thank you. I'd love a glass.'

'Bad day?'

Alain blew out his cheeks in a mute whistle. 'What the hell is going on? The social-worker woman, who, by the way, was a total idiot – I wouldn't have her give an opinion on a dog – appeared to be implying that Agnès and I were in some sort of sadistic baby-abusing partnership. I mean for Christ's sake – sorry, Paul – for one thing, I hardly know Agnès. I merely took her out for Sunday lunch. For another she plainly dotes on the boy. It's sheer fucking madness. Sorry.'

His host made a gesture as if to brush aside any suggestion of offence. His hands, Alain observed, were, for a man, unusually fine and slender. 'I'm afraid it may be worse than that.' He got up and went over to his desk.

When the Abbé Paul had finally opened the envelope that had been thrust into his unwilling hand by Madame Beck, he had experienced something of an anticlimax. The articles she had been sent by Mother Véronique were scarcely damning. They did not even name Agnès and, even if it were the case that she was the unidentifiable 'minor' in the newspaper report, all that could be deduced from that was that the poor benighted girl had spent some time in a psychiatric hospital.

His first impulse had been to tear up the photocopies but on second thoughts he had deposited them in the locked inner drawer of his bureau. He unlocked it now.

'I'm not sure I should show these to you but some instinct made me keep them.' He handed the papers to Alain.

Alain read them and snorted. 'Is this supposed to be about Agnès?'

'So I've been told.'

'She's not named.'

'No. But the, er, person who gave them to me claims they came from a source which –'

'That vile old nun?' Alain interrupted.

'Yes. She does seem to have caused a stir.'

'I knew her for a bad lot. She had the room next to mine in the hôtellerie and she snored fit to wake the dead.'

The Abbé Paul, who sometimes suspected that he himself might snore, felt bound to suggest that snoring was not, as far as he knew, a sin.

'I don't know. I don't follow the modern notion that you can't judge a book by its cover. She looked a fright. And the old cat that hangs round the restaurant? She's another fright. Bet she gave you this crap.'

The Abbé Paul allowed himself the luxury of a laugh. 'As you say, Madame Beck.'

'So that's why they're questioning Agnès.'

'I'm afraid it's a case of no smoke without fire, a particularly loathsome and fallacious proposition.'

'I tell you what. If Agnès harmed that baby, I'll smash every glass window in your cathedral.'

'Not mine,' said the Abbé Paul mildly. 'And for many reasons, including the preservation of our beloved cathedral, I pray that it won't come to that.'

Professor Jones, now truly concerned, was racking his brains for the name of Agnès' friend who minded dogs. An English girl, short, a Northerner but with frighteningly good French which made him blush a little for his own. He'd met her a couple of times when Agnès had stayed late and she'd come to his apartment to pick her up. Rather a terrifying young woman, the professor had found her. But Agnès had referred to her as a friend.

Remembering that Agnès had mentioned that she and this friend sometimes ate at the jazz café, the professor put on his winter coat, which Agnès had patched, and strolled over to the café.

It wasn't a jazz night, so the café was quiet and inside only a few customers were eating. The professor approached the young woman behind the bar. 'Good evening. I'm looking for Agnès Morel. I believe she dines here sometimes.'

'Agnès? Sure.'

'Have you seen her?'

'No, Professor. Not since . . .' Monique shook her head sadly.

Surprised that this woman knew who he was, the professor took up her silence. 'Since?'

Realizing that he must be ignorant of the scandal, Monique simply said, 'Oh, since last Wednesday.'

'Oh dear,' said the professor. 'I wonder if she's ill.'

'Maybe.'

'You don't happen to know the name of her friend?'

'Terry?'

'That's it. Do you have her number?'

'Sure.'

The professor, who had no mobile, nor any intention of owning one, had to return home to ring Terry, who did not answer her phone. He left a slightly querulous message and spent an uneasy evening translating the final chapters of *The Secret Garden*.

With nothing to occupy him – the now healthy Colin having been reunited with his father, and the untended garden, along with Mary Lennox's fate, having been fully restored – the professor found himself doing what he had had half a mind to do since finding the old children's book from his past. He began a letter to his cousin Gwen at the last address he had for her, which he found, neatly filed by Agnès, among his family correspondence in one of the yellow boxes at the top of the wardrobe.

48

Chartres

Three other people in Chartres were perturbed about Agnès that day. Robert Clément, who had gone to seek advice about the steps required for his proposed change of life, heard the news late, in fact from the restaurant by the Eure where he had seen Agnès with Alain. Like the Abbé Paul and Alain, he first rang Agnès and, getting no answer, went round to her house. Failing to raise her there, he used a resource unavailable to the two other men: he called Madame Badon.

Madame Badon said she had not seen Agnès since the last weekend she had spent in Chartres but she was in fact proposing to visit Chartres again that coming weekend. In her way, she too was fond of Agnès, who had served her elderly mother faithfully and been of great assistance in the management of Madame Badon's affair.

And now the unreliable lover had developed Parkinson's and Madame Badon was considering moving them both back to Chartres. She did not confide this to Robert but it crossed her mind that it may be no bad plan to revive their old tenderness. She suggested she could come from Paris a day earlier in case by chance Agnès was ill in bed and in need of care.

The following day Robert met Cécile Badon at the station. She was looking rather well, he thought: slimmer than formerly and more chic in her dress. Her hair, now a fashionable silver bob, suited her better than when it was long and she had used to colour it.

The old lovers walked the few metres from the station to Madame Badon's apartment, where she suggested, in the light of his concern over Agnès, that he come inside.

The apartment was, as always, orderly. Everything was in its proper place and there was no sign of missing human life other than the slight wilt on a vaseful of golden lilies. Agnès' bed appeared quite unslept in, but then, as Cécile Badon remarked, on the few occasions that she'd been in the room it always looked that way.

A red nightdress was folded under the pillow. A pair of crimson, gold-worked slippers sat neatly on the rag rug by the bed. The wardrobe was full of Agnès' colourful clothes but if anything had been removed there was no way of telling. Her toothbrush was still in the bathroom but it was impossible to say if she had taken a spongebag – none was visible but, then, what did that amount to?

Passing her own bedroom door, Madame Badon touched her old lover's arm. 'Shall we?'

(In years to come, Robert Clément was to recall this moment as his farewell to an old life.)

Philippe Nevers was also worrying. The force of his sister's reaction, one of hysterical anger and violent accusation, had initially steamrollered him into supposing Agnès was implicated in the injury to Max. Brigitte had shouted and raved on the discovery of the fracture, so much so that the hospital had had to offer her a sedative. She was now, thank God, in a bed beside Max, who was still under observation for a possible head injury.

Withdrawn from his sister's destabilizing orbit, however, Philippe began to ponder the logic of the event. That Agnès would attack a baby, never mind one for whom she had shown such loving care, seemed to him less and less likely. Bit by bit, he became convinced that there was something amiss and the feeling was strengthened by a conversation with the doctor in charge of Max's case.

Philippe had gone to the hospital to see how Max was doing and to take Brigitte some of the things she was fretting about: her cosmetic bag, for example, about which she seemed absurdly possessed. She was asleep when he came by and on leaving the room he encountered Dr Moreau.

Dr Moreau stopped to talk to Philippe and, with a casualness which he later questioned, asked him about the events of the evening before Max's injuries were discovered.

It transpired that Agnès and Brigitte had given slightly different accounts. Agnès had spoken of a problem with the train that had led to Brigitte getting back later than expected, at nine, while Brigitte had claimed she was home that evening by seven. Perhaps, Dr Moreau carefully suggested, his sister had, in her anxiety, misremembered the time? Might he perhaps be able to clarify?

Philippe explained that he had not, unfortunately, been present that evening but, although he kept this to himself, Agnès' version of the evening, as reported by the doctor, sounded to him the more plausible one. In his experience, Brigitte was careless, even wantonly irresponsible, where Max was concerned. And she had, after all, been engaged in the business of 'reconnecting' with a potential new boyfriend. Nor could he see any sound reason for Agnès to lie about the time of his sister's return: it could hardly further her innocence to have been longer with the baby than Brigitte's account suggested. He had not forgotten the look of concern on Agnès' face when he told her that Max had been admitted to the hospital. There was, when he considered it, no trace of guilt, or guile.

Like the Abbé Paul, the professor, Alain and Robert Clément, Philippe rang Agnès' number, and like them he got no reply.

★

The third person to be in a state of worry about Agnès that evening was her friend Terry.

Terry had not owned up to Madame Picot that it was Agnès who had found Piaf. The omission was not entirely intentional, or maybe even conscious. If asked, Terry would have said that she was planning to give her friend the credit once Madame Picot's ire had died down. But the moment for that admission had not arrived and hearing Madame Picot's excited account of her friend's supposed crime produced in Terry a severe pang of remorse.

Hastening to repair her lapse of loyalty, she said, 'Oh, but Madame, I should have told you, it was Agnès who found Piaf. She adores babies and animals. I know her very well. She just couldn't have done such a terrible thing.'

While a part of Madame Picot did not like to hear this, for it threatened to take the edge off a gripping drama – one in which, through her friend Madame Beck, she had if not a part at least a ringside seat – another part of her was obscurely relieved. Her sojourn with her daughter had reminded her of merrier forms of relationship. She had her own guilt over Agnès. And she had begun to find her friend's febrile jubilation over her former cleaner's past disquieting.

'You said you found Piaf in the cathedral crypt.'

'I know, Madame. But it was actually Agnès who found her. She was taking care of that poor old nutter, you know, the one who topped himself.'

Madame Picot clicked her tongue. 'I wish you had told me, Thérèse. I should have liked to thank her. And maybe give her a little reward.'

'I'm sorry, Madame, but you were so angry and I . . .'

It has been said that the leopard cannot change its spots, but human beings, just occasionally, can make a shift, if not in their habitual actions then in their perceptions. The loss and recovery of Piaf, following the episode with the broken china doll, had stirred something in Madame Picot's gluey soul.

She waved Terry's apology aside in an almost regal manner. 'It's all right, my dear. I can fly off the handle. Julie ticks me off about it. I'm sorry your friend is in trouble.'

Fear is not always bad, though no one welcomes it. From it, a frail frond of fellow feeling for Agnès had sprung up in Madame Picot. In addition, she felt a need to punish her old friend.

49

Chartres

It was very dark in the crypt but that was what Agnès wanted. Not the dazzling darkness of the upper cathedral but the older, deeper darkness of its ancient antecedent. It was cold too. But she had on her father's heavy coat, and carried in the basket, her one-time crib, a bottle of water. Also a torch, which she would switch on only if she had to. For now, she wanted total darkness, utter obliteration.

Agnès had no clear idea why she had fled to the crypt, but for her, unlike Father Bernard, it was the very opposite of the haunt of the diabolical. On the contrary, it had always seemed to her a hallowed place. Old and still and unjudging. Unjudging was what she most craved. She opened the door on the north side of the cathedral and walked, like the old pilgrims, for about seventy metres until she came to the replica of the statue of Our Lady Under the Earth.

Her first thought had been that she would go there to die. It was where the pilgrims had assembled in the past looking for help, hoping to be healed. In the pocket of her father's coat she had old Madame Badon's sleeping pills, prescribed at a time when barbiturates were still readily available (the more so to troublesome old people who fretted if they couldn't sleep), which she had taken from the bathroom cabinet which had never been cleared. There were enough tablets there, with the help of some codeine, to 'heal' her, to put her to sleep for all time.

But, reaching the seated replica of the Virgin, something dented her resolve.

During the few months before she came to Chartres, Agnès had spent some weeks in a doss house on the shabby outskirts of Evreux. There she had met an old woman – maybe not so old, she calculated now, but the woman had had the face of an eighty-year-old and trembled like an aspen leaf when Agnès helped her to the bathroom. Her doss-house companion, whose name was Iris, had told Agnès a little of her life. She had once had money through a wealthy husband, but had left the husband for a sax player who had regularly attacked her until she had finally found the strength to leave. Iris told Agnès this story one night when Agnès had confided that she felt there was nothing left for her to do but die.

'I felt that way, my dear,' Iris had said. 'I felt it many times after I left Honoré and the other fellow was pummelling me fit to break my ribs. But then, I said to myself, what about the times when you don't feel it? What's true now isn't always true tomorrow and tomorrow I might feel life is good and if I die now I'll miss that feeling. You're young, my dear. You shouldn't say no to life if some of you thinks tomorrow you might say yes.'

Standing before the replica of the lost Virgin, Agnès thought, I can't die yet. I have to find Gabriel.

But she must flee. All the former safety promised by the great cathedral had been destroyed, as if by one of the catastrophic fires that had wrecked the former buildings. Take flight as she might, and had done for the past twenty years, somewhere in her being she had known this day must arrive. The long index finger of Time had finally marked her out.

She walked on, round the long crypt, past the Well of the Strong, and down into the most ancient depth of the cathedral, the chapel of St Lubin, where she had gone with poor Father

Bernard. She would wait there, gather strength and resolve, and then steal away in the hope they would not find her.

But they will find you, said the voice in her head. And then you will never find Gabriel.

The Abbé Paul and Alain were at that moment drinking wine in the Abbé's warm study. They had been conversing most amicably but a lull had fallen on their conversation – a lull of the kind that usually implies a long and mutual ease.

Alain, trying to put himself into Agnès' skin, broke the silence. 'She'll have wanted to run away.'

The thought so followed the Abbé Paul's own that he blinked a little at his guest before answering. 'It's unlikely she'll get far. The police –'

'It will be better for her if she doesn't try to leave. I wonder . . .' Alain fell silent again, leaving his thoughts to divine, unshepherded, Agnès' possible whereabouts.

Suddenly he said, 'If you wouldn't mind, I think I'm going to take a look round the cathedral. It's large and she knows it so well.'

'It's where I'd go,' agreed the Abbé Paul. He would have liked to suggest that he accompany his new friend but he had a feeling that the young man preferred to undertake this mission alone. 'If you do find her, will you bring her here?'

'Sure.' The younger man, already impatient to be off to follow his hunch, had jumped up. 'Could I borrow the keys to the crypt? I only have the ones for –'

'But of course.'

A shrewd guess, thought the Abbé Paul as, alone once more, he returned to his fire-lit study and his wine. It was the holiest part of the cathedral. The place where for centuries men and women had brought their sorrows, their shames, their terrors, their harrowing

memories, their own unique darkness, to the ancient comprehending darkness of the Virgin's underworld domain.

The crypt smelled of darkness and damp. In the darkness,
Agnès crouched remembering. What she remembered was
the day she had run for her life back to the clinic and hidden
in the old laundry, which was boarded up and out of bounds.
The laundry was also dark and also smelled of damp. She had
been there before, to hide things, and she knew it was alive
with silverfish and riddled with mice droppings. Possibly there
had been rats as well. There were sinister scuffling sounds
behind the walls and a putrid smell.

She had crouched there, her heart pounding, waiting, waiting. Waiting as she waited now, for discovery and exposure,
thinking of Mother Catherine's saying 'God takes His time.'

There was another memory too, one that she did not want
to entertain. The hand on her bare thigh as she stood, balancing on the ladder in the apple orchard, the hand that had then
wriggled its way into the serviceable knickers the convent had
provided and poked about. She felt again that probing finger,
the sharp nail which had scratched her inside. She no longer
recalled the sharper pain which followed.

Hunkered down in the dark, she relived again the horror of
the crushing weight, the wine and garlic breath in her nose, the
rough beard grazing her averted cheek. And a hard-palmed,
heavy hand, smelling also of garlic, and nicotine, and something worse, which had held her mouth and stopped her
screams, while another hand scrabbled at her skirt and brutally
yanked her knickers down.

She only felt him, never really saw more than a fat white
hairy belly and a revolting black fuzz of wire wool hair out of
which there stuck a disgusting red and purple-veined thing,

and then she had shut her eyes tight against the horror and the pain.

She had crept back to her bedroom, quietly changed her underwear and gone in secret to wash her skirt. The knickers she wrapped in a newspaper and threw away in the convent dustbins.

And after that, the growing sickness in the mornings and the slow, at first imperceptible, swelling of her belly, until the day Sister Véronique had her in for questioning and yelled at her and banged the desk and shouted, with a red face and furious eyes, 'You cunning little whore!'

Who he was she would never know. He had gone, she supposed, as unremarked as he had arrived. A passing farmer or workman, maybe.

God alone knew. Only God alone would ever know, that is if there was a God to know anything – if anything could ever really be known.

50

London

Dr Denis Deman had never forgotten his patient Agnès Morel. How much his conduct in her case had propelled his flight to England was something about which, over time, he had come to brood.

His initial treatment of her was, he could reassure himself, effective. The nourishing food and rest he had prescribed had, at least superficially, rescued her from the damage wrought at the hands of the nuns by the loss of her child. And, later, the fresh air and the walking regime had seemed to strengthen her.

But the matter of the alleged attack over the little boy, and his part in her apparent involvement and subsequent treatment, remained an acutely sore spot in his memory. To be sure, from what had seemed a disastrous error on his part some good had come. He had managed to free her from the hospital in Le Mans and the attentions of Inès Nezat (for whom, however, he retained an amused partiality), and his patient's years spent on the farm with Jean Dupère had been, he was sure of this, happy ones. But then she had been ousted from that oasis of security and to his shame he had lost touch with her.

His flight to England had hardly been a success. The relationship with Pauline, the girl he had impulsively married on the strength of her resemblance to his fictive fiancée, had not fulfilled his fantasies. The initial attraction, brought on by the chance to be of use, however slightly, had not been sustained. He had wanted, he recognized now, to be of use to someone.

Pauline was not a bad woman. But she lacked the kind of strength his own character needed. It was, he had concluded, a combination of the flight from his handling of Agnès and his disappointment in his marriage that had led to a growing tepidness in his medical practice.

His belief in the therapeutic virtues of trust and respect, his faith in nature and the remedial power of hope, had never entirely vanished, but they had, he was bound to acknowledge, been set aside. He had found his English colleagues more hidebound than his French ones. With the memory of his terrible error still fresh in his mind, some part of him had given up, had not wanted really to try. He had bowed to the unspoken distrust of his methods – indeed to his own mistrust in them – and resorted to drugs, in which he did not believe, and even to ECT, which he had always abhorred. The truth was, he acknowledged that morning, sinking into an armchair to read his post, he had lost heart.

But, on opening the letter which had been forwarded from the hospital from which he had lately retired, the lost heart palpably stirred.

Mother Véronique was writing, she confided in her elaborately florid hand, to give him the news that in a recent visit to Chartres she had come across Agnès. 'She looks well,' the letter went. 'And she appears to be doing well too. She was quite overjoyed to see us (Sister Laurence accompanied me).' The letter, in purple ink, ran on for a page and a half, outlining various improvements that the Mother was planning for the convent. It concluded with an invitation to visit them any time he should find himself near Evreux.

Denis Deman gazed round the drawing room, tastefully furnished and decorated but in a style and colours that he thoroughly disliked. He had always been so particular about colour, but he had allowed Pauline her taste, perhaps because it was something he could fairly give her when it appeared – for, to their joint regret, they had remained childless – that he could give her little else. She was away now seeing her mother. Pauline saw quite a bit of her mother these days, and it had crossed his mind that she returned home with a degree of reluctance which suggested that perhaps it was not only her mother she was seeing. It would not, he suspected, pain her were he to suggest that they part.

He reread Mother Véronique's letter, walking now into his study.

Back in the Rouen days, he had had a sense of what mattered, of what a life – his life anyway – might amount to. He had loved his work and if he had not always been wholly successful with his patients, he had, by and large – with the exception of Agnès – felt he had done his best for them. Could he put his hand on his heart and declare that the same was true of his career since?

Looking at the curtains of his study, a heavy maroon weave, chosen for him by Pauline, he reflected how he would like to find Agnès, if only to satisfy himself that he had done her no lasting harm.

Time had softened certain things in Denis Deman but not his tendency to be impulsive. He went to his desk and fumbled in it till he found his fountain pen.

'Dear Mother Véronique,' he wrote, hung fire for a moment, crushed the paper to a ball, tossed it in the bin and began again.

'Dear Sister Laurence . . .'

51

Chartres

Turning the key in the stiff lock of the door to the crypt, Alain felt a cat shoot past his legs. He had searched the upper cathedral first. But his stronger instinct had been to come here. A scared animal, he knew, will seek the shelter of a cave. The beam of the torch moved before him as he walked down into the darkness.

'Agnès. Wake up.'

She was hiding now with Max. She was to meet someone. Someone, not a friend, maybe even an enemy, but he would take them into hiding.

'It's me, Alain. Wake up.'

But she had forgotten something. Something vital to Max. Some medicine he had to take. Without it he would die.

'Agnès.'

But Max was dead already. She had forgotten. He was dead and she was responsible.

'Agnès, listen to me.'

No point in running away. She had done this thing. They would get her now.

'Agnès, *Agnès.*'

They had found her. She knew they would. She always knew they must.

'Agnès, for God's sake, *wake up!*'

'Agnès, for God's sake, *wake up!*'

What was Alain doing here?

'Why?'

'Because you must.'

'What?'

'Wake up.'

'I can't.'

'You can.'

'I don't want to.'

'You must.'

She felt him grab her shoulders and drag her to a sitting position. 'Listen to me, Agnès. Have you taken anything?'

'Let me sleep.'

Now he shook her. 'Answer me. Have you taken anything?'

'Only . . .'

'Only what? Only *what*, Agnès?' He shook her again. 'Speak to me.'

'Only one.'

'One what?' Only one *what*, Agnès?'

'Sleeping pill.'

'Only one sleeping pill?'

'Yes. Please let me –'

'Are you sure?'

In spite of the dazzle of his torch, and the longing to return to sleep, she made out the concern in his eyes. 'Yes.'

'Sure? Just the one?'

'Yes. Two maybe.'

'OK. We're going to the Abbé Paul's.'

'No, please.'

'He told me to bring you there.'

'No, I don't want to.'

'Yes.'

'No, no, please.'

'I'm sorry. But you're coming with me, Agnès.'

52

Chartres

When Agnès woke, she was in a strange bed. The room was warm and peacefully dark, but she could make out from the familiar tatty tapestry of a heraldic shield hanging on the wall that she was in the Abbé Paul's spare bedroom.

There was a man's dressing gown at the foot of the bed and she put it on over her underwear. She had no recollection of having got undressed or of getting into the bed.

The Abbé Paul was washing up in the kitchen when she entered. He turned round briefly to ask, 'Tea or coffee?'

'Coffee with milk, please.'

Wordlessly he made coffee, heated some milk in a small pan and brought it to the table, on which bread, butter and jam were already laid. 'Will that be enough?'

'Plenty, thank you, Father.'

'The jam is damson. I'm rather proud of it but watch out for the stones.'

When she had finished, he took away the plate and cutlery, washed and dried them, and offered her more coffee.

'I'm having some. We can take it through to my study.'

They walked through to the study, where the Abbé Paul was in the habit of sitting with none but his few intimates.

'What day is it?' she asked.

'It's Saturday. My day off.'

'Mine too.'

'Excellent. We can take our day of rest together.'

Agnès looked out of the window towards his garden at the last frail white blossoms on a windblown rose. 'There's no rest for the wicked, isn't that what they say, Father?'

'Are you wicked, Agnès?'

'Yes.'

The Abbé Paul, reaching out, refilled her cup with coffee and milk. 'I'm assuming you wanted more.'

They sat without further words. The Abbé Paul allowed his mind to fill with the nothingness that long practice had taught him. After many mute minutes Agnès said, 'A long time ago I did something.'

'Ah.'

'I had a baby when I was very young. Just fifteen. The nuns who brought me up made me give him away.'

'Did your baby have a name?'

'He was called Gabriel.'

'A good name.'

'I never wanted to give him away. He was taken from me and adopted. I had I suppose what you call a breakdown. I was sent to a clinic. St Francis. A nice place, for what it was.'

'I'm glad of that for you at least.'

'I was glad to get away from the nuns. And there was a doctor there. I suppose I must have been in love with him.'

'Not unusual in those circumstances, I'm told.'

'He was very kind and quite handsome. He had a photo of the labyrinth – our one – on his wall. It's because of that I came here.'

'A man of taste.'

'He had all these ideas about how to treat people who were sick like me – we had special food and he liked us to sleep in airy rooms but he also liked us to go walking in the countryside. He thought that nature and exercise were good for us.'

'He sounds splendid.'

'He was. He was bit absent-minded – actually very, though I don't think he knew that about himself. I knew it. I knew quite a lot about him.'

The Abbé Paul nodded. He was all too aware that even those who see clearly into the souls of others rarely see themselves quite as they are.

'One day he had my file on his desk and when he got up to get something in another room I took it and hid it under my skirt. It was a long skirt so it wasn't hard. I couldn't read but I had this idea that it would say where my baby had gone.'

'Not a bad supposition.'

'Yes. And it did. Or I thought it did. I showed the file to another girl there and she read it for me. She said the only thing that might be a clue was this address that was written there. She told me where it was and I found out that it was not that far from the clinic. I was used to finding my way about the countryside and Dr Deman, that was his name, had told me to walk. I put the file back on his desk – he never locked his door and his desk was always untidy so that was easy – and walked there.'

'To the address on the file?'

'Yes.'

'And you found it?'

'It was a big house, old, and I could tell the people who owned it were rich. I kept thinking just because they've got money they've got my little boy and he was taken from me because I'm poor and can't give him anything. That wasn't the reason, of course, I know that now. Anyway, I hung around, in these trees by the road near the drive of the house, just watching and then I saw this young woman pushing a buggy with a baby in it up the drive. He was a sweet little baby boy with black hair, just the age my Gabriel would have been and she was blonde so I knew she wasn't his real mother.'

'That must have been a shocking moment for you,' said the Abbé Paul, feeling some shock himself.

'It was. Anyway, I walked back to the clinic and two days later I went back there with a knife. I had this thing about knives. I used to cut myself at the convent and although I mostly stopped doing it at the clinic I was always after knives. I had places I hid them. They never seemed to notice.'

'So you were planning an attack?'

'I don't know what I thought I was doing exactly. I stole a scarf from a nurse at the clinic and wrapped it round my face. I don't know if I meant to kill the woman but I don't think I cared if I did. All I knew was I was going to get back my baby.'

Dear God, thought the Abbé Paul.

'I went back to the trees and waited. It seemed hours. I thought she wasn't going to come and then I saw her. Pushing my baby. He was asleep. I waited till she was passing the trees where I was hiding and then I must have stabbed her. Stabbed her in the back. I don't really remember this bit properly. I suppose I just went mad.

'Someone driving past saw me and pulled the woman away and I ran off and got back to the clinic. I put the scarf back on its hook and hid in the old laundry where no one ever went, but nobody said anything. Nothing happened for ages and then one day Dr Deman asked me about it and I still thought the little boy was my Gabriel, so I said so. I suppose I was off my head.'

'But he wasn't your child?'

'I only found that out later. Anyway, I was very confused and I kept saying that the baby was mine. Dr Deman reported what I'd said – he had to, I don't blame him – and the police questioned me but I never admitted to attacking the girl. I just went on about Gabriel. I'm not sure what I was saying, really. They weren't either. I don't think they knew what to believe so they had another doctor examine me. I don't remember him at all or what I said to him, but he sent me to a secure psychiatric hospital, which was awful, I hated it. There was this big woman psychiatrist, not at all like Dr Deman. But Dr Deman came to see me there and took me, and I don't quite know how he worked this, but he took me to see the man who found me when I was a baby, who I called "father" . . .'

The Abbé Paul got up to fetch a box of tissues.

'I can't believe I'm telling you all this.'

'It's good that you are, Agnès, I think.'

'Anyway, I don't know how but Dr Deman arranged for me to come back to stay at the clinic and there was this Australian nurse there, Maddy. I really liked her, and she told me how to get out of the other hospital. "Just say you didn't mean it about him being your child and you didn't know what you were saying," she told me. "Keep saying it. Just stick to your story." It was Maddy who'd given Dr Deman the address that was in my file. She'd been a nanny to the couple who'd adopted the baby that wasn't Gabriel, and the girl I attacked was the new nanny. I guess Dr Deman must have thought for some reason that the baby was Gabriel too. Otherwise, why would he put the address in my file?'

'And you did what Maddy said?'

'Yes. I just kept repeating that I had not known what I was saying before but I knew now the little boy wasn't mine and in the end it worked. They let me go from the secure hospital and I went back to the clinic for a bit and then I went to live with the man I called my father. And everything was good for a while.'

'You had no father of your own?'

'No. Nor a mother. I was found. The man I called my father found me.'

'And you lived with this man?'

'For just over two years. And then he died.'

'I'm sorry.'

'I really liked it at the farm.'

Not for the first time, the Abbé Paul reflected that it was not surprising that people had trouble believing in a merciful God. 'And then you came here?'

'It was because of the labyrinth. Dr Deman gave me a photo of it for my seventeenth birthday. He had it on his office wall and he knew I always liked it. I used to try to do it, get to the centre, with my eyes, but I never could. I left it behind when my father's niece and her husband took over the farm. I was in a state, I suppose, and they were so anxious for me to leave I forgot to take it with me. They told me when I rang to ask about it that they had burnt it. If they hadn't, I mightn't have come here.'

'It's called Providence, I believe,' said the Abbé Paul. 'Agnès, have you told this to anyone else?'

'No, Father. I couldn't have told anyone but you. Because . . .'

There was a silence in which the Abbé Paul waited. Agnès got up, looked down at her bare feet and made an odd wriggling movement with her long toes. 'I would never harm a baby.'

'How about an adult?'

She smiled, which was a relief to him because he saw that she had read his mind and grasped the irony, and in his view the ability to correctly read another's mind and interpret irony was a sign of health.

'I'm not off my head now.'

'No. I don't believe you are. What would you like to do, Agnès?'

He observed her, quite literally, straighten her shoulders. 'Should I tell the police, Father?'

The Abbé Paul also got up but he walked over to the window and seemed to be looking out. In the garden, still alive with fiery colour, a goldfinch was balancing on a long spray strung with rose hip beads. The red on the berries did not quite reflect the spot of red on the bird's head. Lord, he thought, what a conundrum you've set me.

With his gaze still averted, the Abbé Paul said, 'I think what is important is that you have told me. I am not God, and would never claim to speak for Him, but if God is, as I believe Him to be, all comprehending and merciful, He would, I think, say you have been punished enough. I don't see what good could come of a further confession to the police. You were beside yourself.'

The berries that autumn were truly magnificent. It was going to be a hard winter.

'She was in hospital for ages.'

Of course, thought the Abbé Paul. All of this is why she cleans. It crossed his mind to refer to the Prodigal Son but another story came to his aid. 'I wonder,' he said, 'have you maybe come to the story of Ajax in my book of myths?'

'It's one of the names they list at the front. It's an easy name to read.'

'You might like to read his story. Ajax was one of the Greek heroes who went to fight in Troy. He became possessed by a demonic anger and tried to kill his colleagues – it was over something far more trivial than a baby, some armour, in fact, but that isn't why I mention him. The goddess Athene made sure that he didn't slaughter his colleagues in arms but some cattle instead, which is another way of saying that Ajax was beside himself. Not in his right mind.

'I think you too were beside yourself. The young woman did not die and you cannot take back what you did to her by serving a prison sentence. You are not mad or out of your mind now, so nothing would be gained by your return to a psychiatric hospital. Indeed, much may be lost.'

It was the longest speech the Abbé Paul had made to a living soul since as a young man he had joined a philosophical society and discussed Spinoza. He turned and levelled a long look at Agnès, the image of the red hips still in his nether sight. 'Ajax committed suicide when he found what he'd done. There was, is, no need for anything like that. Have you noticed, there are no tombs in our cathedral?'

'No.'

'You perhaps wouldn't. The human mind doesn't deal well in non-events. We tend not to notice what is not there when often absence is the more vital thing. All the great and famous cathedrals have the dead interred there save ours. Not ours, in honour of Our Lady, and I like to think it's because she is for life, not for death.'

Words, words, words, as the afflicted young prince said, what were they worth? But, letting his mind go free, the Abbé Paul found himself adding, 'There are forms of justice which override human law. I propose that the telling of this to me is your means to forgiveness, Agnès. Agnès, my dear . . .'

But she was crying and words were no longer needed.

53

Chartres

Madame Beck had been most put out to receive that Saturday morning a letter from Mother Véronique. The letter was written in violet ink on notepaper embellished with a quotation from St Thérèse of Lisieux. Below the saint's maxim about following the example of 'the poor in spirit' Madame Beck read these words.

'I have been thinking and praying' – 'praying' was underlined three times – 'and, with God's help, I have reached the conclusion that I was at fault in sending you the press cuttings. Nothing was ever found to connect Agnès with the terrible event described there.'

Madame Beck, frowning, took a disbelieving sip of coffee.

'I sent them to you to give you a better idea of what the poor girl has been through,' the violet ink continued, 'but I fear now I have been precipitate and unwise. I would ask you, dear Madame, to destroy the copies and not to repeat their contents or to let the story fall into the wrong hands.'

This kind of reversal, had Madame Beck known it, was typical of Mother Véronique, who drove the Sisters of Mercy almost crazy with her inability to stick to one line.

Madame Beck was, as a consequence, not in the best of moods when she opened the door a little later to Madame Picot. 'I must say you might have rung first, Jeanette.'

'I'm sorry, my dear, but I have something on my conscience. I felt it could not wait.'

This potentially enlivening prospect did not somehow sound well to Madame Beck's ear. 'Yes?'

'May I sit down, dear?'

'Don't be silly, Jeanette.'

'It's about your china dolly. The little coloured girl.'

'Lulu?'

'Lulu, yes. The truth is, you see, well, the truth is, dear, I took her. I broke her, you see, and wanted to get her mended and then you became so angry about it all I felt abashed. But it was wrong of me to let the blame fall on Agnès.'

The news of this perfidy from a friend almost succeeded in dumbfounding Madame Beck. '*You* took Lulu?'

'I brought her back, though, all mended. She's tucked away at the bottom of your bed. I'm surprised you haven't found her but I suppose without Agnès here you haven't had the strength to turn the mattress.'

Madame Picot found to her surprise that she was enjoying this revelation. Rather than remorse, or fear, she seemed to be feeling unusually blithe. After all, what could Louise do to her but drop the friendship? And that prospect no longer seemed so very dreadful.

'Frankly, I'm speechless, Jeanette.'

'Well, dear, there it is. We all make mistakes. If you go and look . . .' But Madame Beck had already flown to her bedroom and was scrabbling like a terrier at the foot of the bed.

'It's just that,' said Madame Picot blandly when her friend returned, inspecting the recovered doll in her hand, 'I felt you should let the Abbé Paul know that you've been mistaken and Agnès is not a thief. Of course, the dear little baby boy is another matter, but I do hope it turns out to be another mistake. She seems such a nice woman, Agnès. I was thinking I might ask her to clean for me. Now, dear, take a look at Lulu's neck and tell me if you can see the join.'

Philippe said, 'Brigitte, what train did you catch last Sunday?'

'How do you expect me to remember that?'

'You remembered when you spoke to the doctor.'

'So?'

'Only Agnès apparently said you got back at nine and you told the doctor it was seven.'

'You're not going to believe her?'

'I can't see why Agnès would lie about it.'

'She would, wouldn't she?'

'Why's that, Brigitte?'

'You know what I mean.'

'I don't, in fact,' said Philippe, who knew perfectly well and hoped to be able to control himself enough not to slap his sister. 'You see, I was thinking that if, as you told Agnès, the train was cancelled and that was checked, and it turned out that it wasn't cancelled after all, wouldn't that show you up as rather unreliable? And you might not wish to come across as unreliable in the circumstances. You see, what's bothering me is you've tried that trick about trains on me before.'

'What are you saying?'

'I'm saying that you might need some help, Brigitte. I'm saying that I doubt Agnès did this terrible thing to Max. Brigitte?'

Her strained white face stared up at him, and he thought – hoped – that perhaps she might turn to him, embrace him, maybe, and even cry. For a fraction of a moment her lips trembled and then the past superseded the possibilities of the present and they became hideously distorted. 'You've always had it just the way you wanted it, haven't you, mother's little darling?'

'Brigitte, you need help. You can't punish Max because he reminds you of me.'

'Get out, get out of here, mother's little queer boy.'

'Thank you, Brigitte, you've just managed to convince me of Agnès' innocence. And if you don't mind I shan't be leaving my own apartment.'

54

Chartres

Alain had not forgotten his promise to Agnès over the silver chain. He had borrowed a wetsuit for the purpose from a colleague who liked to scuba dive and had already spent a morning trawling the river by the watermill where the body of Father Bernard had been found. Saturday also being his day off, he reinstated the search.

It had been his hope that the chain with the earring on it was not too light to have been washed away. But it was a hope which was waning as he sifted through another clump of waterweed and dead sycamore leaves.

A gang of children, old enough to be out alone but too young still for café life, had congregated on the bridge to observe this operation and pass whispered insults among themselves. After some giggling one of them questioned him. 'What you doing there, mister?'

'Searching for treasure. Want to help?'

'What we looking for?'

As Alain explained the face of one of the girls turned knowing. 'Is there a reward?'

'Absolutely.'

'How much?'

The girl's expression became more arch. Alain did a swift calculation and decided it was best to pitch the reward high. 'Fifty euros.'

The crowd made approving noises indicating that they were

impressed. The girl fiddled in her pocket and produced something. 'This it?'

'My dear child. What is your name?'

'Chantal.'

'Chantal, you have just performed a miracle. Let me get this damned frog suit off and fifty euros is yours before the sun goes down.'

Later that afternoon, the astonished Chantal having been paid her dues, Alain called round at the Deanery.

Agnès had retired again to bed and the Abbé Paul was ironing. 'I don't know why people complain about doing this. I find it soothing.'

'I wouldn't know, I never iron.'

'People like their clergy ironed.'

'How is Agnès?'

'Better, I think. She's resting. My own view is that we must back her up in simple denial.'

('How will I cope?' she had asked him and he had answered, 'Do as Maddy advised. Stick to your denial. It worked before . . .')

'I don't want to disturb her. I came to give her this. She gave it to Father Bernard and a child found it in a grate by the river. It must have fallen out of his gown when they pulled him from the river. Poor old boy.'

'Yes,' said the Abbé Paul, who was missing his dead friend and aware that in time he would come to miss him more. 'Thank you. I'll give it to her. And I'm sure she'll want to see you, so do, please, call again later.'

The enthusiasm in the Abbé Paul's voice as he issued this invitation was not, in truth, squarely matched in his heart. He could hardly fail to notice that the young man had a more than ordinary fondness for Agnès. The Abbé Paul was not the jealous sort but had he been he might have been experiencing some discomfort.

The young woman with her lithe form and expressive eyes, even before she had made her brave revelation, had come, he had been recognizing, to inspire in him a new and quite delightful emotion. And that she had chosen him to confide in seemed to affirm the rightness of this feeling. Unlike the Abbé Bernard, the Abbé Paul had not lost his faith, but he had grown in the belief that fidelity to God might bear a larger, more human, interpretation than he had once supposed.

He had not embraced celibacy as many of his colleagues had: as a refuge from heterosexual uncertainty, disinclination or downright distaste or dislike. He had undertaken the state because as an ardent youth he had felt that loving any mortal woman might stand between him and his love of God. It was a belief that over the years he had come to find callow. Mistaken. Even possibly damaging.

He had therefore braced himself to meet, with sufficient warmth, when he answered the door again early that evening, the tanned face of his new young acquaintance and was startled to encounter instead the pallid face of Madame Beck beneath her grotesque bonnet of hennaed hair.

'Good evening, Madame.'

'I have something I must discuss with you, Father.'

'It is not,' said the Abbé Paul, 'terribly convenient.' Accustomed as he was to the practice of ready accessibility, he surprised himself at the bluntness of this statement.

But it took more than a departure from established form to deter the zeal of Madame Beck. 'Just a brief word, Father, if you please.'

'As you wish, Madame. Come in.'

The tenderness that Agnès had inspired in the Abbé Paul had been expressing itself in his cleaning of her recovered treasures. He had polished the chain with the cloth bought by Agnès for the candlesticks, and when the doorbell rang he had been busy with the decorative silver surround in which the single turquoise earring was set. Having had it in his hand when, expecting Alain, he went to the door, he now laid it carefully on the coffee table in his receiving room.

Madame Beck had not come with any intention of retracting her revelation of Agnès' past. The discovery of Madame Picot's treachery had awakened in her a desire to get back in with the Abbé Paul. She had come on the pretext of discussing Mother Véronique's letter and to ask the Abbé, with no intention of taking his advice, what she should 'morally' do about it.

But before she could broach this subject her eye was caught by the turquoise drop.

'How did that get here?'

'What is "that", Madame?'

'My earring. There. On your table.'

'That? That is not yours, Madame.'

Madame Beck started up from the blue chaise-longue, slightly disarranging her wig. But some swift instinct in the Abbé Paul led him to pre-empt her. He rose from his chair and retrieved the earring.

'Father, be so good as to give that to me.'

The Abbé Paul had a tendency to stoop but when he straightened himself he was an unusually tall man. He positively loomed now over Madame Beck. 'Why should I do that, Madame?'

She looked up at him, her bloodless face gleaming with righteous ire. 'I must insist, Father. That is one of a pair of earrings given me by my late husband. The silver work is quite distinctive. I lost one of the pair in Evreux but I . . .'

'Madame Beck, stop a moment –'

But she was not to be stopped.

'. . . have always treasured this remaining one because I too, Father, am the sole survivor of a pair.'

The Abbé Paul looked down into his visitor's livid little eyes and with a sinking heart observed in them a most acute and horrible distress. For half a second, and maybe for the first time in their acquaintance, his heart was wrung for her. She was a sad old woman, maybe once attractive but clearly going bald – a part of the Abbé Paul longed to straighten the crooked wig – who had found nothing better to do with her considerable intelligence than sow rumour, discord and strife. It was, he allowed himself to reflect, an appalling fate.

But the general manqué in the Abbé Paul was never wholly mute and dictated where his higher duty lay. With what might have been construed as a gesture of menace, he placed a hand on Madame Beck's shoulder.

'Madame Beck, I'm afraid you have made a mistake. I assure you, indeed' – he directed his straightest look at her flinching eyes – 'I take my oath as a priest of your Church, Madame, that this is not your earring.'

55

Chartres

When Alain turned up half an hour later, the Abbé Paul made no mention of his encounter with Madame Beck. Instead, when Agnès came down from her room, he let Alain give her the cleaned necklace with its little turquoise drop, only remarking, as he poured his guests wine, that such things were providential and it looked as if it was Agnès' lucky day.

The three of them ate a rather awkward supper at which conversation did not flow smoothly and when the meal was finished the Abbé Paul insisted on doing the washing up. He left his guests together in his study.

Alain said, 'So now, we've recovered your necklace. As Paul says, that's a sign. You're going to be all right, Agnès.'

'Am I?'

'I think so. People, the police, are not daft.'

'No?'

'Sometimes they are. But over all not. People by and large know the truth of things even if they don't always admit it.'

'Do they?'

'I think so. Who do you think did this thing to Max?'

She waited a little before saying, 'Brigitte, I suppose.'

'And she'll be the first police suspect. If she is responsible, believe me, it will come out. You must simply stick to your story.'

At which, to his pleased surprise, she laughed. 'I can do that.'

'The truth is consistent, you see.'

'Sometimes.'

'Do you feel up to walking to the cathedral, Agnès?'

'If you like.'

'Get your coat, then – it's cold. I'll tell Paul.'

The Abbé Paul was mopping the floor when Alain looked into the kitchen. 'Good Lord, Paul, you *are* a domestic bird. You'd make someone a good wife.'

'Really?'

'Agnès and I are going out for a brief stroll.'

'Fine.'

Oh dear, Alain thought, as he collected Agnès from the hall. I must have offended him.

The cathedral, though dark, was lit well enough by the light of the lamps outside filtering through the windows. Alain said, 'Let's visit the Blue Virgin.'

They climbed and this time she went first. Up on the scaffolding Alain switched on his lantern torch.

'Look at her. She won't let you come to any harm.'

'But you don't believe in her.'

'No. I do believe in her. I just don't believe she's the Mother of God.'

'Then who is she?'

'The image of the spirit of all mothers – of motherhood. That which holds us when we're hurt or angry or afraid. She's a cosmic pair of breasts – there's a lovely window with her breastfeeding, have you seen it in the South Clerestory? – and a great wide lap in which I for one have sat many times and been comforted. You can be too.'

'Maybe because I never knew my mother –'

'I know. That makes it harder. But you have her earring back. And, see, it's blue, like the Virgin. Maybe that's why she left it with you.'

'It would be nice to think so.'

'Listen. We found the necklace and the earring. When this is over – all this foul business about Max – you'll have unwedded yourself to misfortune. Luck is a strange phenomenon.'

'I don't know that I will ever be lucky.'

'To be lucky all you need is to believe you are lucky. I was lucky in a mother who, simple soul as she is, believes in luck. Even when her man, my dad, died she went on believing she was lucky. And she made me feel so too.'

'I don't know – is being lucky something you can learn?'

'With help, I think so. And one way to be helped is to be around a lucky person. Like me, for example.'

A hush fell. Somewhere in the depths of the cathedral she heard the faint cheep of a bird. Then she said, 'I'm not sure what you're saying.'

'I'm saying come live with me and be my love.'

'I'm older than you.'

'Only by a year. And I like older women. They know more about love.'

'I'm not very good at love.'

'You haven't tried.'

'I don't even like sex much.'

'You will with me. I'm a terrific lover.'

At which she laughed. 'How you have the nerve, Alain Fleury?'

'It's true. How many lovers have you had?'

'No one you could call a proper lover. I tried it with a few people. I didn't like it much with any of them.'

'Was Robert one? Don't answer that. And listen, I've had more lovers than I can count and I promise you they were all very happy with me. Merry as midsummer larks. Until I left them.'

'But then you might leave me.'

'I might. But I doubt it. I like you, I admire you and I fancy you like anything. In short, I'm in love with you.' And all in an instant Alain understood that that was what had been eating the Abbé Paul. 'Poor Paul,' he said aloud.

'Why?'

'Never mind.'

Behind them, the Blue Virgin sat in enigmatic witness of their conversation. Somewhere below, the cloistered bird had found a companion. 'Sparrows,' Alain said. 'They're in the choir. I guess it's the right place for birds.'

'They used to drive poor Father Bernard wild.'

'Well, he's saved from that, at least, wherever he is now.'

'Maybe with his mother. Though she sounded as if she was more of a weight on him.'

'You must wonder about your mother.'

'Yes.'

'And your father?'

'You know, I don't bother my head about him. I always feel, even though she abandoned me in that way, that it was my mother who loved me.'

'Well, there you are, then. That's not a bad start.' The wind outside whined, wrapping itself round the cathedral, and he pulled her towards him. 'Remember how the gods come in through the door of winter? The door that lets in the light.'

'Alain.'

'I'm here.'

'I want to tell you something. Or, I don't want to at all, but it's that, it's that –' How could she say it? But how could she not say? It would be there for ever waiting to destroy her all over again if she did not say it now. She looked across at the Virgin, flanked on each side by angels brandishing swords. 'It's like this. I can't come with you until I tell you. And when I tell you, you may not want me.'

'Try me.'

She got up and went over, apparently to examine the angels' swords.

'I tried to kill someone.'

'Ah.'

'I didn't kill them but that was just luck. I wanted to and I might have done.'

'What happened?'

'They ended up in hospital very badly hurt.'

'No, I mean why did you do it?'

'I thought this woman had my baby. I was wrong. It was another baby and she was just the nanny anyway.'

'You'd lost your child?'

'Yes.'

'And you thought she had it –"it" – sorry – boy or girl?'

'A boy. Gabriel. Yes.'

'And?'

'They took him from me. They thought I was too young.'

'Of course losing your child made you murderous. Who's "they"?'

'The nuns. You don't mind?'

'Come here.' She turned back to him, hesitating. 'Come and sit down. Please.'

She slowly went over and knelt beside him and he put both arms round her shoulders. 'Listen to me. I did the same once.'

'What?'

'Tried to kill someone and like you by good fortune I didn't succeed. We're two of a kind. It's probably why I fell in love with you.'

'You're making this up.'

'I'm not making anything up. In my case, it was a drunken British lout trying to carve an obscenity on a beautiful ancient column in a poorly supervised site. I tried to knock his block off with a bit of scaffolding. He had a hard British lout's skull and recovered, otherwise I'd have probably been incarcerated in a Turkish jail.'

'It doesn't sound –'

'Agnès, if you never listen to me again listen now. Everyone has a murderer in them. That's the point of the Ten Commandments. But that doesn't make them murderers for all time.'

'But I don't –'

'Shut up, will you. This is something I know about. You are not going to murder me because I am going to give you a baby and not take one away from you, and you, as far as I can judge, are unlikely to try to deface an ancient monument. So I think we're both safe. Hey, darling, don't cry. Or rather do.'

She did cry until Alain said, 'Now you're going to stop crying, or go on if you like, but we are going to start on that baby because we mustn't waste any time and I'm going to show you what it's like to be made love to before the eyes of the Mother of God.'

The Virgin's expression looked no less serene when, sometime later, they eased their bodies up from Jean Dupère's old coat, which Alain had spread out on the wooden platform.

'Was I right?'

She laughed, shaking her head, but not in denial.

'Go on admit it. That was the best lay ever, wasn't it?'

'There wasn't much competition.'

'That's another reason for loving you. You're droll. As well as wise.'

Agnès said, 'I remember you calling me a savant. I thought you were laughing at me.'

'I would never do that. Shall we visit the Minotaur's lair?'

Down in the body of the nave the lights illuminating the

Western Front were making darkly brilliant sapphires of the great rose window. Agnès squatted down, peering at the floor.

'What are you doing?'

'There's gum here.'

'Dear God. I tell the woman I'm in love with her and want to spend a lifetime with her and she's worrying about chewing gum. Where is it?'

'There.'

He bent down and scraped with his knife at the centre of the open rose. 'It's probably another reason for loving you. You're like me – obsessional.'

'Am I?'

'Fastidious, is maybe what I mean. All I know is that we're two of a kind. Where shall I put the gum?'

She took out a tissue. 'Here.'

'I suppose you'll always be a cleaner at heart.'

'Yes.'

'Me too, I expect. Agnès?'

'Yes?'

'The Minotaur is dead.'

'Maybe.'

'Yes. It's dead.'

She smiled up at him. 'But you're not Theseus?'

'But I don't mind being Dionysos. And since you may have the makings of our baby inside you, I think I shall carry you off.'

Picking her up in his arms, he carried her out of the cathedral and down the southern steps before the bleak gaze of Madame Beck, standing sentinel and alone in her watchtower.

56

Chartres

The moment Madame Beck got in from her abortive visit to the Abbé Paul, she went straight to her dressing-table and her jewellery box.

Compared with her other jewels, the earrings were not valuable but Claude had given them to her when it was clear that they had finally begun to make a go of the restaurant. They had had a party with all their best customers to celebrate. A publicity event, Claude had called it. They had agreed on such things, she and Claude. She had found the earring gone from her ear when, way past midnight, they finally tipped into bed and Claude had said not to bother to go and look, and she would be sure to find it on the floor in the morning. And then they had . . .

Denuded of her wig, Madame Beck allowed herself to remember the embraces of the man she had loved and once believed herself loved by. Too happy at the success of the evening and Claude's sudden desire for her, she had not taken the usual precautions and it had led to the one and only pregnancy of her life – the pregnancy that they had both decided was better discreetly terminated by a private gynaecologist who was prepared to take the necessary risk with the law.

Claude had not wanted children. Had she not wanted them either? She had wanted, or she had believed she wanted, what he wanted, what he said was best for the business. But, Madame Beck allowed herself to muse – pulling from her jewellery box the soft cloth bags in which she kept the tokens, the pearls, the diamond clips, the costly rings and bracelets, that Claude, over their long marriage, had also given her – it might have been nice sometimes to go, as Jeanette did, on shopping sprees with a daughter.

For all she had searched the restaurant the following morning, she never found that missing earring. That pert Algerian waitress with the long black hair took it, she was sure of that. The one she had had to fire for taking the restaurant linen. The one she found that time with Claude. The woman had had the nerve to write to him some months later asking for 'help' with some trouble she had got herself into. Lucky that she had intercepted the letter before he read it. Claude had had a soft side.

Alone on the wide matrimonial bed that her husband, in later years, had so rarely occupied, Madame Beck found at last the small white box where she kept those earrings which, over the years, had lost their partners. But, tipping them out on to the bed, to her amazement, when she had sorted through the jewelled jumble, she found the solitary turquoise drop, set in the distinctive silverwork, that she had been so convinced she had seen on the Abbé Paul's table.

A horrible fear began to overtake Madame Beck. Perhaps she was going demented, losing her mind? Hadn't Jeanette made a comment about that only recently? Despite their recent coolness, she rang Madame Picot, who was, after all, her closest friend; but she got no answer.

An hour or so later, after a dispiriting frozen 'single' meal and an unamusing TV programme, Madame Beck went to her bureau, sat down and took out a box of scented notepaper.

'Dear Mother,' she wrote beneath a spray of honeysuckle. 'I would be glad to take up your kind suggestion of a stay in your Retreat Wing.'

★

Madame Picot was out on a mission of her own when her old friend failed to reach her. She had taken Agnès' address from Terry and put sixty euros into an envelope, along with the card which Auguste had brought back from the Courtauld in London, the picture by Gauguin of the young woman asleep on a yellow pillow, whom Agnès so resembled.

On the card she had written 'A little "thank-you" for finding Piaf. Affectionately, Jeanette Picot.'

Putting the card through the door of the Badon apartment, Madame Picot felt the peculiar warmth of unmerited self-satisfaction. Walking back into town, she thought that Louise may not approve of what she was doing, but, as she murmured to Piaf, Louise could 'go fuck herself!'

Professor Jones had popped out to post a letter when he observed the figure of Alain carrying Agnès down the cathedral steps. An awful thought had beset the professor. He had never paid Agnès, and although she had never referred to this oversight he had concluded that this was why she had disappeared. The money he had so lavishly distributed; none of it had gone to her. What had he been thinking?

About to hail her, in an attempt to correct this dreadful omission, the professor held back. The couple were laughing; his presence would perhaps be an intrusion.

An association of ideas led the professor to thoughts of his cousin Gwen. The letter he had been about to post to her was still in his hand. Maybe he should have suggested that his cousin pay him a visit? Or should he propose visiting her? He hurried home with the letter unposted to add a postscript.

About to reseal the envelope, a further thought struck him. 'P.P.S.,' he wrote. 'I wonder, did we, as children, know anyone, can you remember, who had a parrot?'

57

Chartres

When Alain and Agnès got back to the Deanery, they found a note stuck in the letterbox: 'Key under geranium pot. Help yourselves to wine.'

'He's not afraid of burglars, then?' Alain suggested.

They let themselves in quietly.

'Do you think it's really all right for us to help ourselves?' Agnès asked as Alain poured her a glass. 'I generally wash these for him.'

'I'm sure it's all right. He's a very generous man. Exceptionally so.'

'Yes.'

He sat down next to her on the blue chaise-longue, running his hand over the dark silk. 'Paul has taste. Listen, no need to now but sometime, my darling, you might want to tell me how you came to have Gabriel.'

'Yes.'

'No hurry. Or compulsion. Never let that be the case with us. You know that?'

'I think so.' She thought a moment and then said, 'I will tell you. But – but now is too nice to spoil.'

'When you're ready.'

'You know, when I said I didn't like it much?'

'Yes.'

'I didn't like it at all. Not at all.'

'And now?'

'You're making me blush.'

'Good.'

Much later he said, 'I don't want to leave you but I think it's politer to Paul if I go. And you should rest up.'

'Alain . . .'

'Yes?'

'You will. . .'

'I'll come and fetch you without fail but not before you've had time to rest.'

So it was only the Abbé Paul and Agnès who sat over their breakfast coffee together in his fire-lit study the following morning.

The goldfinch had long left the spray of hips but a jay was performing a raucous solo in the garden.

'You look better, my dear,' suggested the Abbé Paul. Better than 'better', he thought.

'Father Paul –'

'Paul, please.'

'I'm not sure I can call you anything but "Father", Father.'

'If you must, then.'

'When I was in the cathedral with Max, the day I fainted and you brought me here, I saw something.'

'Yes?'

'Yes.' She sat there a moment. Then, 'I saw the Virgin. At least I think, no, I know it was her. She came through the wall of the South Transept in a blue light.'

'Ah.'

'That's all really. I wanted to tell someone.'

'Thank you for telling me.'

'I've not told anyone else.'

'Not even Alain?'

It might have been the closest the Abbé Paul could come to a reproach, but if Agnès felt that the mention of her lover had more behind it than the simple question suggested, she ignored this. 'I think, I can't explain, but I think, I feel, that I should only tell you.'

'It's a great honour.'

'I know.'

The Abbé Paul was not a visionary. Nor, on the whole, did he take much account of reports of such occurrences. But he had lived long enough in and thought deeply enough about the world to know that the fine mesh of what is called 'reality' was also made up of exceptions. 'I meant that it's a great honour that you do me.'

She sat thinking some more. 'It's like this. I *think* it's like this. I found a "father". He died but he gave me love and care and his coat and my silver chain. I think, I know this sounds odd, but I don't know how else to put it, but I think in a way, you've been my "mother".'

The Abbé Paul said nothing to this but he smiled. If this strange pronouncement from the young woman, who looked that morning, in his shabby dressing gown, so unbearably radiant, hurt him at all no mortal soul could have detected it.

Looking across to him, Agnès said, 'I know it sounds odd. You don't mind?'

He stood up and went over to embrace her. Holding her close, so she should not see that his eyes were unsuccessful in holding back tears, he said, 'My dear Agnès. How could I possibly mind?'

Afterword

There are no true endings but there are places where any account comes to a natural halt. Those who have followed this story may like to know that Max Nevers was eventually given into the care of his uncle, Philippe, and his civil partner, Tan.

Denis Deman did return to France. With the help of Sister Laurence, he finally tracked down his old patient Agnès Morel. But he never learned the full truth about the events he had triggered.

Agnès continued to help to look after Max while she and Alain remained in Chartres. After they left, they were frequent visitors at the Deanery, where they were the guests of their friend, the Abbé Paul, godfather to their son, Jean-Paul.

So far, Agnès has not found her first child, Gabriel. She lives in hope.